THE
SCROLL

A novel by

CAT LE DÉVIC

The Scroll
© Cat LeDévic

Book cover design and text layout:
Jaquetta Trueman, Graphic Solutions
Front Cover image: Lascaux cave painting, Photographer
Larry Dale Gordon, licensed through Getty Images.
Book text set in ITC New Baskerville Roman 11 on 15pt

First published in 2006 by Ecademy Press

Contact:
Ecademy Press
6, Woodland Rise
Penryn, Cornwall, UK
TR10 8QD
info@ecademy-press.com

Printed and Bound by Lightning Source UK and USA

— DEDICATION —

To Mom, I only wish you were here to see this. And to Dad,
without whom this book wouldn't be a reality.

— ACKNOWLEDGEMENTS —

Thanks to my two main editors, Kiana and Dustbunny2. You were with me from the start. Jaquetta, you did a stunning job on the graphics and the typesetting. Ecademy Press has been a joy to work with, this book would be lesser without them. I'm grateful to Dr. Tom Campbell, whose idea it was to go on and finish this book. You always had faith. Many thanks to Debber, who educated me on all things regarding Carbon 14C dating. Any errors are mine. Rabbit, your knowledge of the Bible was invaluable. And thanks to my Beejay, who gave me such wonderful insight into leukemia, and then succumbed to it herself.

The entire Jokers Updates site has been behind this book from the start. Guys, I love you.

∨

— PROLOGUE —

Dust puffed from beneath the man's road-worn sandals as he walked steadily onward. He ran his tongue over his dry lips, thinking of the Gaul village he'd passed early that morning and the cup of water he'd been so generously served. He smiled, a white flash in his tanned, sun-wrinkled face.

Behind him, the dirt road stretched for countless flat miles, then flowed through the bright summer afternoon. Reluctantly, he stopped and looked around. Green flatlands met a ruffled forest collar off to his left, and just to his right, a low hill rose black against the brilliant sunlight. He stopped and stretched. Soon his need for water would become overwhelming. Perhaps if he were to gain the height of the hill, he could spot another village or even a pond.

Panting slightly, he made his way upward. As he attained the summit, one sandal slid and a stone flipped under his toes, and he hurriedly reached toward a dead tree for support. Rough bark warm beneath his hand, he gazed upon the land rolling to the skyline—green, verdant, and pulsing with birdsong. He sighed and lifted one foot, trying to dislodge the pebble.

His shoulders slumped: there was neither a village nor water in sight. The bone-crushing beating he'd taken from the length of his journey was slowly sapping the strength from his legs, as well as his will to go on.

Finally, he succeeded in prying the stone from under his bruised foot, and he kicked it over the side of the hill. He watched as it skittered through clumps of grass, hit a stump, and went briefly airborne. Then it vanished, landing with a peculiar echo.

He frowned, perspiration running down his cheeks and into his dense heavy beard. Stones don't simply disappear. Curious, he made his way over the lip of the hill and began to descend. As he reached the stump where he'd last seen the stone, he stopped and leaned forward. Just beneath yawned a large cavern.

Favoring his sore foot, he gingerly made his way around the loose stones that topped the cavern. A cave could mean water, and water would mean an end to his raging thirst and maybe even the completion of his mission. A small cloud swept across the sun as he hopped the rest of the way to the bottom of the hill.

Close enough to the cave's entry to feel its cool wet breath on his face, he stopped. He inhaled deeply, squinting into the darkness, and saw them—graceful horses running across the rough walls. A vibrant brown, the horses appeared to be freshly drawn. Instinctively, he knew the hands that had painted the horses, and the bulls that pranced nearby, belonged to an artist dead for eons.

He ran a hand over the slightly raised paint, marveling. Then he sniffed. Behind the earthy, rank cave smell … was that a hint of moisture? He sighed heavily, then was startled at the explosion of small yips resonating from the depths of the cave in front of him.

Conscious of the darkly shaded and uneven cave floor, he moved slowly down the steep clay incline. A large pillar-like stone appeared through the gloom, and just behind it, a mass of grayness seethed and whined. He leaned around the pillar and squinted.

Four very young puppies lay sprawled in a slight depression. Dark as the depths of the cavern were, he could make out no details of their appearance, save their minute size. He stared, hearing one small yip rise above the others—one with a high, scared timbre to it. Hoping his eyes would adjust to the blackness, he stepped with care beyond the pillar.

Just beyond the slight depression where the four puppies lay, a portion of the floor dropped to a thin ledge where a large body of water gleamed in the dim light. A small, dark form huddled, whimpering, on the ledge, and the man gingerly dropped to one knee, thrusting his arm downward.

Instantly rewarded by the sharpness of baby teeth sinking into his palm, he lifted the pup and placed it with the other four. Moving a slight distance from the animals, he leaned over, cupped his hands, and brought the water to his lips. It was icy cold and sweet.

He sank to his haunches and reached behind him. Slipping a hand into his backpack, he felt for his wooden ink bowl and withdrew it. He dipped it full of water, walked back to where the light gleamed off a herd of horses, and sat.

He pulled a little sack of finely ground lampblack out of his pouch and poured a handful into the water. With one finger he stirred until the grains were completely dissolved. Adding a small ball of gum from another pouch, he again stirred the ink until the texture was smooth. After unrolling the fine sheepskin to the correct spot, he took his reed, dipped it in the bowl, and began making careful marks on the soft leather.

As he wrote, his emotions rose. He paused for a moment and looked up as a drop of ink fell to the bottom of the sheepskin. Thoughts filled his mind—visions of those in the future who would find his missive. There would be a red haze of violence wavering over those distant times.

Shuddering, he prayed they would understand the words he so painstakingly scribed. As he prayed, he looked down, saw the small puddle of ink, and relaxed. He dipped his reed and began a design.

Nearly done, he heard a bird startle and fly away outside.

He stood with alacrity and peered at a dark indentation in the wall beneath a regal black bull. There, a perfect hole to contain his work. He wrapped the leather into a roll and inserted it into the opening, and soon found a right-sized rock to plug the hole.

For a moment, he stood in front of the wall. He laid a hand on it, breathed deeply, then turned and walked back to the front of the cave.

A looming shape awaited him, silhouetted against the sunlight behind. As he stepped forward, he recognized the figure as a large female wolf, swollen dugs hanging close to the ground, hackles raised, fangs bared. A low growl vibrated through her throat.

Joyfully, he walked forward, and she sprang to meet him. At the last possible moment, she turned her body and landed at his side, the growl turning to high yips reminiscent of her young cubs inside the cave. Then she was scooting between his legs and flipping on her back in front of him, four massive paws in the air and a distinct plea on her elegant face. He smiled and kneeled to scratch the soft furry belly before taking his leave.

He expected the journey back to be equally long and grueling, with a fearsome death at its end.

✕

— CHAPTER ONE —

WEDNESDAY, JULY 15

When her cell phone rang, Maggie stiffened. The sharp scent of French tobacco floated into the back of the taxi, and she breathed through her mouth as she fumbled through her travel case. She found the phone, held it as it rang again and again, and counted the rings, as always, until just before the voice mail would answer at the sixth. She flipped it open, read the small screen, sighed and responded. "Maggie Purcell."

She listened for a moment, then turned to look at Reeve Hawkins, one eyebrow lifted. "I see. Well, that's certainly a different way to arrive in Paris … It was fine, considering Reeve was green most of the way." She chuckled. "Yes, that's the taxi you're hearing—guy has to be doing eighty. We're about ten miles outside of Paris—okay, yes, we'll do that. Thanks for the warning. Talk to you then."

She folded the small phone and placed it back in her bag,

turning to her seatmate. "Well, this is a fine state of affairs," she said. "That was Francois. Xcorp, Paris has had a bomb threat."

"You jest." Reeve's dark face grew solemn, then broke into a grin. "Does this mean we actually get a day off instead of an imminent arrival at Xcorp?"

"Nice to know you're so worried about them." She rolled her eyes. "Yes, they said the police were already there, and it's probably a false alarm. Else I'd be nervous about going in at all. On the bright side, we'll be able to go through the French system manuals before we tackle the problem. And at least Mom didn't call. Every time that phone rings ..."

The taxi swerved around a slower truck, then moved back into the lane of traffic, throwing Reeve briefly into Maggie. He reached out and propped himself on the back of the driver's seat, winking at her. "You and that phone. Girl, you need to lighten up. I know it's hard, but you simply can't spend every waking moment in dread."

She took a deep breath. "Yes, I can, as well you know. But really, I should be concentrating on the job at hand. First thing, we need to find the range of ports on the computer servers that Xcorp uses to access the Internet. On each port we put a special sniffer, which will check incoming and out-going traffic. We'll nail the problem."

As a New York-based security engineering team for Xcorp Corporation, Maggie and Reeve consulted for clients wanting the most secure Internet applications possible. The current assignment was Xcorp's own Parisian office. During the previous week, the logs had shown a security breach.

"Where's your sense of fun? We just got to Paris, and all you can think of is work?" Reeve poked her arm playfully. "Me, I intend to get a little bit silly—hit a café, have a croissant ... " The taxi driver slammed on his brakes then abruptly shot forward. " ... If I live through the next five minutes." He grinned.

"I just believe in being prepared," she responded.

"Tell you what. Why don't we hit the flea market, see if we can't buy Beth a fairy, then find a café?"

Maggie hesitated, considering. Once the bomb threat was resolved, their time in Paris would be brief. And finding a gift for her little sister was imperative.

Twelve now, Beth Purcell had been diagnosed with chronic mylogenic leukemia five years earlier. The disease had wasted her already thin form to nearly skeletal proportions, but her gentle spirit and positive outlook never waned. Maggie was often awed at her sister's courage through the painful treatments and their dreadful side effects. Beth herself claimed she had help from fairies, else she'd never endure. She had a lovely collection of the glass and porcelain creatures, and Maggie always managed to find a new one on her travels.

Maggie shook her head. "Okay, but *then* you have to help me go over the manuals."

"Done deal."

The taxi soon deposited them at the Hotel Régina just across from a large statue depicting Joan of Arc mounted on a prancing horse. Maggie gave the familiar gilded statue a salute as the doorman came out to fetch their bags. She told Reeve she'd meet him in the lobby in an hour, time enough to shower and try to melt away the jet lag.

Following the bellboy, she took the elevator to the top floor of the venerable old hotel. The bellboy slipped the keycard into her door and put her bag on a small stand. She turned to tip him and noticed that his gaze hung on her chest. In irritation, she shoved the money into his hand and closed the door in his face. Her overly-large breasts had always been a matter of concern to her. Ever since school, she had hated the ogling looks.

She walked into the room, relaxing, as always, at the sight

3

of the fabric-covered ceiling that sloped toward the large windows. Wasting no time, she stepped out of her suit and padded naked into the bathroom.

I could stand a work-out, she thought, running a hand over a flat stomach that had no defined muscles. *Face still okay, though*. The face was "good enough" with its straight nose above a wide mouth. Back in college, she'd had offers to model.

She bent over the tub and turned on the water.

Somewhat revived after a long, hot shower, she dressed in comfortable khakis, a golf shirt, and her favorite Adidas tennis shoes. She quickly ran a brush through her short, straight black hair and noticed that her deep green eyes were red with exhaustion from the long flight. She brushed her hair back from her face, the widow's peak falling into a natural part.

Calculating that she still had a few minutes to spare, she moved out of the bathroom and picked up the phone to dial Nashville. Her sister Beth answered on the first ring.

"Hi, cutie! How you feeling today?" Maggie said, cradling the phone between her neck and shoulder. She again ran her hand through her hair, shaking it dry with her fingers.

"Maggie! Wow! Are y'all in Paris already?" the light voice came over the line.

Maggie concentrated. *Does her voice sound weaker?* "We sure are. And I get a day off ... Xcorp had a dang bomb threat."

Beth gasped. "Oh my gosh! You sure it's safe? I reckon it is. The girls haven't said anything and I know I would have heard—"

"We're fine. We're going to the flea market, and I might pick up a thing or two. Now tell me, how'd the treatment go?"

"Oh, the usual. A needle with my name on it, and that nice burning feeling." She laughed, then choked and tried to cover it. "Really, I'm fine."

Maggie's own throat closed. "Honey, is Mom around?"

There was a brief pause. "She just ran out to the store."

"Oh well, I'll catch her tomorrow then." Maggie furrowed her brow. "So, who won at 'Animal' during the treatment? You didn't try to use 'platypus' on her again, did you?"

"Uh, we didn't play 'Animal.'"

Yes, Beth did sound as if she was weakening, and though she was loathe to press the matter, Maggie simply had to know. "Beth, did Mom take you to your treatment?"

"Actually, Linda did. But it's okay, Mags. It really is. Linda's the coolest neighbor on earth." Beth paused, started to say something, then went silent.

"What is it?" Maggie's stomach began to roil with nerves.

"Linda's moving next week. Her husband got transferred to Houston."

"Oh ... that's bad news for sure." Now their mother *had* to slow down her headlong flight into the bottle. "Well, I'll be back in a few days and we'll figure something out ... Tell me. Is Mom behaving?"

"I think so, I really do. But I don't want you worrying about us! You take care of yourself and say hi to Reeve for me. Besides, Mom gets so upset if I get sick. You know how she is."

Maggie bit back a harsh remark. "Yes. Well, love, I have to meet Reeve in about three minutes. I'll call you again tomorrow. Try and get some sleep, will you?"

"Yes, I will, and you be safe! I'll send Zaddie over to guard you."

"You keep that fairy right there with you. I'll be just fine."

"I'm sending her anyway. I love you, Mags."

"I love you too, sweetie. Bye."

Maggie stood, sighing deeply. She walked back to the full-length mirror and checked her short shaggy hair. Soon she'd need a cut. But she couldn't keep her agitated mind off the conversation with Beth, and a flush of anger reddened her cheeks. She had a feeling about why Mom hadn't taken Beth to the hospital, and she only hoped she was wrong.

Anna Purcell, a whip-thin bottle blonde with a deep Southern attitude, resented her life. The small house bought so lovingly by Maggie's father wasn't large enough to impress "the afternoon Annies," as Maggie called the group of women who gathered every day to play tennis, shop, and drink with her mother.

Maggie stood and walked to the slanted window. Just beyond the stone rear end of Joan of Arc's horse, the Louvre rose elegantly into the Paris afternoon. She stared at the beautiful old palace.

The fact that Anna could neglect Beth's trip to the hospital for an afternoon of shopping or drinking didn't surprise her. Instead, it offended her on a level she kept fiercely under wraps. Not even Reeve, as close a friend as he was, knew the depth of her rage and anguish over her mother's violation of trust.

Determinedly pushing the fury out of her mind, she transferred her wallet and passport to a small shoulder bag, then took the aging elevator down to the lobby.

Reeve was, as usual, impeccably turned out in a wine-colored short-sleeve Dior shirt and light gray Sergio Valente slacks. The color of the shirt set off his black skin and indigo blue eyes. Maggie gave him an approving grin as they set out through the revolving door and hailed a taxi.

Reeve asked for the flea market in fluent French, and the taxi took off with a sharp jerk. Maggie's teeth snapped together and she frowned. Reeve laughed. "Now I know we're back in Paris."

Not listening, Maggie turned to face the stone expanse of the Louvre.

Reeve watched her, wondering. "Mags, you okay?"

"Yes. No ... Well, I'm not sure. I just talked to Beth. She had her chemo yesterday, and Mom didn't take her."

"Now, there could be any number of reasons—"

"Or she could be drinking," Maggie finished for him. "She waited until I was out of the country, didn't she."

"You can't assume that from what little you know. Give her a break. And you know Linda will take care of Beth."

"Not for long," Maggie said, taking a deep breath. "Linda's moving next week—to Houston. I don't know what I'm going to do without her. We need to find something really neat for her while we're at the Flea Market."

Linda, the Purcell's neighbor, cared deeply for Beth, often staying with her while Anna was otherwise occupied. Now, Beth wouldn't have that very beneficial backup.

Maggie leaned back against the seat, drained both from the long trip and her tight nerves. As she closed her eyes, the sound of the taxi's engine seemed to rise and wane rhythmically. It was mesmerizing, and she felt herself relax.

Then the drone of the engine seemed to blend into a mass of voices, speaking together. She couldn't quite hear what they said. Not sure whether she was awake or slipping into a dream, she strained to listen. The voices grew louder but remained indistinguishable.

Alarmed, Maggie sat straight up in the taxi, startling Reeve.

"Did you hear that?"

"Hear what?" He said, raising a brow. "For a minute, I thought I was going to hear you snore."

She glared at him. "I must have dozed off. Oh look, here we are," she said, spying the winding streets of the flea market. "Fare thirty-nine francs? Wow! It's robbery." She hurriedly rummaged through her purse and extracted several large notes as Reeve opened the door.

Reeve stood waiting and sniffed. "Ahhh, smell that smell!" A grin grew on his face as Maggie joined him. "Please tell me we can stop for a coffee and croissant. I don't think I could stand it if we don't."

Looking at his pleading dark blue eyes, Maggie grinned. "You and your food. I have to admit, I'm starving. Croissants, here we come!"

The café was just across the road, blue and white Cinzano umbrellas hanging over wrought-iron tables on the narrow terrace. Maggie sat and was soon pouring hot milk into her rich coffee from a small steel pitcher. Reeve put a piece of sugar into his tiny espresso, then inhaled and let out a heartfelt moan.

"How do they do it? Did you ever smell anything this good?"

"How does anything that smells so good taste so bad? I don't know how you stomach that stuff." Maggie blew on her own light coffee, then sipped cautiously. It was delicious, the flavor exploding to the back of her throat. She extracted a warm croissant from the nearby basket, then broke it in half and knifed a dab of butter onto it before dunking it into the coffee.

"I have to admit, this is the best. How do they get them so flakey?"

"If you knew how many layers they make, each one buttered separately, you'd understand. I've made croissants, and it's a giant pain in the ass." He bit the entire end off his own croissant and munched with gusto.

"It's totally worth it." She chewed slowly, watching the passersby. Older women in head scarves carried large cloth bags as they walked alongside business women in suits and heels. A little boy walked hand in hand with an older man wearing a beret. The sky was a soft cloudy blue, and the air was a blend of exhaust, coffee, and wonderful perfume exclusive to Paris in early summer.

For a moment, Maggie was disoriented. Was it really just yesterday she'd been in her small office, eradicating the last of a nasty virus on GE's servers?

"You're not worrying again about your sister, are you?"

"Not at the moment," she said. "But it's not good, Reeve. I have a bad feeling about this. I think Mom uses my absence as an excuse to hit the bottle even harder." Maggie looked into her coffee, swirling it in its large cup.

Reeve's lips tightened. "I'm afraid she uses any excuse at hand, Mags."

"It's got to stop. What if something happens to Beth, and Mom's unable to care for her? I should've stayed. Mom's getting worse."

"You're needed here, and you've done all you can. You have Linda watching, and Mags?" He caught and held her gaze. "You have to live *your* life, as Anna has to live hers."

"But Beth needs her. She's not stupid—she knows when Mom's loaded. It's an awful, helpless feeling … you're supposed to be able to depend on your mother.

"Beth sometimes has to call Linda to come get Mom off the floor and into bed! That's not something she should be dealing with, even if she weren't so sick. She's only twelve. It's the height of selfishness for Mom to allow herself to get that drunk with Beth right there." Maggie suddenly had to choke back tears.

Reeve leaned forward and laid his hands on each of her shoulders. "Sweetie, there's not a damn thing you can do about it from here. You've got Linda keeping a close eye while you're gone—you know nothing really bad will happen." He considered a thought for a moment. "Maybe it's time you decide to bring in home health care. After Grand-mère Amelie had her stroke, she refused to recuperate anywhere but at home. We found a girl who would feed her take care of her, and do general cleaning. Smartest thing we ever did."

Maggie nibbled a nail and looked at the fanciful stone carvings above a window across from the café. "I thought about moving back to Nashville myself, but the tech market is so soft there."

"Mags, I'm telling you," he said emphatically, "Grandmère Amelie's back to normal now. These people are trained in everything from CPR to physical therapy, and they generally don't charge more than ten to twelve dollars an hour. If you find someone young and fun, Beth will enjoy life. And *you'll* finally get some peace of mind."

"I guess I'll look into that when I get back. I know you're right. Something really has to be done." She turned and looked down at the checked tablecloth, dabbing a tear she hoped he didn't see.

"But it'll have to wait until you're back. You don't have a choice in the matter! Now, come with me." He held out his hand in a grand gesture. "There are fleas to find, and fairies to buy."

Maggie straightened in her chair and took a deep breath. "And no doubt, handmade silk shirts, eh?"

Reeve brushed a crumb off his maroon shirt and smiled. "As a matter of fact, there happens to be a shop not far from here with a killer tailor. You go in, get measured, pick out a fabric, and a day or so later, presto. Sometimes I order them right from New York. It's going to be a treat to actually see Alphonse again. Mags, you really should pamper yourself and hit a nice dress shop."

"Give me *Au Printemps* straight off the rack. And right now, the last thing I need is another suit."

"Not a suit—a pretty, feminine dress. The fall fashions just came out." He eyed her appreciatively, her still-damp black hair shining in the sun.

"In late spring?! Forget it. I'd roast. I'm after a fairy and maybe some calligraphy for Beth."

"Sugah," he drawled in an exaggerated Southern accent, "y'all just don't know how to live."

"Yeah, yeah, well. If you must know, I'm pining for a new laptop. Come on, let's go hit the market. My butt's going numb in this little chair."

"If we get separated, meet me right back here in two hours at the corner of Rue Marie Curie and Rue des Rosiers."

They strolled down a small street in the Marché Biron. Lined with various vendors, the street took several bends, then wound back on itself. Layers of postcards hung in front of little kiosks selling magazines and papers. Through the dense crowds, hawkers blared their wares. Among all the clothing shops that dotted the streets, birds chirped, sang, and spoke from hanging cages in front of one noisy shop.

Maggie and Reeve stopped in front of a large window filled with delicate porcelain and long-stemmed roses next to finely-woven baskets, all shining in the morning sun. Then she saw it.

A tiny fairy stretched upward on one toe, veined golden wings partially spread as if she was just taking flight. The bright blue eyes seemed to stare right at Maggie, and even the parted lips, with their minute white teeth, were lovingly detailed.

"Reeve, look! Did you ever?" She pointed.

"Oh, that's most definitely it. Now remember," he insisted, "haggle! That's what it's all about."

"Yes, sir. Be right back." She entered the store quickly, hoping he wouldn't follow. As she walked up to the register, she looked over her shoulder. Reeve stood facing the opposite side of the street. Grinning, she quickly pulled out her wallet and paid the exact price quoted on the tag.

The delighted proprietor wrapped the fairy in layers of

tissue, chattering away in French. Maggie leaned over the counter, concentrating. She caught a few words and smiled as the woman promptly pulled out a larger fairy from a nearby case. Maggie shook her head, and pointed to her own purchase. The woman shrugged, placed the wrapped fairy in a small bag, and handed it over.

When she walked out of the shop, Reeve was nowhere in sight. She grinned. No doubt he was visiting his favorite tailor shop. Judging by the number of women he dated, the clothes must have been a success.

Rapid-fire French prevailed over a smattering of English and other languages. As she walked, she heard a low drumbeat start up somewhere close by. Uneasy but unsure why, she looked around, but saw no musicians. The somehow familiar beat grew steadily louder, and she felt chills run up her spine. She spun on her heel; the sound lessened a bit. Turning in her original direction, she began to discern voices chanting in no language she'd ever heard.

The sound rose as she walked a few steps. She spotted a young couple walking toward her. "Excuse me," she asked. "Do you speak English? Can you tell me where the musicians are, the ones playing the drums?"

Eyebrows raised, the couple looked at each other, then at Maggie. "No music here." Embarrassed and more confused, she walked on.

By now the voices pounded a definite rhythm in her head. Her heart beat right along with them. Frightened and feeling increasingly alarmed, she saw a small side street leading off to the right. She turned and walked down it, and the voices seemed to rise with joy.

She looked around her, but the crowds didn't seem to notice anything amiss.

The fine hairs on the back of her neck prickled as the deep voices rose and fell to the steady throb of drums. Shaking off her apprehension, Maggie strode down the side street. She was on a mission. She had to concentrate.

The shops here were far tinier than those she'd just left, and the narrow street was dark from age. Perhaps she'd find a bargain here, maybe even calligraphy for Beth's wall.

A large cloud swept across the sun, and the sky darkened. Maggie looked up, her sense of unease returning and deepening. As she walked farther down the cobblestone street, the chanting pulsated more strongly until it physically beat against her thin frame.

In near panic, she stopped and looked in every direction. Surely there *had* to be musicians. She saw no street players, but just across the street from where she stood was a small window hung with various quotations and poems in calligraphy. She breathed a sigh of relief. It was exactly what she wanted for Beth.

Determined, she crossed the street. As she walked up to the shop's window, the chanting abruptly cut off. For a moment, she scanned the street again, puzzled, but nothing was out of place.

She shook her head. *I must be hearing things now. It sounds sort of familiar ... like that weirdness in the cab on the way down here.*

She turned her attention to the shop window, impressed by the many styles of writing displayed in *Ancienne Écriture*. In the center of the display, brown velvet surrounded a lovely faded paper covered with delicate calligraphy. She leaned forward to try to make out a signature, but couldn't read the spidery old script. Next to it hung a long piece of papyrus brightly decorated with birds and plants.

Excited, she pushed open the door and entered to a soft chime. The shop smelled wonderful, the scent of old paper overlaid with perfume from the many candles scattered about. Maggie stood in the center and looked around.

One narrow wall was hung with more calligraphy samples, each covered in a protective plastic sheet. The wall to her left was divided into bookshelves, displaying what appeared to be hand-sewn books. She began to walk toward the books when she heard footsteps from the back of the shop.

"Hello! American, yes?" Walking through a narrow door behind the counter was a dark-skinned, heavyset man with a faint blue smudge on the side of his elegantly hooked beak.

"Yes, indeed. How could you tell?"

"The shoes. All Americans wear the Adidas. Where you live?"

"I'm from New York," she grinned. "You have a lovely shop here." Maggie walked toward the counter.

"Thank you. I am Achmed Kiyat. It is interesting, writing, yes?" He leaned both arms on the glass counter. "My daughter, she is visiting in New York. I am wanting her to come home to Paris. She is artist with calligraphy." His teeth flashed white as he smiled.

"Oh, really? Do you have some of her work here?"

"You already have seen it. You have seen the centerpiece in window outside? That is Fatima's most favorite piece. It is part of a letter written by Molière to his lover. Very rare indeed."

Maggie grinned, delighted. "Amazing. It even looks old. How did she manage that?"

"Eh, that is, how you say? Trick of trade. But look, you must see my favorite. It too is the romance. Fatima, she copied with perfection a letter from Napoleon to his Josephine." Achmed reached into the case and pulled out a book and a piece of parchment covered with strong, sloping script.

"And here, look. In this book, you see the original." He opened the book, flipped to the back, and turned it to face Maggie. "Even the signatures, they match! But see at bottom left, the little FK. Fatima, she put initials there so the world know it is fake. But good fake, yes?"

Maggie was fascinated. "That's incredible. She even dots her i's the same. She's really talented. I have to have this for my sister. She'll love it. How much?"

Placing a blue and black stained forefinger against his nose, he winked. "For you, two thousand francs."

Maggie pulled out her wallet and extracted her credit card. The shop owner rang up the sale, then laid several layers of tissue paper on the counter. He placed the letter on top and began to roll it into a protective tube when the shop door banged open behind her.

Achmed, hands poised to roll up the paper, glanced over Maggie's shoulder. His smile dropped briefly. Seeming to ignore whatever it was he saw, he reached under the counter. "You are so nice, I have souvenir for you," he said to Maggie. "You take to America, and remember Achmed to all your friends." His eyes flicked beyond her, then he picked up the paper, turned partly away from Maggie, and put something on top of the letter, expertly rolling it all into a neat tube.

Maggie caught a movement out of the corner of her eye and felt a sudden unease. She turned toward the door and saw an Arab in full white robes staring directly at her. In the brief second before she hurriedly turned back to Achmed, she noticed how his left eye bulged from his face.

Achmed handed Maggie her card and the tube, then frowned and leaned toward her. Confused, Maggie took a step back from the case. Then her ears rang as a gunshot tore through the shop.

Achmed's eyes went wide with surprise, and in horror, Maggie recognized the spreading red flower on his forehead as he slipped out of sight behind the counter. She felt a jolt run through her, like she'd grabbed a live wire.

Instinct kicked in, and she ran.

— CHAPTER TWO —

Maggie fled behind the counter and pushed through the bead-covered passage behind it. Leaping the legs of the fallen Achmed, she heard a guttural curse.

Hearing quick, running steps behind her, she picked up speed, knocking over a table in her path. Ink jars, pens, and assorted papers scattered as she spotted a door at the back of the workroom. To her enormous relief, it opened onto an alley.

She flew down the short alley and turned back onto the crowded Rue Biron. Frantically weaving in and out of clumps of people, she was grateful it was now the busy lunch hour. She ducked down a quieter street that angled sharply away, and flat out ran the short distance to the heavily crowded Rue Voltaire. As she slowed to a walk among a group of German tourists, she risked a look backward. No men in robes. She heaved a sigh and left the group only when they entered a large café.

Again she looked back, and to her horror saw the slim, robed Arab scanning the scene from less than a block away.

Instantly, she ducked into the first small shop she saw, realizing where she was only when she heard chirps and screeches from the many birds that lined the wall. She pretended to study one large white bird while keeping a close eye on the window for followers. No one stood out from the slow moving crowds—perhaps he had gone the other way up Rue Voltaire, toward Rue des Rosiers, the main thoroughfare.

The large bird made a strange, almost purring, noise and hopped close to the bars of the ornate cage. Still terrified, Maggie walked quickly around the cage, effectively putting it between herself and the window. The bird muttered, then clawed its way around on the perch until it faced her again.

"*Allo! Viens ici, coquette. Viens ici!*" it said in a surprisingly deep voice.

Relaxing slightly, Maggie smiled. "Hello, yourself. Sorry I don't speak French, but aren't you a beauty." She dabbed at the beads of sweat that had formed on her forehead.

The cage formed the centerpiece of the small shop. Built like a Chinese pagoda, the cage stood on a low table, its sloped green roof right above Maggie's head. The brass plaque read "*Le cacatoès Cocktail.*"

Still nervous, Maggie leaned around the cage. People paused in front of the window, but no one seemed interested in the shop. She blew out a breath, and the bird once again made its low purring noise. As she looked down at it, the bird extended his white head and bowed through the cage like a cat asking for a stroke. Obligingly, Maggie reached down and rubbed around its soft head as the bird trilled.

Immediately, she heard a spate of worried French from behind her. A small woman in a blue smock walked rapidly toward her, gesturing Maggie away from the cage. Understanding, Maggie moved backwards as the bird squawked a protest.

"I'm sorry, I shouldn't have touched him," she confessed. "He just looked so cute. It was hard to resist."

"Is never safe to touch odd bird! He bites, the bird." The small woman smiled. "He like you. He offer you the head! Only to me, he offers the head." The woman's expression softened. "Oh, yes, I am Syvlie."

Maggie offered her hand. "Hello, I'm Maggie. Wonderful shop you have here." She leaned around the cage, heart still pounding, and scanned the street. A child and several adults were looking at a display of parakeets in the window.

"Thank you. The family of my husband has this shop since the war."

The bird muttered again, and as Maggie looked down, he seemed to look her right in the eye before once again lowering his plumed head and extending it through the bars. She looked at Sylvie, who gave a Gallic shrug, hands in air, and said, "I warn, he bite."

Once again Maggie stroked the warm feathered head. The bird purred and pushed into her hand, turning his head sideways so she could reach the soft throat. Entranced, she scratched, keeping an eye on the large beak.

"*Henri, viens! Faut que tu voies ce'qui ce passe!*" the woman called softly. A much older man in a blue coverall that matched Sylvie's limped out the back of the shop and paused, eyes widening at the sight of Maggie still stroking the bird.

"My husband, he too must see. It's not normal, Cocktail!"

The man, filterless cigarette dangling from his lip, limped up to the cage. The bird whipped his head back into the cage and emitted a raucous "*Va t'en! Va t'en!*"

Sylvie grinned. "You see? He say 'Go away.'"

Her husband shook a fist and growled something in French, to which Sylvie laughed. "He say, one day Cocktail make good soup for the table!"

"No, no, no!" Maggie shook her head, then tentatively held a finger near the ornately tooled bars of the cage. Instantly came a guttural purr, and the white head rubbed gently against her fingernail.

On impulse, Maggie asked, "Do you ever ship birds to the States?"

A delighted grin spread across Sylvie's face. "With sureness. We deal with bird shops in Boston and New York. They send to us, and we to them. Normally one month the bird must rest in … quarantine?"

Maggie nodded to indicate she understood. Again she glanced at the window, then at Sylvie who didn't seem to notice anything wrong.

"But he has passport, so one week—only if you buy today. But, I have a word of caution. You realize for how long these birds may live?"

"No, I hadn't thought of that," Maggie responded.

"They may live until ninety years old. And Cocktail, he is already in his thirtieth year so he may well have sixty more. Is not a casual pet, you understand?"

Maggie's gaze drew inward. Sixty more years. That would be Beth's entire life, assuming … She didn't want to think farther than that, but tears rose to her eyes.

Then she shook herself. Life would be unbearable if she didn't remain optimistic.

The shop woman broke in on her thoughts. "You find bird in one week in New York or Boston, as you want."

Maggie thought quickly. Had the horror of what she'd just endured made her slip a mental cog? She'd never had a bird nor had anything to do with birds, much less a large exotic specimen like Cocktail. She could imagine that the care and upkeep of the creature would be an adventure in itself, and yet … Beth was alone so often.

No collection of porcelain or imaginary fairies could keep

her company, while Cocktail actually communicated. And he was such a loving bird. He'd be grand company and perhaps keep Beth's mind off the miserable side-effects of her treatments. And she owed him: it was possible he'd saved her life by giving her a place to hide.

As she eyed the bird, Maggie heard distant sirens. It was time to decide and to move.

I have to, for once, make a major purchase without over-thinking it, she told herself as she pulled out her credit card. The arrangements weren't as complicated as she thought: she signed several documents and was soon at the front door scanning the street carefully.

The lunch crowd had thinned somewhat. Maggie now spotted a taxi stand across the street. No men in robes were anywhere in sight. She walked quickly to the taxi stand, jumped in the first one, and requested the Hotel Régina.

Reeve was standing in his favorite tailor shop, Chez Alphonse, looking at a rack of silk bolts. One deep green pinstripe gave him pause, though it wasn't one of his preferred colors. The green was, however, the exact hue of Maggie's eyes—the color of late summer on the New Orleans bayou.

He fingered the silk and imagined she was that soft. She was everything he'd always wanted in a woman—something he only rarely admitted, and only then to himself.

She was beautiful, with those green eyes and her fine figure. She was also one of the most highly respected trouble-shooters at work, and he'd seen, when snooping in one of her photo albums, that she'd graduated magna cum laude from Columbia.

But, unlike most other women, she doesn't respond to me at all. I'm not that hard on the eyes. He turned slightly to view himself in a long mirror. *I've even caught her with a wary look when she doesn't think I see.*

I know she's not seeing anybody else, unless you count that artsy-fartsy guy who picked her up at work a few months back. That can't be her type, all bushy hair and teeth. Dude had no substance to him, either. Thin as a rail.

"*Ça y est?*" The tailor's voice broke into his thoughts.

He looked with longing at the green material, but instead he selected a stunning blue and his favorite deep wine. "Yes, I'll have one in this, and this." The tailor slung the bolts onto a bench and stood Reeve on a little platform before asking him to strip to his briefs.

Alphonse chatted steadily as he expertly ran a tape measure across Reeve's stomach and chest. Reeve stood motionless as the short, balding tailor moved the tape to his shoulders.

"M'sieu Reeve, I would not want you angry at me," he said with a smile.

"Why so?"

"Evidently, M'sieu is very good with karate. Look at these flat muscles on the shoulders. They show the sport every time."

Impressed with the man's powers of perception, Reeve looked at himself in the mirror. He certainly didn't have the thickened neck and heavy muscles of a body builder. His muscles were taut and flat, from his broad chest down to his narrow waist. Deep blue eyes, courtesy of a Frenchman several generations back, were set off by his dark, coffee-colored skin.

He frowned then tensed slightly, the feeling of deft hands running across his back teasing him, not unlike an overseas flight spent in close proximity to a desired woman who thought of him as a brother. Maggie's face rose softly in his mind, her dense black hair falling over one green eye as she leaned over his shoulder to point at his monitor.

Consciously, he relaxed—first one muscle, then another, using several techniques he'd studied for years. His breathing became slow and regular, and the tailor's voice faded.

He hardly noticed the man had stopped speaking, when a familiar sound intruded—that of approaching sirens. Many sirens. Though still deep in meditation, he felt a visceral unease. He leaned forward, and the tailor scolded him. But soon, the grumbling Alphonse himself was rushing to the front of the tiny shop, followed by his customer.

The sirens peaked, then fell silent. Reeve stood, undecided. Sirens weren't a rare thing in Paris—quite the contrary. However, Alphonse had all the measurements he needed and Reeve had already chosen his silks. There was no reason to wait around in the shop, and the hairs on the back of his neck were already tingling. Reeve saw people moving in a steady stream up Rue Paul Bert, and his feeling of discomfort increased. He might just have been overtired from the trip, but his faint twinge of dread intensified when he realized the stream of people was moving slightly faster in the direction of the last spot he'd seen Maggie. She'd been looking into a shop window at the corner of Rue des Rosiers and Rue Villa Biron, and the crowds were rushing toward that same area.

Suddenly, he made up his mind. With a quick word of apology to Alphonse, he handed the man his credit card and said that if he didn't hear from him, to please ship the shirts to his home address. He waited impatiently while the tailor processed the card and talked about crime in the neighborhood and the cost of doing business in such a populated spot. Reeve grew more nervous, and when the tailor finally gave him back his card, he nearly ran out of the shop.

He quickly covered the two short blocks back to Rue Des Rosiers, looking toward the café on the far corner. No shaggy black hair. He glanced at his watch and saw he was fifteen minutes early. He sighed and walked toward the Marché Biron, where he'd last seen Maggie in the porcelain shop. As he drew nearer, the crowds grew thicker, and people were murmuring as he pushed through. Just as he was within sight of the porcelain shop, he saw flashing lights down a small street to the left. He stopped for a moment and took a deep breath.

Policemen had formed a barricade in front of what he realized, to his horror, was a small art shop, its window filled with calligraphy and hieroglyphics—exactly the type of shop Maggie had been hunting.

The crowd collectively gasped as paramedics carried a still form covered in a sheet out the door. Reeve pushed himself frantically through the tight bodies, but as he reached the front, a policeman roughly pushed him backwards.

"Excuse me. Can you tell me who has been hurt?" Reeve asked.

"Not your business, M'sieu. Now please stand back." The policeman already had lost interest in Reeve and was scanning the rest of the crowd alertly.

"It's just that I was supposed to meet my girlfriend here, and she's very late," he improvised.

The dark face softened. "M'sieu, it's not a woman. I'm sure your friend will be fine."

Reeve thanked him and walked the short distance back to the café, making his way through the throng of gawkers. He sat and ordered a pastis, and wondered why the sirens had worried him so much. Grandmère Amelie would tell him to respect his senses and take much care. The old Cajun had a highly developed sixth sense with which she'd often impressed Reeve when he was a child back in New Orleans.

His thoughts shifted to her jambalaya, a thing of wonder. It took twenty-four hours to "build," as she'd say. The results were an ever-changing mix of chicken, sausage, seafood, and hot spices. Reeve licked his lips at the thought and realized his glass was nearly empty.

Maggie was already twenty minutes late and still had not arrived. Reeve's misgivings returned, and he made his way swiftly to a pay phone inside the café. The phone rang with the peculiar French double drone, and he declined to leave a message when Maggie didn't respond.

For a moment he paused, indecisive. Should he wait longer, or follow Grandmère Amelie's dictate and act? He ran a nervous hand over his short, tightly curled black hair and headed toward the street. He'd hail a taxi and go back to the Hotel Régina. At most, Maggie would realize she'd missed him and take a cab back later.

Sighing heavily, he held an arm up and whistled.

A slim, dark man in a well-tailored business suit stared up at the enormous gilded statue of Joan of Arc. Slowly, he stepped away as if to get a better view of the flag-bearing warrior, while his concentration on the Régina never waned. He slipped his cuff over a thin gold watch, and pursed his lips. Reaching into his leather satchel, he searched until he found his compact camcorder. As he closed the satchel, he noticed a corner of white robe hanging out and hastily shoved it back in.

"Masood! I am here." Masood jumped slightly, then relaxed as his brother strode carefully across the busy square. "Sorry I was so long, but the traffic on the Champs ... pah!"

"Ebbi," he said, "I was beginning to wonder. And I have so many questions ..."

"Not now," Ebbi replied, taking the camcorder. "For now, we play the tourist. Look now at Louvre." Taking the lens cover off, Ebbi aimed the device at the stately stone museum across the way and pretended to film with enthusiasm. Masood helpfully pointed out details with one hand.

His heavy brows knitted together over nearly black eyes—

Masood simply couldn't wait. "I have to know, my brother. Why did the girl shoot Achmed? To steal it?"

"I do not believe she killed him, but I am nearly certain it is in her possession. Others entered after you passed to the rear. One had a bad eye … something wrong with his eye." Ebbi panned the camera across the busy intersection.

"I do not understand this, Ebrahim," he exclaimed. "Yesterday I am studying in peace at the Sorbonne. Today brings gunshots and the death of very close friend." His voice cracked with emotion.

Transferring the camera to one hand, Ebbi threw an arm around his young brother and drew him close. "Myself, I am not clear about why this has happened. But we must keep our heads sharp. I will contact the Council—and soon. But all will be well. You have my word."

"All isn't well for Achmed Kiyat," Masood said, near tears. "And who will tell Fatima? Oh Ebbi, remember that summer they came to Badu Tanar, and she pushed me in the water?"

"Of course. But we cannot permit ourselves to think about Achmed now. I am sure Father will inform Fatima. For now, we have a job to do."

"I feel you know much more than you are telling me …"

"That may be. It is not the time for you yet—you are still in school. For now, we do as directed." While talking, he turned on one heel and appeared to be aiming the camera up at the large horse. In truth, he was scanning the windows of the elegant hotel, paying attention to those at the top of the building, surrounded by whimsical domes.

"Masood, she's on the top. I heard her request her key. She should be second room from the corner, if I counted correctly. Ah! Look," he pointed. "She just passed in front of the window. And again. Oh, she is looking!"

He slowly panned to the base of the horse, then once again turned toward the Louvre. "That is unfortunate. She may have seen us. I believe we should wear our robes soon. You go to that little café just off the Rue de Rivoli and put yours on. I'll wait, she may leave. You have your phone if we get separated."

Masood, slightly pale beneath his dark olive complexion, reached into the satchel and extracted a bundled-up robe. "I am very much not liking this, Brother, and I hope you are here when I return." He waited for a pause in the traffic circling the island where he stood, then walked quickly across the street.

Maggie paced. She felt an unfamiliar, bone-deep shaking, and the only way to keep it at bay was to stay moving—from the bathroom, to the front of the double bed, as far as she could, until the deeply slanted roof met the cloth covered walls, and she turned back again. She was wearing a pattern into the carpet.

Over and over, she saw the hole appear in that poor man's head, and herself running out the cluttered back of the shop into the marketplace. The shaking grew worse with each visualization, and her breath was coming in ragged gasps as she turned one last time toward the bathroom. She caught sight of herself in the mirror and was horrified: her green eyes were sunken, her face so pale her freckles stood out like tiny bruises. Suddenly, her stomach lurched—she made it to the toilet just in time.

After being thoroughly sick, she eased her way slowly back into the bedroom and rummaged through the small bar.

She sat herself in one of the low chairs near the window and began sipping a ginger ale, when a sharp knock startled her. She stood, wary, and moved lightly across the deep carpeting. The knock came again, followed by Reeve's voice calling. "Mags? Are you there?"

She let him in, moved back to the bed, and sat heavily.

"Maggie, are you okay?" he asked, crossing to her.

Speechless, she burst into tears.

Reeve was stunned. In the four years they'd worked and traveled together, he'd never seen her cry—not even when her sister was undergoing another treatment. She never let her emotions show. Horrified, he sat on the bed and gathered her into his arms.

"Okay, now, it's going to be alright, but you need to tell me what happened, girl."

Maggie burrowed into his chest and simply let go. Between sobs, she told him about the shop and its owner.

"And he talked about his daughter in America, how she did much of the calligraphy and writing for him, and how proud he was of her!" She sniffled. "Oh Reeve, it just isn't possible. One minute we're discussing calligraphy and the next ... bam! It blew him backwards into a glass case. There was blood ... so much blood!"

Reeve stiffened, then consciously relaxed. "Mags. Did you see who did it?"

"Yes! I heard the door slam open ... and I turned ... and it was an Arab, Reeve, white robe and dark skin. Something was wrong with his left eye; it was swollen, all bugged out, like that." She demonstrated, cupping one hand beneath her eye.

"I looked him right in the eyes!" she continued. "I saw something in his hand but I, I didn't know ... maybe if I'd known, but I didn't! Then Achmed, the owner, was saying something about a gift he wanted me to have. What a wonderful man ... It just isn't right!" She stopped to catch her breath, tears flowing.

"Sweetie, the important thing is, are you hurt?"

"No, no." She went to the bathroom for a tissue. "But Reeve, I never ran that fast in my life."

27

"Are you sure you weren't followed?" Anxiously, he rose and strode to the window, bending over to look out.

"No. I ran into a shop and bought a bird for Beth, but that isn't important now." She blew her nose and took in a deep, steadying breath. "I feel better now that I'm not alone. I'm so glad you're here."

Reeve turned from the window, sat down beside her, and wrapped her in a tight hug. For a moment, Maggie felt a deep internal spark, quickly squashing it with determination.

"I should at least check out the gift Achmed gave me. Giving it to me was the last thing he ever did." Gently, she untangled herself from Reeve's arms, oblivious to the faint regret passing over his classic features.

She sat on the bed, found her travel case with its laptop in one side, and began rummaging through it. She found the tightly rolled up paper, laid it out, and stared.

"This must be it. What on earth?" On top of Napoleon's letter lay a piece of rolled-up leather tied together. She untied it and held it up.

To her uneducated eye, the scroll looked ancient—but it could have been a "trick of the trade," as Achmed had pointed-ed out. The writing was on a rough leather-like surface that had turned a mottled cream with age. Here and there, portions were missing or simply blackened. The writing was unfamiliar to her, like a series of straight marks jagged across the page. She ran a hand over its old softness, wondering.

"Well, his daughter really is good. Looks like hieroglyphics to me, and check out how old it seems to be," Reeve noted.

"I'm not sure. Beth is really into this, and I'm thinking this might be some ornate kind of Arabic ... no, you've got to be right. Oh, I don't believe this has happened!" She pressed her hand to her head. "I feel sick about the whole thing."

"I'm sorry it ended like that, but I think you should go on and give that letter to Beth," Reeve said. "Minus the story."

Maggie shuddered. "I certainly won't tell her about poor Achmed. But I don't know how I'm going to ever sleep again. I can't stop thinking about it."

He reached out and gently touched her cheek. "I know it's awful but you'll get past it. You really will. You have so much else on your plate, girl. Once we get home this will be a blip on the horizon."

"I hope you're right." She wiped away a tear. "Wait!" she exclaimed. "You haven't seen the Napoleon letter. Check it out." She handed it to him.

Reeve went silent for a time as he read the French, lips moving. "Oh, it's a love letter. How pretty."

"See the bottom right corner? The little 'FK'? Those are Fatima Kiyat's initials. Evidently, she's so good that her work can be taken for real. Oh Reeve, she's going to be heartbroken to find out about her father."

"Try not to think about it, sweetie." Reeve handed the letter back. "Wonder if she ever thought of counterfeiting for a living."

"Only you," Maggie said as she carefully re-rolled the old leather, tied the laces around it, then placed it on the tissue paper. "Don't you think we should contact the authorities?"

"Listen, when in a foreign country, my motto is 'Don't get involved.' You don't know what was going on in there. And I have a really bad tingle about the whole thing."

Maggie stood, padded to the window, and stooped. "Listen, it's getting dark. We should consider ..." Her voice trailed off. "Oh no. Reeve. He's here!"

"Who's here?"

Her face turned stark white. "The guy from the shop! Walking into the Régina right now!"

Reeve was in motion faster than Maggie thought possible.

"Get a move on. We're leaving. Now! Got your passport? Good. At least we haven't unpacked much."

Maggie backed away from the window and was once again shaking. Reeve gently took her by the shoulders. "Come on, we need to get the hell out of here now. We're going home."

The word "home" did what nothing else could, and Maggie was suddenly rushing across the room after Reeve. They opened the door, and after Reeve checked quickly, fled down the hall. He pulled her past the elevator to the glowing "*Sortie*" sign.

They opened the door onto a dark set of steps and ran down all six flights. Maggie was slightly out of breath as they emerged into a short corridor. At one end, a glass door led back into the lobby. At the other, a heavier door appeared to open onto the street.

Reeve pushed past her and shoved the door open. They emerged into the soft sunset of a Parisian summer night. Lights were coming on down the arcade-like walkway on the Rue de Rivoli, and they briskly walked several blocks to the Metro.

Reeve purchased two tickets, and consulting a lit map on the wall, led Maggie to the proper train. Once seated, Maggie wiped her damp forehead.

"This isn't happening. You need to tell me this isn't happening."

"I don't have a clue what's going on, but one thing is for sure: we are out of here. We're going straight to Charles DeGaulle and hopping the next flight home."

"What about our luggage? The hotel? My God, the job?"

"The hotel is on the corporate account, and we'll have the luggage shipped. It's all going to work out. I'll talk to Todd when we get back. He can send another team. It's not life and death for them."

Maggie relaxed, but still watched each face as passengers got on and off the train.

Their luggage sat in the hotel hall, tags hanging, address side up.

— CHAPTER THREE —

THURSDAY, JULY 16

A day later, Maggie was sitting at her small kitchen table
sipping coffee. Still in her robe and giant puppy dog slippers, she leaned back and stared at the leaden New York sky.
If not for the souvenirs she'd brought back, she'd have
thought the entire trip had never happened.

At least she had several unique gifts for Beth. The Napoleon letter would delight her, and Beth's French was excellent. Then a thought struck. Beth would surely ask what the
piece of leather meant. It should be translated. She smiled
and stood. It would just take a moment to scan the artwork,
and then she could send it to an old professor at Columbia
who specialized in Eastern languages. Maggie had transferred to Columbia from Vanderbilt for her senior year.

Professor Royce Stevens had done the impossible: he'd
developed in Maggie a love of history, a subject she'd

previously only tolerated out of necessity. He taught a class on Ancient Egypt, which she'd taken merely for the credits. Eventually she found the subject matter fascinating, as taught by the short, hyperactively thin Stevens, who brought flair and high energy to the subject.

Unfortunately for Maggie, Ancient Civ had been at eight a.m.—not her best hour. Professor Royce, bounding from blackboard to lectern, would note her drooping eyes there in the first row. He'd make a point by slapping the lectern just to enjoy her startled face.

He had done it so many times that Maggie, bent on revenge, brought an enormous dictionary to class one day. She waited patiently until Professor Royce was facing the chalkboard, then slammed it loudly onto the desk.

He jumped, then said without looking back, "Purcell, I knew you were up to something."

After that, Maggie joined his study group, mostly grad students, and was invited on field trips, including a trip to examine a mummy found in the Valley of the Queens.

She took another class from him her final semester, and the friendship was sealed when he invited her to his son's graduation. There, Maggie met his elegant, if prudish, wife Marie. She'd had to stifle a grin when she was introduced to the well-dressed older woman with her designer bag and matching shoes. Quite a difference from Professor Royce and his plaid jackets with the worn-away elbows.

Now, she eagerly expected that Professor Royce could translate the piece—or at least know someone who could.

She walked the few steps to her computer desk in the dining room. Before sitting, she sipped her coffee and stared at the picture hung just over her monitor. A favorite piece of her own artwork, it pictured an enormous tree with gnarled branches and a man's body growing out of the trunk. His outstretched arms grew into two branches, and his barely visible head was crowned with leaves. His legs stretched downwards into roots that snaked toward a city at the bottom of the painting. In the city, a silver dome dominated over warm, Mediterranean plaster walls.

The man's head was thrown back in ecstasy—or pain, Maggie was never sure which, although she'd painted it herself. Some days she saw a powerful man stretching in bliss, perhaps after a bout of satisfying sex. On other darker mornings, she saw a man being tortured on the rack of the living tree.

Today, she thought perhaps he just had gas pains.

Maggie had been painting since she was small. During the time when her parents fought almost nightly, artwork was a form of release. As she grew older, it became a way for her to calm down after a lousy day of work, or just to relax and lose herself in creation.

When she was at Vanderbilt, she'd learned how to build wire frames and add plaster for a unique look. Somehow it was even more satisfying to smooth layers of plaster into place, then carefully paint the entire creation.

She grinned, turned back to the computer and caught a glimpse of her dusty work table from the corner of her eye. Before she'd had to pack for Paris, she'd only had time to mix the plaster and mold it to the frame, then fix the whole thing to a prepared canvas. *Soon I'll find the time to paint it*, she had promised herself with delight. Painting was her favorite hobby—her only one, actually.

She busied herself with the scanning. The image came out fairly dark but the first few sets of characters were at least legible. She attached the image to an email and sent it to Royce at Columbia, along with a brief explanation.

Then, with a pang of guilt, she called Xcorp and explained that she and Reeve were no longer in Paris. Todd, her boss, cut in before she could explain further.

"Yes, Reeve informed me that once again, you have family problems. We sent Andy and Jee, but I don't need to tell you, they weren't my first choice."

"Wait just a minute. Reeve must not have told you the whole thing. My life was threatened in Paris—I inadvertently witnessed a murder, and the killers actually came after me."

"You're kidding. What the hell were you up to over there?"

"I was shopping for my little sister at the time."

"Why the hell didn't Reeve tell me that?" Todd's voice sounded peeved.

"I guess he figured the part about my sister would be sufficient," Maggie said dryly, suppressing a much nastier response. "In fact, I need to request a few personal days this—"

"You don't have any more personal days," he interrupted. He blew out a loud breath into the phone. "Just take until Monday, but you'd best be here for the Monday meeting." Abruptly, he hung up.

Maggie sucked in a deep breath and considered calling Reeve, though he'd surely still be asleep. She decided to go ahead and fly to Nashville. She had the impression from the call she'd made in Paris that all was not well at home. She had to visit and ensure Beth's well-being, no matter Todd's attitude at work.

As she was stepping out of the shower, the phone rang. Reeve's sexy deep voice, sounding exhausted, told her he'd called the Régina and arranged for their luggage to be shipped.

"And you called Xcorp already! What did you do, leave a message on Todd's machine last night?"

"Hey, I'm nothing if not efficient. I only told him about Beth, I figured if you wanted him to know the nitty-gritty you could tell him yourself."

Maggie sighed. "Todd's sick of excuses about Beth. I went ahead and told him the truth." She nibbled a nail. "He's giving me grief about missing so much work. Speaking of Beth, I hope she's not going to be sicker, now that we used her as an excuse …"

"Not a chance. In fact she's going to be a happy young lady. Hey, she's got herself a new fairy and a romantic letter. And wait till she sees your cool leather scribble!"

Maggie laughed as she packed a bag, phone clenched between her ear and shoulder. "Whatever it is, I sent a scan of it to my old professor at Columbia. I didn't want Beth up for days trying to translate the thing."

"Why's that kid so into languages? She's only twelve."

"She's one of those rare people who instantly picks up new languages. Plus, she loves studying how people express themselves. When she was little, Mom used to take her to the beauty salon. The woman who did Mom's hair was Mexican. Beth was fascinated by her accent, and got the woman to teach her Spanish. At six years old, Reeve! Mom got her a Spanish primer—this kid who was just learning to read English."

"She really is something of a genius, isn't she?"

"Without a doubt," Maggie said. "Now that she's sick so often, she tells me she escapes through reading websites in different languages. She says to understand a people, you need to read about them in their own lingo. Pretty deep for twelve years old, wouldn't you say?"

"Incredible. Just incredible. So now you're off to Nashville? Did the Todd God actually give you some time?"

"Unwillingly. He made sure to tell me I'm out of personal days." She took a deep breath, hoping Reeve wouldn't pick up on the stress in her voice. "I'll spend tomorrow and the weekend there and be back Sunday night. Can't miss that sacred Monday meeting."

"No, you better not," Reeve said. "Have a good flight. Better you than me. Me, I'm back to bed for the day."

Maggie hung up and made one last call to her travel agent. There was an early afternoon flight to Nashville and she promptly booked it.

She was glad she'd left herself sufficient time to get to the airport, as the gray skies produced a steady rain. Steam came up off the streets as they drove out of Manhattan, and Maggie wrinkled her nose. The clear air of Nashville would be a treat.

She leaned back and closed her eyes, still feeling disoriented from the jet lag. As the cab turned onto the expressway, the sound of rain tapping on the roof was nearly hypnotic. Traffic was miserable and horns blared, but to Maggie, everything seemed distant.

As the taxi crept through the dense traffic, she tried to relax. With so much on her mind, her neck muscles felt as taut as strings on a violin. She reached back and gently massaged the tight knots, her mind insistently recalling the conversation with Todd.

She had the sinking feeling that he'd start requiring her to come to the office every day, instead of allowing her the freedom of working from home.

And that would make life almost impossible. What if Mom slipped farther into the bottle? Maggie knew Anna loved her youngest daughter. *But Mom is weak. She doesn't always have her priorities straight.*

It was absolutely vital that Maggie have the freedom to fly to Nashville whenever she was needed. The only thing that seemed to keep her mother in check were her visits—those and the actual checks she wrote every month. Anna Purcell's income was nowhere near enough to provide for herself and Beth, especially when she had to maintain both the house and her affected lifestyle with the Afternoon Annies. Just the thought of the perfectly-coiffed group of Southern biddies was enough to give Maggie a pounding headache.

The taxi braked for a light, and its rough, idling engine was so loud it practically rattled inside with her head. She moved her hand to her temple and began lightly stroking it.

Ah, the relief.

She felt the tension drain from her neck as her headache receded, leaving the faint rumble from the taxi's engine. Drowsily, she noted that it sounded almost like an off-beat drum. But little by little, she became aware that she was indeed hearing a steady rhythm. Several drums beat in a familiar pattern that alarmed her, and then the chanting began.

The voices chanted faster and swelled until she felt them in her bones.

With a small cry she jerked herself to full wakefulness. The cab driver gave her a nervous glance over his shoulder.

Great. I've alarmed a New York cabbie.

Embarrassed, she sat up in her seat and ran a hand through her hair. Then a screech, several enraged honks, and a loud bang behind the cab had her twisting around, startled.

She saw that a large truck had jackknifed across the expressway behind her cab. Several other cars had plowed into it, and one vehicle was pinned halfway under it. She gasped, and her cab driver muttered something under his breath.

Maggie rubbed her eyes, wondering. The odd chanting she'd first heard in Paris was becoming increasingly frightening. She was sure she'd read somewhere that hearing a rhythmic sound like that could be a sign of grave illness, maybe even a brain tumor. The thought sent a chill down her spine.

She didn't feel sick, however. She never even got colds.

Other than exhaustion and nerves—nothing new to Maggie—she felt like her usual self. *All the same*, she thought, *if I hear those voices again, it'll be time for a doctor's appointment.*

Her pulse accelerated. What if something was really wrong? Who would take care of Beth?

She took a deep breath and pulled herself together. *No reason to panic. Just overtired from so much travel in such a short time—that has to be it ... has to be.*

Forty-five minutes later, they pulled into LaGuardia, and Maggie grabbed her carry-on and made her way into the airport.

Stalled behind the wreck, Masood and Ebbi were incredulous.

"This is an amazing country!" Masood said, straining to see through the windshield. "Look at size of that truck. It covers the road entirely. Can you believe it?"

"Yes, I can. I am only glad we are not under the thing." Ebbi was nervous, hands clenched on the steering wheel of their rented Toyota. "I suppose we will not catch her now. It would take a miracle."

"We are taught miracles happen, Brother. Forward, I say!"

They were forced to admit defeat when nearly an hour passed before the truck cleared the highway. Masood took advantage of the down time to grill his brother.

"Ebrahim, I believe it's time you inform me of our real duty in this. I have seen guns, chased a woman halfway across world, and I am now missing exams at Sorbonne. Uni exams are impossible to make up. I believe you have something to explain to me."

Ebbi tensed. This wasn't the way his brother should learn of these things. There were no elders, no ceremony, no brightly lit tents filled with luscious foods. Nothing but this cursed traffic jam of outraged Americans, each glued to their horns like old men pounding a table in hunger.

"Masood, the Council has given me permission to tell you of things you would not normally know for several years. You must promise to me not to ask details."

Masood inclined his head, his eyes never leaving his brother. "I will not ask, my brother."

Ebbi continued in his native Amharic. "How much do you recall of the early days of the Sons of Light?"

Masood leaned his head back, closed his eyes, then responded in the same language. "Chased by the Romans, we carried the writings to Qumran and protected them near the Dead Sea. But the group was divided in thought. Some did not believe in marriage or women, so several of our ancestors decided to part and practice on their own in peace. As they prepared to go, Romans attacked Qumran and killed most of us. Those remaining escaped into Africa, and we lost several more.

"Always, we knew if we were found, it meant giving up the location of the scrolls. Finally, we landed in Badu Tanar, in what is now Ethiopia, where the thirteenth tribe took us in. We established the Sons of Light enclave, thanks to their generosity."

"Very good," Ebbi responded. "However, other members of that brave final group went elsewhere. Safety lay in them scattering to save that which they carried. Unfortunately, we lost touch. Through the years, we have watched everywhere for signs of our people. That is why we encourage the young to leave and live elsewhere, so that Sons of Light shall never be broken nor forced to run again. Never starve ... Above all, never lose family." Ebbi was rigid behind the wheel, his eyes staring straight ahead.

"What you do not know," he continued, "is we are everywhere. We are in police service throughout the world. Always, we protect Badu Tanar's location. Always, we search for scrolls and the Chosen."

Masood silently visualized his people running, seeing their terror as the Romans slashed and killed. As the pictures of horror faded, he remembered his boyhood in the tribe: the laughter, the games, the trips through the flatlands stalking the ebok. Then, in more recent days, studying and living in the grand old city of Paris.

He thought for a moment. "So, you believe the shopkeeper was part of the tribe that split off?"

"No."

"He must have come by a ..."

"Enough!" Ebbi was angry. A spot of color appeared on his high cheekbones. His cheeks sunk under his proudly arched nose, and for a moment he frightened his brother. "We are finished. You now know more than is safe. You must never breathe word of these things. It threatens the tribe's existence."

Masood nervously bobbed his head. Knowledge was a great burden, and this ... this would take time to assimilate. He frowned. "Ebrahim, I must ask. Why do we not surround the woman with tribesmen and take what is ours?"

"Our duty is not to take—do you not see this? Our duty is to find. What is our credo? 'Seek and protect.' The world is harsh, Masood. It would take with greed. It would destroy. That is the way things are. That is why we go into the world to learn its ways and learn yet we always return to Badu Tanar—to privacy, secrecy, and safety."

Masood shook his head slowly. A feeling of uncertainty welled in his chest. So much was unclear, and he felt shaken from his foundations. How he privately wished to give up this unasked duty of watching the unknown woman. He wanted to go home.

He looked away from his brother, lest his eyes give away

his discomfort and misery. Badu Tanar. The mystical Tississat Falls, and all the mornings he'd sneak down to the pool below.

The power of the great falls caused clouds of fog in the early morning, and he could almost believe that mythical creatures were descending to drink. But the rarest of all creatures in the region was no myth: the leopard. It was said that he who saw the leopard would enjoy great enlightenment and wisdom. The only person in the tribe ever to have seen one was his grandfather, the wisest man he knew.

But he was far from Badu Tanar. He had so many more questions about the current assignment they were on, but they'd have to wait. He reached into the backseat of the Toyota and withdrew the camcorder, turned it to VCR mode, then rewound until he saw the gilded Joan of Arc. He went frame by frame until he saw the woman crossing to the window, then he hit the pause button. He studied the distant face under its dark gleaming hair. Always another question. Was it the woman they were to protect? Or that which she carried?

Beth Purcell lay across her bed, the nausea rolling through her in waves. *Won't get sick, can't get sick, won't get sick*, the mantra Maggie would always chant with her—oh, how she missed Maggie. She looked out her window, trying to project herself into the soft Nashville summer afternoon. The sounds of the cicadas' monotonous wail echoed through her shaky stomach, and she turned her attention to the always-safe writing on her ceiling.

Lovingly, her eyes caressed the careful markings made so many years before. She could almost see the people drawing their brushes over the papyrus, creating the hieroglyphics. The ancients showed such artistry in communication.

Everything communicates in its own way, she believed.

Her cracked lips parted in a small smile as she thought of human language, birds chirping, even plants spreading their spores. She'd always loved language in its many forms. Often, she'd pull her laptop on its mechanical arm—adoringly installed by Reeve, over her bed—and surf websites in various tongues. The always active brain inside the thin, wasted body delighted in finding similarities in languages, then running the pages through a translator to see how close her guess had actually been.

Anna Purcell knocked softly, then entered the frilly blue bedroom.

"Honey, how are you feeling? I brought you some sweet tea." Anna's thin face was an older mirror of her youngest child. Bloodshot eyes regarded Beth warily as she set the beaded glass on a small table near the bed.

"Oh, I'll be fine. Thanks Mom, I think I'll wait a bit to have a sip though." Through the roiling nausea, Beth scanned her mother's face. She noted the flushed cheek color and sucked in her breath. Those red spots high on Mom's cheekbones signaled that she'd had several stiff Scotches.

"We're going to have to get some Ensure down you, later. Have to be strong for Maggie! She should be here soon." Anna reached down, fluffing the pillow behind Beth's head.

"Who should be here soon?" Maggie grinned as she walked in the door.

"Maggie!" Beth struggled to sit up. Maggie crossed rapidly to the bed and hugged her.

"Hi, sweetie. How are you doing? Wait till you see what I brought you this time!"

Beth buried her face in her sister's shoulder, inhaling the familiar scent of clean hair and soap. Something inside her relaxed—it always did when Maggie was home. She exhaled heavily.

Anna Purcell heard the small sound, looked at her

daughters entwined on the bed, and left the room quietly.

Maggie whispered, "So how is she?"

"She's—she's okay, Mags," said Beth, gazing at her lap.

Maggie sat next to her on the bed. "You don't sound sure of that."

"Really, we're doing fine here. I don't want to make you worry or anything."

Maggie reached out and lifted Beth's chin until she was looking her in the eye. "I get the feeling you're not telling me something."

"Okay, but it's no biggie, Mags. The other night, I went to the kitchen for a glass of water, and it was so hot, it felt like an oven. I looked at the stove, and the back left burner was glowing bright red, right next to the spice rack! Mom had left the back burner on all night long. I wouldn't say anything, but Mags, sometimes I can't walk." She blushed with shame.

"Oh my God," Maggie said, lips pressed tightly together.

"Promise you won't say anything, Mags! She'll know I told you and—"

"I should just let her burn the house down? And you in it?"

"I told her at breakfast and she looked scared to death. She won't do it again. She just wasn't thinking."

"And she wasn't thinking when she didn't take you to your chemo, either?"

Beth didn't answer for a moment, her thin hands fidgeting with the comforter. "She just can't stand to see it," she burst out. "It's hard for her, Mags!"

Maggie's heart clenched. At twelve, her sister Beth had so much wisdom and grace, but she was so desperately ill. Her pale blue eyes looked warm under the straggling wisps of blonde hair, mostly gone now. Fine bones showed through her pasty white complexion. Maggie loved her fiercely and felt such guilt at having to leave her with the weak woman

44

their mother had become, now frequently drowning her stress in a sea of extremely expensive single-malt Scotch.

"We'll discuss this later. For now, look at this." Maggie rummaged in her purse and extracted the neatly-wrapped box. Beth took it and gave it a gentle shake. "No, you don't want to shake it!" she laughed.

Beth carefully undid the pale blue paper—the delicate fairy appeared, with gossamer yellow wings stretched behind her. She faced forward, masses of long, curly blond hair surrounding her tiny face and bright blue eyes. Beth gasped and hugged the tiny figurine to her chest.

"Oh Mags. She looks like my Zata fairy!" She studied it closely, turning it over and over. "It also kinda doesn't look like a fairy at all."

"That isn't all, either. Wait until you see this." Maggie took the tube, turned her back to her sister, and extracted the Napoleon letter.

Beth took it and gasped. "Mags! Does that say 'Napoleon' at the bottom? You never should have done this—it must have cost the entire earth! And look, it's to Josephine. *'Je t'aime.'* Oh, it's a love letter!"

Maggie grinned. "Not exactly by Napoleon himself, though. The shop owner's daughter was the artist, but it looks just like the real thing. I have one last thing to show you— something he gave me before … well, something he gave me. Look."

She plucked the scroll out of her purse, turned her back to Beth, and unrolled it slowly to present it with the greatest possible drama.

Beth reached up and pulled the string attached to her miniblinds. The sun, bright and low, shone directly on Maggie's face.

"Maggie, can you bring it just a hair closer?" Illness forgotten for the moment, Beth reached for her digital camera and took several fast shots of the piece. The flash half-blinded Maggie and she blinked, then laughed.

"Warn me next time you're going to do that!"

"Wow, Mags! Check out the fairies! Zata and Zaddie are dancing all around that thing. Wow!" Beth glowed. "You *have* to be able to see them. They're twirling right near your hands."

Maggie grinned and angled the leather so Beth could better see it. As she did, a thin beam of sunlight briefly pierced the Levalour blinds, illuminating the scroll with thin stripes of light. The old leather glowed in the light, the black characters floating across it.

Stunned, Maggie stared. In the dim glow, she could almost believe she saw two small figures flitting about the old scroll.

Beth erupted into a hoot of laughter. "Maggie! Look, they're holding hands. They must really be happy with this scroll. This time you have to see them."

Maggie quickly replied that she saw nothing but sunshine through the blinds. *Only one fairy nut per household.* Then she looked down at her own two hands holding the scroll. That's all she'd seen—her own two fists.

The sound of Beth's door opening surprised Maggie, and she quickly rolled up the scroll and popped it back into her purse. Anna walked into the silence and stopped, looking from one girl to the other.

Maggie stood and embraced the older woman, saying she needed to complete a bit of work and was going to fetch her laptop out of the rental car. Anna Purcell nodded and followed her from the room.

Feeling knots of tight muscles in her shoulders, Maggie was glad to escape the house and walk into Nashville's gentle late afternoon. Soon, she'd have to confront Anna about the burner, but not yet.

She stood for a moment, drinking in her childhood home.

The crickets were just starting their evening chorale and she relaxed to the familiar sound.

The weeping willow she and Beth had found for Mother's Day some ten years back now reached from the curved crushed-rock drive all the way to Beth's window. Around it, Anna had set ornamental white rocks. Last year Anna had placed a short white fence around the beautiful tree, and the year before that, she'd had a small bench built just under the green canopy. Maggie sighed. Still, the tree remained and grew, its lovely green fronds hanging nearly to the ground.

Planted by Maggie and Beth's father, roses climbed next to the large front door. Maggie frowned at the windblown red blossoms partially eaten away by bugs. Evidently no one had used the special rose spray insisted upon by her father. Growing things required help, he'd insisted. Provide a loving, healthy atmosphere, and they couldn't help but flourish.

Maggie heaved a sigh. Even with a healthy atmosphere, Beth certainly hadn't flourished. Along with Anna's constant carping over Dad's failed career as a musician, Beth's illness had undoubtedly served in pushing their father from his family. She didn't care to reflect on how he'd escaped from so many plans gone wrong. He'd taken the easy way out.

Maggie inhaled deeply, the crisp scent of pine helping to clear her head. She strode to the small car and retrieved her laptop from the front seat.

Back in the house, she placed the computer on the kitchen table and set to work searching for Home Health agencies in Nashville. Anna stood behind her at the counter and leaned forward, cheeks glowing a hectic red.

"Maggie, I've been thinking. Wouldn't it be a wonderful thing if we had a pool for little Beth? Think of the exercise she could get."

Maggie raised her head to regard her mother before speaking. Finally, she responded in measured tones, "Mom,

Beth doesn't care for water. She's so weak I'd be afraid she'd get in and not be able to get back out on her own."

"Oh, but you know I'm always here to watch out for her!" Anna grinned, pleading.

Before Maggie could stop herself, it was out. "Mom, remember the new sunroom, not even two years ago? *I'm* still paying that one off. Come on, you have to admit ..."

"I don't have to admit anything! It's me here with Beth all day. The room provides her so much pleasure. She uses it all the time ..."

Maggie raised an eyebrow. "Yes, as long as it isn't time for the Afternoon Annies to make an appearance."

Anna jerked backward. "And what is that supposed to mean? Do you begrudge me that small pleasure, after what I go through on a daily basis? Would you prefer I lock myself into this house permanently and have no joy at all? I suppose you would ... you who's almost never here."

Maggie swallowed her fury. Now wasn't the time. She needed Anna amenable to the idea of a health care worker. "Yes, I've been thinking about that, and I might have an idea that will work all the way around. I've been thinking of hiring home healthcare—a companion for Beth. Someone who knows a little about nursing and would stay here eight hours a day ..." She trailed off, unsure how the unpredictable Anna would take this.

To her amazement, Anna leaned against the counter, smiling brightly. "What a wonderful idea! Beth would have someone to talk to, someone to see to her during the day. Do you think it's possible?"

Maggie bent over her laptop, beginning the search. "Oh yeah, Mom. It shouldn't be hard to find at all."

Anna stiffened. "Wait. Are you insinuating that it's too hard for me to take care of Beth? That I'm lacking some-how?"

"Sometimes I wonder. After all, you're the one who left the burner on all night," Maggie said.

"That little monster. She had no right! I'm going to march right in there and—"

"You'll do no such thing. She's just worried about you. At her age, to have to worry about her own mother!"

For an instant, Anna's eyes dropped and a flush came from beneath her chin. When she raised her eyes to her daughter, they were glassy with tears. "It's hard, Maggie, without your father here."

Maggie melted, crossed to her and gave her a quick, firm hug. "I know it is, and I don't mean to make it any harder. Hey, this new healthcare worker will just give you more time to live your own life. Of course, it won't be cheap and you'll have this person underfoot all day. Do you think you could deal with that?"

"If you can afford it, I really think it's a wonderful idea. The constant stress of dealing with this kind of illness, I don't think you can imagine! The trips to the doctor, the treatments. Up all night with a sick child. Maggie, sometimes I don't think you see it from my point of view at all."

"Better than you think," Maggie muttered as she located a few agency names. She took advantage of Anna's furtive reach for the Scotch bottle and placed the call on her cell phone. The woman at Nashville Cares was warm and understanding, promising she'd call first thing in the morning with a list of available people.

After a dinner of Anna's overdone beef stew, Maggie retired to the guest bedroom with a book. Every now and then, she checked on Beth, who barely moved in her sleep.

Around eleven that night, Maggie got up for a cup of tea, and walking past Beth's bedroom, noticed light streaming from under the door. She tapped gently and Beth invited her in.

Beth was propped against a large floral pillow, laptop

swung in front of her. The room was neat as always, its eggshell blue almost matching Beth's eyes.

"Mags, I loaded the pictures of your scroll onto my laptop. Guess what! The writing is Aramaic." Lower lip caught in her teeth, she was the picture of concentration.

Maggie pulled a chair to the side of the bed. "Aramaic? Now where have I heard of that?"

"It's the language of the Dead Sea scrolls."

She turned her laptop to face her sister. "Look at how it's smudged. Can't even make some of it out. I'd love to meet the guy who did this."

"Wasn't a guy—was a girl. Her father owned the neatest shop in the French—Beth?"

The girl had gone a pasty white that even her lips shared. Maggie leaped forward and caught her just as her eyes slowly rolled up into her head.

— CHAPTER FOUR —

FRIDAY, JULY 17

"Beth? Beth?" Maggie leaped to the bed, reached over, and stroked Beth's face. "Beth? Oh lord, hang on. I'm getting you to the hospital."

She raced into her room to grab her purse, yelling for Anna as she went. Anna didn't respond. With no time to waste, she ran back into Beth's room, picked her up, and carried her to the rental Ford.

Her heart was thumping in her ears as she drove swiftly down the dark road. There was little traffic until she made a fast turn onto Trousdale Road, where a slow pickup made her grit her teeth and curse under her breath until she finally passed it. She reached Harding Place and took a left on two wheels, heading for I-65 toward downtown. Beth moaned softly.

"Beth! Beth, hang in there. It won't be long." Concentrating on the road, she reached over and stroked Beth's soft blond wisps of hair. Tears threatened and she forced herself to bring both hands back to the wheel.

Ten minutes later, she pulled into the Emergency Room at Baptist Hospital, grateful she'd remembered how to get there. She ran inside and called for help. A young paramedic raced out to the car with a stretcher. Maggie began to follow, but the paramedic told her to park the car first.

Cursing again under her breath, she obediently pulled into a nearby spot. She ran into the hospital and asked at the desk for Beth, only to be forced to sit and fill out paperwork. Beth was no stranger to the old hospital, and the woman at the desk rapidly accessed her records.

Maggie sat and watched the woman type, a feeling of dread crawling its way up her stomach. She'd never known Beth to faint before. It couldn't be good news. *Just one more time*, she prayed to herself. *Get us through this just once more. I won't curse anymore. I'll be so good.*

She gulped back tears as the woman finally told her to go through the door on the left and continue to Room 10.

The room was small and paper-white in the glare of the fluorescent lights overhead. Beth looked tiny on the bed, barely wrinkling the sheet. To the left of the bed was a counter, several cupboards, and a sink with foot pedal controls for the water. There was one rolling stool next to the bed. The room smelled of alcohol and grief, and Maggie shuddered as she entered.

Beth was awake and smiling at the nurse.

"Mags! I'm so sorry. I don't believe this. It's never happened before, I swear."

Maggie strode to the bed and took one of Beth's little pale hands. "Don't apologize, silly," she said. "It's not like you did it on purpose."

"The doctor will be right with you," said the nurse, exiting the room.

"Wow, Mags. I don't even remember the ride down here. How weird is that? One moment I'm in bed, the next I'm here. I think Scotty beamed me up." She smiled, and Maggie felt her stomach clench in anguish.

There was unusual color in Beth's face. A faint blush ran over her cheeks up into her hairline. Her eyes were wide and sparkling. Maggie put a hand against her forehead, thinking she had to have a fever. Her skin was hot and dry to the touch.

"I actually don't feel bad at all. Go figure! This is the best I've felt in ages. Maybe I need to faint more often."

Maggie scowled down at her. "You scared the hell out of me. One more like that and you'll be carrying me in here ... Oh, here's the doctor."

A tired looking doctor walked in. Maggie noticed how young he was. His tousled, unkempt hair gave him an anxious look. Stethoscope dangling, he smiled when he saw Beth. "Hello there, young lady. I'm Dr. Goode. What seems to be the problem?" He had her file in his hand and flipped through it as he spoke.

Beth looked up at him and smiled. "I'm not sure. I think I fainted."

"As you probably see there, she has leukemia, Doctor. Her latest chemo treatment was three days ago, and I'm worried she's having some kind of a reaction. She's never fainted before. Oh, I'm Maggie Purcell, her sister." Maggie extended her hand and the doctor shook it.

"I haven't seen Beth myself," he said, "but I've seen her at a distance. Right, Beth?" Beth smiled and he continued. "If you'll step out for a moment, Ms. Purcell, I'm going to examine Beth. We'll call you when we're ready."

Maggie started to protest, but Beth urged her to call Anna. Mom would be worried if she woke up and her daughters weren't in the house.

Maggie walked slowly back through the reinforced door to the waiting room. A woman in a baggy dress held a sobbing toddler. An older man, asleep, had his head cocked back against the window, mouth agape.

Rummaging through her purse for her cell phone, she realized she'd left it charging at home. She walked to the short corridor where the pay phone stood, then dialed home. The phone rang unanswered until Anna's voice mail picked up. Exasperated, she left a brief message detailing where she and Beth were, then went and sat a safe distance from the woman with the toddler. The child was coughing, great snotty barks from deep within his chest.

Maggie clenched her purse and looked down. She had many reasons for loathing hospitals, not the least of which was her fear of catching something. Then there were the feelings of helplessness and dread. She could do nothing to affect the outcome, and she hated the powerlessness. She was almost afraid to go back to the small room where Beth lay, afraid to hear the news that was almost always bad.

Five years ago, while in grade school, Beth had caught a bad case of flu. Originally, Dr. Coles had her rest for a week. When the symptoms did not get better, he'd had Anna bring her in for some tests.

Dr. Coles had been their family doctor for as long as Maggie could remember. Tall, with dark hair always falling in his eyes, he had a gruff way of speaking that nearly concealed the caring person underneath. When he called Anna to come in for Beth's test results, however, he was anything but gruff. His unusually gentle manner set off alarm bells for Maggie.

Dr. Coles' office faced a street in the older part of Nashville, and the trees outside it were large and mature. Maggie had gone with Anna, who was worried—normally results were given over the phone. Both were seated on a deep couch facing Dr. Coles and the window over his shoulder.

Maggie was staring at an enormous tree trunk as the doctor seated himself and began talking. It was a windy day, and every now and then a leafy branch would blow in front of the window. There was a deep hole in the trunk, and Maggie could have sworn she saw something inside, moving. She applied all her concentration to that trunk as the doctor began to speak, feeling on some subconscious level a sense of dread that made her sick to her stomach.

He informed them that Beth had tested positive for acute myelogenous leukemia, a disease where cancer invades the bone marrow. Anna had gasped and grabbed Maggie's arm so tightly that later, Maggie found a ring of finger-shaped bruises there.

For her part, Maggie felt as if all the air had been sucked out of her lungs. Her ears began to ring so loudly that it drowned out the doctor's low voice, and she was forced to take her attention off the tree trunk and look directly at him to try to understand the words coming from his mouth.

The man's eyes were suspiciously bright, and she saw that he was close to tears. The dread grew tentacles in her belly, clawing up into her throat.

"Chemotherapy, followed by radiation ... We will hope for remission. But that's where we'll want to start. I'm sending you to the best oncologist in Nashville, Dr. Wagner. Dolly will call his office before you leave, and we'll try to sneak Beth in tomorrow morning. He needs to see her as soon as possible."

The words stuck in Maggie's ears. "Chemotherapy ... radiation ... As soon as possible." It couldn't be happening. If only she stared long and hard enough at the tree trunk, maybe she could project herself out the window and into the black depths of the hole in it. Sink right in, and maybe whatever was in there would eat her.

"Maggie Purcell, they're ready for you now." The nurse's voice broke into her thoughts, and she stood slowly. Taking a deep breath, she walked back to the small exam room. She steeled herself and forced a brave smile for Beth.

Beth was alone and smiled as she saw her older sister walk in. "Oh, this one's so nice, Mags. He told me he likes to go mountain climbing. He's going to do the Himalayas soon. How cool is that?"

"He must have some pair of legs. Did he say anything while he was examining you?"

"Nope. He had the nurse take a bunch of blood, then he poked around on my belly, as usual."

Maggie pulled up a little stool and sat. "Hey, you cold or anything?"

"Not at all. I swear, Mags," Beth said brightly. "I really do feel okay. Can we just leave? I want to get back home and hit the computer."

"Not so fast, kiddo. Let's see what the doctor says first." Maggie paused. "Listen, while we're away from the house, let me ask you something. How's Mom doing? Other than the burner."

Beth looked away from Maggie. "She's not all that bad. Really she isn't. She just worries so much, you know."

Maggie bit her lip. "Yes. I know that I probably shouldn't be bringing this up right now anyway."

"Yes, you should. It's okay. I am feeling … better. Weird, but better. Anyway, Mom's been worrying me more lately, Mags. I just didn't want to say anything. You know how you get."

"Never mind how I get," Maggie grinned through the tightness she felt. "Come on. What's been on your mind?"

Beth sighed and began picking at the sheet. "I'm pretty sure she's drinking a lot more. She takes long naps in the afternoon, after the Afternoon Annies leave. Oh, and one time ..." She turned a deep red.

"It's okay—whatever it is, sweets," Maggie encouraged her. "I need to know."

"Well, one night last week, I heard this noise, really late. I got kind of spooked, and called out for Mom. Usually she comes when I do that, thinking I'm sick or something. This time though, nothing happened." She took in a deep breath and rolled onto her side under the sheet, facing Maggie. "It was three a.m. when I finally got up and went to look for her. I thought something was under the bed. I was scared to move. You know how it goes," she said with a blush. "Anyway, I went to her room and she wasn't even there. She wasn't anywhere, and the car wasn't in the driveway. Oh Mags, I was so scared."

Maggie frowned, then forced herself to breathe. "Did you ever find out where she was?"

"No, I didn't ask, either. But I heard her come in later, when she fell in the living room." Beth's blue eyes blinked back tears and Maggie reached over and gave her a long hug.

"It's better that I know, sweetie. I'm not going to say anything. But, guess what? I have some news for you that should make things a bit easier. I called an agency today, one that handles home healthcare. I figured I could hire someone young and fun to come be with you, do some cooking, and maybe drive if needed. What do you think?"

Beth's little face looked so glad for a moment, then sober-ed. "But that's going to cost a fortune! We're doing fine as we are. Really."

Maggie leaned over and gathered her into a gentle hug. "You might be surprised what I can afford. Geek girls make good money. You know that. And it isn't like these big cor-porations will all of a sudden stop having major security issues on their networks."

Beth giggled. "Not with all the bugs built right in, not to

mention hackers and things."

"Exactly! So, what do you think? Might be fun to have someone around a lot more?"

"What's her name? How old is she? It is a she, isn't it? I don't know that I'd like a boy around," Beth blurted, and she flushed again.

Maggie laughed. "I specified a girl. From what the lady at the agency said, they have several in their early twenties. She was going to make a few calls and then give me our choices in the morning. I wanted to make sure you were cool with the idea."

"I'm such a pain for you," Beth said, looking away. "None of this is your fault, this stupid leukemia. And Mom and her issues."

"Don't you ever think that way. Ever. You're what I live for. You're my only sister, and wherever you are, you carry a large piece of my heart with you. This will actually be a relief for me. I won't worry so much. And …"

The doctor pushed open the door and got straight to business. "Ms. Purcell, the base results are back. Beth's white count looks elevated. I see that as a sign of an infection. These things happen. I'm going to prescribe antibiotics, and if she doesn't improve by Monday, you should get her immediately to her oncologist. The rest of her levels are within normal range.

"Her electrolyte count is good, though she's running a low temp, about one-oh-one. You should keep a close eye on her, but I think you can take her on home. If she gets dizzy again, bring her back in ASAP."

Maggie sagged on the stool in relief. "Thank you. But if it's just an infection, why did she faint?"

"We're not sure. It's probably a side effect of the chemo, along with the slight fever. You did say she was nauseous earlier? Nausea and dizziness are common side effects."

"I hope that's all it was," Maggie said, standing. "Well, we sure thank you. Come on, Beth, get dressed. We're out of here."

The drive home was mostly silent. Nashville was deserted, so Maggie was able to make good time on the interstate. She looked at Beth curled up in the seat. Her color was somewhat improved, a tinge of pink showing in the dim light from the dashboard.

I wish Reeve had been here, Maggie thought. Sometimes this being alone was really difficult. But it was better than the alternative. Togetherness, for her at least, was agony. She cringed at the thought of her last date. *Adrian was more feminine than I am. He's the only person I ever knew who had to have three closets just for his clothes.*

Reeve loved clothing as well, but he kept his wardrobe in one walk-in closet.

Reeve—she felt the familiar small spark in her belly at the thought of his perfect dark face. She glared at the road and pressed her lips together. That spark was a dangerous thing, to be avoided at all costs. These days, she only dated "safe" men, those steady souls who cared more for her than for their own looks. Ones who could accept her frequent flights to Nashville. Not like Arne Ross, who had dropped her over just a few broken dates.

Her relationship with Bruce, her first love, had been a thing of sparks, flame and fire from the first moment he appeared outside that afternoon class in high school. When pressed against him on those rare occasions in his aunt's large old-fashioned bed, she thought her body would actually catch fire for the wanting of him. Even after they made love, the flames would make her toss restlessly against him until he once again smothered her with kisses.

Oh, how I loved him. Almost ten years ago, now.

"It's your problem." Remembering the comment brought

her upright and rigid in the seat, squinting against oncoming lights. They'd had an accident with a condom, and the inevitable had happened. "It's your problem," Bruce had said, and simply walked out of her life.

Her mind veered away from the agony, and she brought herself back to the present with several long, deep breaths. Here and now. Driving down I-65 with Beth sick in the seat next to her.

Beth didn't wake up until they were nearly home. Soon enough they were at the small house in Creve Hall. In the driveway, Maggie cut her lights and sat for a moment, feeling the exhaustion and tension seep from her body. Beth, fully awake now, opened her door and stepped out.

"Oh, crud," she said. "The porch light is burned out again. Good thing you're here—I can't reach it. Could you change it tomorrow?"

"Sure ... You know something? You go on in. I think I'm going to sit here for a moment and collect my thoughts."

"Stop by my room before you go to bed?"

Maggie agreed and watched her walk up the stone path to the porch steps. Once she'd opened the door and gone inside, Maggie sank back into the Ford's seat and nibbled a nail.

Where had Mom been when I came to get her? Passed out, without a doubt. Maggie didn't want to think of the possibilities if she herself had not been available to take Beth to the hospital. Worse, she wondered how many other times she had needed help, called out, and no one came. She had almost expected what Beth had told her in the hospital.

She shuddered in her seat. *Thank God she'd have someone in the house on a regular basis tomorrow.* The thought prompted her to check the car's clock. It was nearly two a.m. and the agency had said they'd call by eight.

With a sigh, she gathered her large purse and Beth's

hospital paperwork and made her way out of the car.

The gravel crunched under her feet as she walked slowly to the porch, rotating her neck and shoulders to free the tension. The night air was sweet and humid, with a hint of rotted wood that always brought Nashville to her mind. She sniffed the air, listening to the crickets and a lonely hoot owl close by.

Out of the corner of her eye, Maggie saw a flicker of movement. She stopped in her tracks and then let out a breath of relief as the neighbor's cat ran across the yard. She chuckled tiredly at her nerves and rubbed her eyes, heading for the front door with thoughts of the comfortable bed awaiting her.

Maggie turned sharply at the sound of footsteps behind her and was blinded by the sudden snap of headlights from a car parked in the driveway across the street. A dark figure raced from behind the willow tree, then blackness engulfed her as she felt something slip over her head.

— CHAPTER FIVE —

Maggie struggled and tried to call out, but her small, squirming frame was lifted and carried back across the street at a bouncing run.

A thick, heavily-perfumed scent rose from the material over her face.

She heard a car door open and two voices speaking softly in a foreign language. Then she was thrown onto slick, cool leather. One of the men said in a deep, heavy accent, "You be quiet now and we will not hurt you. All we want is the letter."

Maggie stiffened where she lay. *That accent. Could it be …*

The car started up and, with a squeal, accelerated out of the driveway. Disconcerted by the covering over her head, Maggie swayed and nearly fell to the floor. As she did, she realized her purse was still over her arm and was hooked on the arm rest. She struggled to get free from it, and the voice came again.

"Be still! Give us the letter. Now. And we will let you go."

Certain that the voice belonged to the attacker in Paris, Maggie pulled at the cloth over her face and cried with desperation, "I don't know what you're talking about! Who are you people? Let me out of here! You've made a big mistake!"

"Not we who are making mistakes, Maggie Purcell. Now give us what you took that does not belong to you!" The voice was sharp and menacing, and Maggie was horrified. They knew her name.

"So help me, I don't know what you're talking about! Whatever it is, you can have it. If you want money, take it. Here's my purse. Take whatever you want. Just don't hurt me," she said, her voice breaking into a sob.

The two voices conferred again, and she heard material shifting across the seat in front of her. Then she felt the weight of her purse leave her side, and heard someone rifling through it. She heard a quiet exclamation from the passenger.

"*In sh'allah*, it is here! This will change the world."

So they were after the scroll. It couldn't be the Napoleon letter because Beth had it, she thought, shaking with nerves and terror. For a moment, she thought she would throw up, then knew if she did, she might strangle in the process, wrapped up as she was.

Now that they had the scroll, what did that mean for her? Surely nothing good. Although she had unfortunately seen nothing of the men, they didn't know that. And she had indeed seen the murderer in the shop in Paris.

Then she realized what the man had said. "It will change the world." *Why had the shop-owner given her such a thing?*

A growing feeling of helpless dread sapped her strength and her mind. Tightly wrapped in some kind of material, she was powerless. Only her feet were free.

All this crossed her mind in a split second as she vaguely

noticed the hollow sound of the Ferrell Parkway underpass. Then she heard the driver say in a reverential tone, "To see such a thing in my life. It is worth more than money could buy..." and there was suddenly an enormous bang, as she was thrown onto the floor of the car, her face scraping badly against the inside of the material.

The other passenger screamed in a high voice, the car hurtled over a series of bumps, and suddenly Maggie realized what had happened.

They'd evidently reached the end of Ferrell Parkway. There, they should have turned either right or left onto Lambert, but the end of the road had always been a problem area, coming as it did so suddenly after the underpass. If the driver had taken his attention off the road for just a moment, it was possible he'd never have seen the stop sign.

They'd hurtled across Lambert, hit a ditch, and launched into the front yard of a house.

As soon as she realized this, the car came to a wheezing stop. She'd been thrown onto her side and into the door, and the material over her head and torso had loosened enough that her right hand was now free. But her head was pounding in agony and she wasn't sure she could move.

She heard fluid dripping and the engine ticking. Moving slowly, she pulled the material off her head.

Groaning with pain, she slowly edged her rear end onto the back seat then peeped forward. The driver was still, his head back, airbag deployed.

The passenger, dressed in the familiar white robe, had his head in his hands and was moaning softly. He rolled his head, rubbing at his eyes, and she stiffened. She'd seen that bulging eye before.

Head pounding and vision fuzzy, she moved faster than she ever would have believed possible. Even with the world going gray around her, she yanked on the door handle, opened it and fell out to her knees. She pitched forward and lay on the ground a few moments, then pulled herself to her feet. Staggering at first, she fled back down Ferrell Parkway. She ignored the left turn onto Regent Drive and instead ran, more swiftly now, through two backyards just behind Anna's small house on Barrywood Lane. Sirens swelled as she ran into the driveway and up onto the porch, where a horrified Beth and Anna stood.

"Maggie! Oh God. Mags, are you okay?" Beth launched herself off the porch and into Maggie's arms. "What happened?"

Blinking sleepily, Anna was wrapping a bathrobe around herself. "Honey, what on earth is happening? Beth yanked me out of bed with some tale of you being dragged right into a car …"

Gasping for breath, Maggie held up a hand. "Hold on, guys. I'm okay. I banged my head and I'm scared to death. Oh, here come the police. Beth, did you call them?"

"You bet I did, and fast, too!" Beth had tears and was trying to wipe them without Maggie noticing.

"You sweetheart." Maggie hugged her.

They were standing arm in arm when one police car shot into the driveway, followed closely by two more. The blue lights lit up the backyard, stippling the willow tree with pale color. Maggie stared at it as the police walked rapidly toward her.

"Ma'am, we had a call from this location. Would you be Beth Purcell?" the policewoman said to Maggie.

"No, Beth is my sister. I'm the one she called about," Maggie said, beginning to shake with nerves.

The other woman noticed. "Perhaps we can go inside to discuss this."

Maggie nodded and saw little stars. She winced and gently rubbed her head. With Beth firmly at her side, she followed

Anna into the living room. The policewoman, her partner, and two other policemen followed. The remaining two stood, talking outside their car.

The tall policewoman introduced herself as Sherrie Adams and her much shorter partner as Brian Delano. Sherrie was at least six feet, with wide shoulders above a thick waist and grayish blond hair curling out from under the blue police hat. Brian, much shorter, was dark and Latin in appearance. Anna offered coffee, which they accepted.

"Mrs. Purcell," Detective Delano said, "can I interview you and your younger daughter?" She nodded, and the three of them walked into the kitchen.

"So, Ms. Purcell, can you explain what happened?" In the living room, Detective Adams flipped open a notebook. "Your sister told the 911 dispatcher that you'd been thrown into a car and abducted."

"Exactly. We had just gotten home from the Baptist ER. Beth went inside, and I stayed in the car a moment ... I don't live here—I just flew in from New York—and I needed a moment." Realizing she was babbling, Maggie drew in a deep breath, then continued. "The porch light was out. I reached it just before this man leaped out from behind the big weeping willow next to the driveway. He forced a shirt over my head, grabbed me, and threw me in the back seat of a car!" She sobbed, taking in short breaths.

Detective Adams took advantage of the pause. "Andy and Craig, why don't you check the bushes and road?" The two policemen quietly walked out.

"I tried to fight, I really did. I think I got in one good kick," Maggie added.

"Can you give a description of the perpetrators?" The policewoman asked.

"No—no. Not a good description. Both were dark-haired, wearing robes. I was blinded by the car's headlights, when he first grabbed me, and then the shirt was over my head. But on my way out of the car, I saw the passenger had something wrong with his left eye." She shuddered. "It bulged out. And they both are foreign, judging from their accents. They were also speaking another language at some point. I hit my head a pretty good lick, so I wasn't thinking straight." She gulped, tears pouring down her face, then felt Beth's arms around her, surprisingly tight.

"And the car? Make? Model? Color?"

"It was a dark Chevrolet Suburban. I saw it briefly when I got out after it wrecked. Oh! It might still be there. The guy driving missed the turn from Ferrell Parkway onto Lambert, right after the underpass, you know? He went straight across, hit a ditch, and missed a house by a hair." She shuddered at the thought. "I think the driver was knocked out. The passenger was also hurt. I guess I was really better off flat across the backseat, because I don't have a scratch. I tore the shirt off my head and got the hell out of there."

Sherrie's partner walked in from the kitchen, conferred quietly with her, then walked rapidly out the front door. Maggie watched him go. Should she tell them about Paris? Her mind went in frantic circles. What would Anna say? Probably that Maggie brought nothing but trouble, and she didn't need that.

Oh my God, the scroll. Suddenly she realized she no longer had it. Her head whirled. Wasn't this good news? Did she need that kind of trouble in her life? The scroll hadn't been a positive influence, for sure.

At the moment, she needed to decide what, if anything, to tell the police.

What choice did she really have. The problem had evidently followed her to Nashville, and now the Arabs knew where Beth and her mother lived. The thought made her nauseous.

She had to speak up, but had no intention of doing so in front of Anna and Beth. She thought fast. Also, she wasn't at all certain she hadn't broken a law by leaving France the way she had. Would they call that leaving the scene of a crime? She reached back and massaged the knot on her head, the horror of the attack still on her mind, wondering how on earth she'd managed to get involved in such a nightmare.

"Is there a reason someone would attack you?" Detective Adams asked.

Maggie looked over her shoulder. As Anna removed several cups from the cupboard, the sound of crockery assured Maggie that her mother was still occupied. "Yes, but let's discuss it outside."

Sherrie's radio squawked, and she walked into the hall. "Excuse me for a moment."

Anna walked out of the kitchen, three mugs of steaming coffee in her hands. "Where did they go?"

"Not sure, Mom." Maggie took a napkin from Anna and blew her nose. "Boy, what a night," she said, and crumpled the napkin in her hand.

"What a way to get jerked out of bed!" Anna said, then set the coffee on the table and grabbed Maggie's head in a tight hug. "You and Beth, you'll be the death of me yet. Is the little one okay?"

"Yes, but she does have a minor infection, they think. Her white count was elevated, and she had a temperature. We just need to watch her and give her one of these three times a day." She handed Anna the bottle of pills.

Beth smiled. "I really do feel better, Mom. Or I did—until this happened."

"You need to get into bed," Anna declared before turning her attention to Maggie. "You better explain to me why two men suddenly grabbed you in the middle of the night, threw you into a car, and took off. It's so quiet around here! If they wanted to do a dirty deed, it would have been much simpler to just … do the deed behind the house, where it's nice and dark." Maggie paled, and Anna stopped. "Well, you know what I mean."

Unfortunately, Maggie did. "Mom, I'm clueless. One moment I was walking up to the porch, and the next I had some guy's stinking, perfumed shirt wrapped around my head and was being hauled down the driveway like a sack of crap! Sorry," she added before Anna could protest her language.

Detective Adams walked back in followed by her partner. "Ms. Purcell, the vehicle is no longer present. Officers located only marks where it left the road and landed in the front yard. There's an emergency vehicle outside. You have a fairly large bump on your head. Why don't you let the EMT take a look at it?" The policewoman stared at Maggie with meaningful gray eyes.

"Yes, good idea. I gave it quite a whack." Maggie followed the policewoman out into the driveway.

"Thank you. My mom is, ah, a bit fragile. She won't take this information too well. I'd rather she not know much of this unless necessary," Maggie explained with a hitch in her throat. The flutter of blue lights against the sky made her feel like she was living in a nightmare.

"I see. Ms. Purcell, we need you to come to the station and make a statement," Detective Delano said.

"Is that really necessary?" she drew a long, shuddering breath. "It's been the worst night. I truly feel ill. Could it possibly wait until morning?"

Detective Adams looked at her closely. "Mostly, it's best to get a detailed report while the facts are still fresh."

"But I saw nothing!" Maggie insisted. "Those creeps had my head wrapped up—" Suddenly the need was urgent. She gagged, leaned over into the bushes, then gagged again.

"In that case, I reckon it can wait until morning," Detective

Adams said with a hasty step backward. Detective Delano nodded.

Maggie sucked in deep breaths to calm her heaving belly. "Let me at least tell you this. I just got back from a business trip to Paris. I saw a man killed there," she said, her voice quavering. She breathed in deeply and continued. "I'm fairly sure one of the men tonight was the killer—I did note a thing with his eye. He was the passenger in the Suburban. It was dark, but I could swear—yes, it *had* to be the same guy." An uncontrollable shiver went up her spine. She spelled the name of the Parisian shop and its owner.

The policewoman said something softly to her partner, then asked Maggie to continue. Maggie told the entire tale, including how they had run from Paris. She wasn't proud of that, she admitted.

"And now, I'm afraid they'll make me go back. They can't do that, can they?" she wondered, frightened anew.

Detective Delano responded, "Ms. Purcell, that's Interpol business. I'm not certain how they'll react, but we'll certainly contact them first thing in the morning. You should be prepared to come in early and let us get this all on paper. We now have the name of the shop and its owner, so we'll make inquiries." He snapped his notebook closed.

Maggie sighed. "This is an unending nightmare. I'll be there. Just please keep an eye on the house tonight, won't you? I really don't want anything happening to my sister or my mom over this."

"We'll ensure that officers drive by frequently tonight," Detective Adams said with a reassuring smile. "Ms. Purcell, we'll talk to you in the morning."

Maggie thanked her for responding so quickly, and they left, the other two cars having already gone. As she came back inside, Maggie saw Anna look down at the untouched coffee and purse her lips, then take the mugs back to the kitchen.

"Sorry to have caused all this trouble, Mom," Maggie said to her departing back. "I hope you'll be able to get some sleep now."

"I may never be able to sleep again! Beth in the ER and you attacked? What is this world coming to? Can't we be just a normal family where nothing ever happens? Sometimes I think your dad got the best of the deal." Her voice trembled.

"Don't even think that, Mom. Come on, sit down for a minute. I haven't even told you all of what happened in the ER yet."

"Beth told me. Just a small infection, right? They gave her pills and let her go. I think we should celebrate that!" Anna walked to the side table, picked up a decanter of brandy and poured a generous measure into a snifter. She motioned with the decanter at Maggie, who nodded and smiled. Anna poured another snifter and carried it to her.

"What about *me*?" Beth said, grinning. Anna took a deep drink and closed her eyes, and Beth looked at Maggie with eyebrows raised. Maggie evaded her look.

"Not a chance, twerp. Aren't you supposed to be in bed?" Maggie reached over and tweaked her nose, then sank back onto the sofa with a little moan. "What a nightmare. I just don't believe this is happening. Mom, why don't you take Beth and go on a brief vacation somewhere, just till we get this figured out?"

"I'll do no such thing. I'm a busy woman. It's my turn to host the bridge meeting next week. I'm not about to leave. And Beth's doctor's appointment in two weeks is for a full battery of tests. Not to mention she's sick right now! There's just no way we're going anywhere. I'm not sure what trouble you're in, but we're not running away, are we Bethy?" She sat in the armchair facing the couch and took a deep drink.

Beth looked sideways at Maggie. "I don't reckon they'll

try again, Mags. At least not here. They've got to know the police will be watching the house now."

"You might be right, but I sure don't want to gamble you and Mom on that." Maggie rolled the snifter between her hands, then inhaled the warm scent. She took a sip and stood. "Guys, I'm totally exhausted. Can we talk about this in the morning?"

"You look beat, poor thing." Anna stood, walked to her and gave her a hug. "Get some sleep. You too, Beth. You've been up all night!"

Shortly after, Maggie was lying in the guest bed under a frilly sheet, sleepless. She stared at the dark window without seeing, and thought.

The scroll was gone now. That poor man had died giving it to me, and now it's gone. She plumped her pillow and attempted to find a comfortable spot for her aching head.

Well, one thing was certain. No more scroll, no more trouble. Right?

— CHAPTER SIX —

After a restless night, Maggie awoke to a loud knocking. Anna cracked the door and told her that a girl from the health agency was on the phone. Maggie threw back the covers and winced, feeling soreness in her shoulders from the night before. Gingerly she put a foot over the side of the bed and felt for her slippers.

Anna was brewing a pot of coffee when Maggie stumbled into the kitchen and picked up the receiver.

"Hello, this is Darla with Nashville Cares. They told you I'd call?" came a pleasant voice.

"Hi Darla. I'm Maggie Purcell, and yes they did. I'm looking for light help with my little sister. She's got leukemia, and mainly needs care when she's sick, occasional trips to the doctor, and, well, a companion." Maggie looked nervously at Anna, who was busying herself at the sink, back turned.

"I'm just so sorry she's sick," said Darla. "Let me tell you a little about me."

Maggie listened as the girl slowly explained that she was

twenty-four years old, and her previous patient, an older man with Alzheimer's, had recently died. She'd been with him for more than three years and considered herself one of the family. Darla's voice wavered as she took a deep breath, then went on to say that she genuinely cared for people and enjoyed her job. She was used to full care, including diapering, bathing, and light physical therapy overseen by a physician. She also drove and ran errands.

She sounded like a godsend to Maggie. Impressed, she asked Darla if she could stop by at two that afternoon to meet Beth.

"Mom, she sounds absolutely perfect," Maggie said, hanging up the phone.

"You better make dead sure you get her references. I don't want just anybody coming into this house. What do you know about her? What color is she? She sound black?" Anna poured them both a mug of coffee.

"Probably, and I have no doubt she'll pass with flying colors. She was with her last patient for three years, and she said they loved her. The old man recently died and she sounded totally broken up over it." Maggie made a sour face. "But exactly what does sounding black have to do with it?"

"Just make sure you make that call. Can't trust people to tell the truth. She could be anybody." Anna looked into her coffee, absently twirling the plain gold wedding band she still wore.

"I'll get the number from her first thing—" The phone rang and Maggie passed it over, then sat up in surprise when Anna answered and handed it right back.

It was Detective Adams from the night before, and she asked Maggie to be at the station at ten. Maggie pressed her lips together, and Anna looked at her curiously. Maggie asked if she was in any trouble, and the detective assured her that that wasn't the case. They just needed to get more information. Maggie hung up and made a face.

"They want me downtown at the police station."

Anna looked at her closely. "Maggie, is there anything you're not telling me? Are you sure you have no idea why those men would do you like that?"

Maggie flushed and looked down. She hadn't wanted to say anything about Paris the night before, when her mother had had far too much to drink. Now there was no escaping it. "Well, there might be a thing or two I neglected to tell you." She began to explain the story to Anna.

Anna sat in silence, thin fingers turning her mug again and again. A dark shade of red climbed up her throat, and inwardly Maggie shrank. "And you brought that mess into our house! Maggie, how could you? My God, the police were here at all hours last night. What will people think? Why couldn't you have just stayed in New York a while, until this thing settled!" She banged her mug on the table with such force that coffee splashed over the side.

Maggie jumped. "Mom, I had no idea anything was going to happen. Believe me, I sure didn't do it on purpose."

"You never do. Like the time you brought home that boy with all that hair. Bruce—remember him?"

"Mom—"

"A real love he was, getting you pregnant. I thought your father was going to have a heart attack. And Mrs. Struthers seeing you walk into that abortion clinic! I thought I'd never live that one down. Never. Dear old 'It's your problem' Bruce."

Maggie winced. Bruce had been only her second boy-friend, a young musician in his first year of college. With his long curly blond hair and electric guitar, he'd seemed glamorous to her as a high school student. She'd loved him beyond all reason.

Then there'd been the accident with the condom. They'd

hoped to escape any consequences, but she found herself pregnant the following month. She'd agonized over the decision to take care of it, but Bruce left her the moment she'd told him.

"It's your problem," he'd said. Only that.

Now she winced at the remembered pain of it—both the physical and the mental agony she'd endured at the choice she'd had to make at seventeen. Of course Anna ignored the negative emotions that were surfacing now, and charged on.

"And that charmer you were with in Florida, Al, wasn't it?" she said, raising her voice. "He hocked that beautiful necklace we gave you when you were sixteen. Another winner. No, it's never your fault, is it?"

"What's going on?" Beth's small face peered around the corner, tears in her eyes. Maggie stood and walked toward her, emotions in turmoil yet struggling not to show it.

"Just Mom being Mom. I think I'll go take a shower. I've got to be at the police station soon." She drew in a sobbing breath and pushed her emotions back down.

"Oh no! Is everything okay, Mags? You're going to be okay, aren't you?"

"Maggie will be fine. She always is." Anna turned her back, reaching for the refrigerator. "Now come on and sit, both of you, while I make some breakfast."

"It's fine, Beth. You never know—they might have something interesting to tell me. Go on and eat breakfast, I'll grab something downtown." She turned and walked out, back straight, head high, and eyes brimming with unshed tears.

Shortly after ten, Maggie met Detective Adams at police headquarters. In the daylight, Sherrie had large, stunning gray eyes. She ushered Maggie into a small room.

"Good morning, Ms. Purcell. I hope you're alright after last night."

Maggie sat, crossed her legs, then leaned her elbows on the table. "I'm fine. I've got quite the lump on the back of my head and my face is a little sore. It feels like a rug burn."

"Or a really bad beard burn," said Detective Adams grinning. Maggie let out a surprised laugh. "Ms. Purcell, can I get you some coffee?"

"It's Maggie, and I'd love a cup."

"Maggie, then. Call me Sherrie. I'll be back in a moment." She turned and walked from the room.

While the detective was gone, Maggie looked around at the institutional green walls, with a view of Nashville outside the window just across from her. She hoped two things: Sherrie wouldn't keep her long, and she wouldn't have to make a return trip to Paris. She also worried about Beth and Anna. She'd feel better if she knew Sherrie herself would keep an eye on the two—the woman looked like she could play football with the best of them.

Sherrie walked back in and slid Maggie coffee across the table. "I hope this is okay—I added a little sugar and cream. Let me start by saying I heard back from Interpol. You're in luck on the murder. It seems the neighboring shop owner recognized the shooter. It was the man's daughter's fiancé, Faod Farazad. That's the good news."

Maggie relaxed marginally, sipped her coffee, and kept her eyes on Sherrie's face while she continued.

"The bad news is that Faod belongs to a fundamental Muslim sect. They're not really well known, but they're believed to have ties to some more serious terrorist groups, like Al Qaeda."

Maggie went white and felt nauseous. Al Qaeda. Her mind played videos of horrors on the news, inserting Beth and her mother as victims. She hunched her shoulders. It just wasn't possible. Perhaps her mother was right, she thought miserably. She did bring these things on herself, somehow.

Sherrie, who'd been watching her carefully, leaned forward. "I ain't sure what's going through your mind, but the main thing now is to identify the driver. We ran Faod through the system, and he was flagged as a member of the Egyptian Islamic Jihad group out of Paris. They're a group of fanatics who want to replace the Egyptian government with a Muslim one. They're a bad group. Back in '81, they were responsible for the assassination of Anwar Sadat. Lately, they've been behind car bombings and other attacks on American interests in Egypt and Europe."

"Faod's not a major player," she went on, "but we'd sure like to know who his driver was. Faod does run in interesting circles. Homeland Security has asked us to show you some pictures. It shouldn't take long. You reckon you'd recognize the driver if you saw him again?"

Maggie considered. She'd not had a good glimpse of the driver at all, more an impression of his size and his deep voice. "I'm sorry. I really didn't get a good look at him at all—I was in such a panic, I just fell out of the car and ran."

"I suppose it ain't no use showing you the book, then," Sherrie said, and leaned back in her chair until it was on two legs. "Well, it was worth a shot. You reckon you'd recognize the voice if you heard it again?"

"It's possible. For sure I'd know the cologne, though. One of them wore something very sweet and rank. It was all over the shirt they wrapped around my head."

"Can you remember exactly what they said?"

Maggie ran a hand through her hair and concentrated. "They said all they wanted was the letter, that it could change the world. They said I took it, and it didn't belong to me. That's a load of crap. I bought and paid for it. I even have a receipt. It's a hand-drawn copy of a letter from Napoleon to Josephine, signed by the artist. The other thing I had is kind of pretty, ancient Aramaic on an old piece of leather. Neither of these things could possibly interest a terrorist! I just don't get it."

"Could I see them?" Sherrie asked.

"They took the piece of leather with them, and my sister Beth has the letter," she said. "I can tell you that the scroll had nothing on it but Aramaic." She had a sudden thought. "One of the guys also said it was worth more than money, now I think about it."

"So the scroll is what they were after?" said Sherrie, moving her chair forward with a small bang. "Do you know what it translates to?"

"Not yet I don't, but I sent a partial scan to a friend who specializes in foreign languages. He should have emailed me by now. I'll let you know when I find out."

"I have to admit I'm stumped," said Sherrie. "The thing sounds too old to be any kind of intelligence. And a letter from Napoleon to Josephine?"

"Actually, they *had* to be after the scroll. Beth had the Napoleon letter. The two losers saw the old scroll and said the words '*In sh'alla*.'"

"Excuse me a moment. I just thought of something." Sherrie heaved her bulk to her feet and walked out. Maggie sighed and looked down at the scarred wooden table, wondering who had sat there before her. A murderer? Drug dealer? Probably no one as notorious as her own personal stalkers, she thought in misery.

But they had what they wanted now, didn't they? Surely she'd be left alone. Or would she? She'd now seen Faod's face, twice. And for all he knew, she'd seen him a lot more clearly the second time.

Sherrie walked back in carrying a fresh cup of coffee.

"Sorry, but I got to have massive infusions of coffee on Friday mornings. Want another cup yourself?"

Maggie shook her head. "No, thanks."

"I wish I had a workable translation of that scroll. Just walked downstairs. We got a guy who speaks Hebrew. Close, but no cigar. You know, they can't just be after the thing for its aesthetic value," Sherrie said.

"So, what happens now, do you think?"

"We're still looking for the vehicle you described. With luck, we find it, pull a few clear prints off it, and get another name. Maybe between that and a translation, we'll know more about what we're dealing with here. I reckon you should go home and relax. Now that Homeland Security's involved, they'll be watching your place and y'all until they're satisfied another attempt on you won't be made." Sherrie stacked the loose papers on the table.

"Honestly, Sherrie, that's going to cause me serious trouble with my Mom. She doesn't understand any of this. Her main concern is that I don't look like a criminal in front of the neighbors, which I truly could if I have an escort wherever I go. Damned if I do and damned if I don't. And what's worse, she'll make Beth's life miserable. If she can't take it out on me, she'll take it out on her." In spite of herself, she felt tears tickle the back of her throat.

Sherrie looked at the stack of papers in her hands, groaned, and placed them back on the table. She leaned over and covered Maggie's hands. "I know this is difficult." The gray eyes looked directly into hers and darkened. "Maggie, we'll figure this out. We're really good at this, and my partner is one of the best."

She blew out a breath. "Our personal catch-22 is Homeland Security and how much they want to get involved in this. They ain't the most subtle when they step into a case."

"You mean they'll be on me like flies on a duck, as Mom

always says. It'll be hard for Mom to explain that to the Afternoon Annies, I'm thinking."

"The Afternoon Annies?" Sherrie grinned, one eyebrow raised. She took a look at her watch, then relaxed into her chair, stretching out her long legs. "We don't have to hurry after all. I just went off-duty. Got nothing better to do than go home and feed the damn cat and my kid." She saw something in Maggie's face and grinned. "Premature gray hair. I ain't that old. Just rising thirty, in fact. Now, tell me about them Afternoon Annies."

Maggie smiled at her and responded, "The Afternoon Annies are a group of old Nashville ladies who play together daily, mostly out of boredom. They go to the country club, go shopping, plan charity affairs. And most of all they gossip. This'll be enough dirt to occupy them for months to come, I'm afraid. Oh yes, this is going to really cause trouble."

"How so? I reckon it'd fascinate them," Sherrie said, watching Maggie curiously.

"I don't know quite how to say this, but ..." Maggie exhaled shakily and looked at the ceiling, hoping the tears wouldn't overflow. "My mom has a slight drinking problem, and serious self-confidence issues since my dad died. These ladies are the yardsticks she measures herself against. They're all wealthier than she is. They all have big lovely houses and maids.

"Mom gave all that up when she married Dad," she continued. "But she was determined. He, ahh—" She looked into the distance beyond Sherrie. "—He was a bartender who played music. He really wanted to make it in Nashville as a musician, but he had a nose candy problem that stopped him." Maggie caught herself and stopped. But Sherrie looked so interested, and she was actually listening. And she had to understand the dynamics of the situation if she were to be any help to Maggie.

"Anyway, Mom always pressured him to make something of himself. She would never be satisfied with just a bartender, no matter how good the music was on the weekends. So when Beth was born, Dad distanced himself further. Between Mom's constant carping about his lifestyle and a screaming, fretful baby, Dad had had about enough."

"And you?" Sherrie broke in gently. "How'd you fit into all of this?"

"If you knew how they fought." She shook her head as she remembered the pain. "Things would go flying against the wall. They'd scream so loudly the neighbors called the police. I was only fourteen at the time, and I was terrified. I also thought it was my fault—Mom told me that often enough. Anyway, I made myself scarce in those days. I'd take Beth out for a walk and never know what I'd find when I got back home."

Sherrie nodded in recognition. "You know, I reckon I can relate to this because I had a similar experience. My dad believed in 'spare the rod, spoil the child.' So that's one thing we were never spared, especially my brothers." Sherrie leaned back in her chair, which creaked under her bulk. "If you don't mind my asking, I noticed that your sister lost a lot of her hair. She got cancer?"

"Five years ago, Beth was diagnosed with leukemia. Our dad never beat Beth or me, but I think that was more pressure than he could stand. He wasn't a bad man, just weak. He'd already had drug problems, and then, after that news, it totally got out of hand. It got so bad, he stole our brand new stereo system and hocked it."

"Oh that poor baby, I just knew it when I saw her last night. That simply breaks my heart. Sorry, go on."

"Thanks. It's been incredibly hard. She's a brilliant, loving kid. Anyway, she was only seven, and she was totally into the whole Barney thing, so we had tons of Barney tapes. They'd already started chemo on her—and she was one sick child. The only relief she had was those tapes, and she'd play them over and over again.

"After a particularly intense round of chemo one month, she couldn't stop vomiting. Mom found her on the bathroom floor, half passed out, still gagging. She sat with her through most of the night. Finally, she talked Beth into going to bed, with the door open so she could hear Barney playing."

Sherrie stirred in her chair. Maggie, who'd been staring down and running a finger over carved initials in the table, looked up to see tears in the large gray eyes. Choking back tears herself, she continued.

"Of course when they left the bathroom, the living room was empty. He'd not only taken the stereo, but he'd cleaned out Mom's purse as well. Took all her cash and maxed out her Visa card, she found out later. Mom was crying. Beth was crying and vomiting again because of it, and oh God, was I pissed."

"How old were you then?"

"I'm twenty-six now, so I was twenty-one then. Studying at Vanderbilt, living at home. Anyway, let me get through this next bit or I'm afraid I won't be able to. Are you sure I'm not boring you to death?"

"Absolutely not, although this sure ain't normal for me. I'm usually sitting across from someone that just done killed someone else."

Through her tears, Maggie managed a small laugh.

"Only transferred to Nashville a month ago," said Sherrie, "so I don't know hardly anybody. This is the longest conversation I've had with anyone except my cat, and his responses ain't the best! Please go on." She set her elbows on the table and propped her angular face on her fists, eyes on Maggie.

"Anyway, Beth finally fell asleep that night, but I waited up for my dad. I knew he'd be back—he had nowhere else to go. And sure enough, at nine a.m., he came staggering in, coked to the gills and grinning like Charlie Tuna. I jumped him immediately. I told him how sick she'd been, that she'd been crying out for her Barney tapes, and asked him if those had gone up his damn nose too. Asked him how he could take the only thing that gave a sick child a moment of pleasure and throw it away. Asked him what kind of man would do that to his own daughter."

Maggie paused. She felt that she shouldn't be telling all this to a total stranger, but felt compelled and could not stop now. She drew a deep, shaky breath and continued. Sherrie watched her calmly, motionless in her own chair.

"Dad broke down and cried. He said he never should have had children, that he didn't deserve them. That since the day he'd married Mom, his music had dried up, and he'd done whatever he could to get back what he considered his life's blood, but it was no good. He told me he was desperately sorry and that we should never have to suffer for mistakes he made, and that he'd always love us. Then he walked out and I never saw him again.

"I went out of town that weekend, and when I got back, I found out that he'd had a car wreck. He hit a telephone pole doing about ninety and died instantly, they told me. I always thought he took the easy way out." Maggie drew a deep breath, aware that tears were flowing down her face.

Quietly, Sherrie pushed her a box of Kleenex. "I imagine your mom was plumb distraught over this."

"I shouldn't be telling you all this."

"Sure you should. What better do I have to do on a scorching Friday? And understand this, I really am new to Nashville. Don't know many people outside the police department at all. Please go on," Sherrie said with an encouraging smile. Maggie noticed she had a chipped front tooth which gave her smile a snaggle-toothed charm.

"Okay," she continued slowly. "Well, part of Mom died with him. No matter how they fought, she truly loved him, I think. She became hard, suspicious. At the beginning, she began to go out a lot, first just on the weekends. Sometimes she'd stay gone all night. I was out most of the day at class, and Beth would call out for me in the middle of the night, terrified. On the few occasions I was studying late on campus, I'd have to call our neighbor Linda to come stay with her.

"I guess that's when Mom began to drink really bad, and she's never let up since." Maggie looked down at her hands. She had dug her nails into her left hand so hard she was afraid she'd see blood. "Anyway, she was fairly well lit last night. When she's like that, she flies off the handle at the least thing. And the more she goes off, the more anxious Beth gets. Beth's in a fight for her life. Nothing takes precedence over that, not this scroll, not terrorists, nothing. You've got to understand that. I'd rather lose my own life than cause her any more hardship or unhappiness than she already suffers."

For a moment, the policewoman looked incredibly tired. The dark pockets under her eyes sagged. "I understand, and I'm so glad you were able to tell me this. We can make it where Anna'll never see us. Our people are the best. They really are. You have my word that Anna won't spot a soul around your house."

Maggie nibbled a nail and looked away, embarrassed. "I'm really sorry to have laid all that on you, but you need to know how vital it is to keep Mom mellow. The doctor says a major part of healing is a positive outlook, and … well, you met Beth. She's special. Even if she weren't my little sister, she's an incredible kid."

"You'll never know we're there. We'll assign the best, I promise you that. Now I've taken up enough of your time." She stood and held out a hand.

Maggie blew her nose, tucked the tissue in her bag, and followed suit. "Thanks for listening to all that. I still can't believe I said it all, but somehow I feel … lighter."

Sherrie smiled, and it transformed her angular face. "I know that was hard, but I'd like to talk to you sometime outside of this setting. It seems we got a few things in common. How about lunch one day?"

Maggie smiled weakly. "I'd like that. It's your turn to spill, for sure."

"We'll see about that," Sherrie laughed her deep, free laugh. Maggie shook her head, gathered her scattered senses around her, and walked slowly into the stultifying heat of the day. She moved down the sidewalk to the parking lot, fishing around in her purse for the keys.

Suddenly, she stiffened and came to an abrupt, amazed halt. She felt something in her purse, something that had no right being there at all … Gently she tugged on it, then stood staring at it in the bright sunshine.

The scroll.

Am I losing my mind?

— CHAPTER SEVEN —

SATURDAY, JULY 18

Ebbi and Masood stood at JFK's Southwest ticket counter, hoping to catch a flight to Nashville. Masood set down his blue carry-on bag in frustration. There were at least twenty people in line ahead of them, and perhaps three times that behind them. If all those people already had tickets, chances were slim the brothers could make the next flight.

Masood rocked impatiently on his feet, one hand in his pocket rubbing his prayer beads. "Ebbi, when is next flight, if we miss this one?"

"Three hours, but we will have tickets on this one."

"All these people. How could that be?"

Ebbi smiled. "It is big jet—a 727. You will see."

"I have much to learn. To think, a week ago, I have flown only from Badu Tanar to France, and now I am in New York to fly Nashville." He paused and leaned toward his brother, lowering his voice. "How did we find out so fast that the girl is in Nashville?"

Ebbi leaned slightly forward toward Masood as a nearby toddler began to wail. "As you will learn, we have tribe members nearly everywhere, including Interpol, both in USA and UK. Father was contacted and told that someone made a query about an incident in Nashville involving Maggie Purcell."

"I see," Ebbi replied, raising his voice slightly to be heard over the toddler's escalating cries.

Captivated, the brothers craned their necks forward to watch as the child and his harried mother engaged in a tug of war over a leather baggage tag. The mother, heavy-set in a pair of bright yellow shorts, hissed, "Timmy. Stop that this instant or I'll put you in time-out right in the middle of JFK. You see if I don't."

"No! No!" the toddler wailed, then gave the tag a sudden sharp tug. When it pulled free from the bag, he fell onto his fat bottom and screamed.

His mother grunted, bent over, and set him on his feet. "See what happens when you're a bad boy?" She took the leather tag from the child and bent to fasten it to the handle. The boy, still wailing, looked at her face, then at the bare leg closest to him. He walked quickly to the leg, a frown on his face, then sank his teeth into his mother's calf.

The woman straightened with a yelp, and Ebbi choked back laughter. As she scolded the child loudly, Masood muttered in Amharic, "If that was us, my brother, we would be dead by now."

They shuffled forward, moving their bags with their feet. "I miss Badu Tanar, Brother," Ebbi responded. "I miss happy children, the Mouth of the Nile, and baboons playing in the sun. I even miss the alligators."

"Me, I miss the eucalyptus, the one in front of the falls, you know? I believed your stories, how it was our great-great grandfather."

"Not my stories," Ebbi said. "Those stories have been passed down in the tribe since we left Qumran. That is what I miss the most."

"The stories?"

"The continuity. The feeling that everything is as it has been for many years. Knowing that everyone everywhere is your family. The love."

"The love! They are a bunch of women, I tell you! I was glad to finally get away, to live where not everyone knows your business." Masood grinned.

"This is something you will learn—the value of family. Look, a place is open. Take my bag, will you?"

Several hours later, they were settled into seats next to the wing. The large plane was only partially full and the brothers relaxed with a cup of tea.

Masood twirled his cup in his hands and frowned. "Ebbi, what was this incident in Nashville involving Maggie Purcell?"

"She was attacked by two men. They tried to take her from her house."

"Is someone after the scroll?"

Ebbi straightened his legs into the aisle, looking casually over his shoulder. Then he leaned forward and scanned the surrounding seats. Satisfied, he leaned back and began. "You know that the scroll surfaced. Achmed Kiyat had it."

Masood nodded.

"You were home and overheard the call that night, didn't you?"

Masood flushed and lowered his head. "Ebbi, I did not do so on purpose. I was there for the winter vacation, just standing in the kitchen when the phone rang. I was only hungry.

I ate some bread and sausage and was walking by Father's study when he called out. I have never heard such a yell. How could I not listen?"

"What is done is done. It is a shameful thing, to listen to others. You do understand that?"

Masood nodded, then trained his eyes on Ebbi expectantly.

Ebbi sighed, then continued in low Amharic. "Achmed told Father that his son-in-law, Faod, had come by what was possibly one of the lost scrolls. It was in ancient Aramaic, not the more recent version. Faod had found it in the caves of Lascaux in the Dordogne where the pictures of the bulls and horses are on the walls.

"Faod wanted money for it—a lot of money. Achmed thought at first that it should be reported to the French government. Then he called Father, as he'd promised he would if he ever came across such a thing. Father had told him a little of our history at school. Anyway, Father convinced him to wait until he, himself, came to Paris to look at it, but of course Achmed sent him a scan of the scroll."

"I don't understand. How did the scroll get to the Lascaux caves? How did it get to Europe at all?"

"Who knows? Perhaps it was found close to the others in Qumran. Then someone took it to Lascaux and hid it until they could retrieve it later.

"Anyway," Ebbi continued, "you saw the girl run out of Achmed's shop. I myself am not sure why Achmed gave her the scroll. Perhaps he saw the two Arabs, recognized Faod, and panicked. We'll never know.

"We do know, thanks to our friends in Interpol, that this Faod is with a rather nasty terrorist cell based out of Paris. Maggie Purcell is a lucky girl to have escaped them."

Masood's eyes were wide. "Terrorist group?"

"Yes, that's why Achmed's daughter, Fatima fled to New

York. She found out who Faod's friends were."

"Ebbi, we, ourselves, should take the scroll from the girl. Why have we not done so?"

"There are things I do not know. But I do know we are to follow instructions—watch the girl, and make sure nothing happens to either her or the scroll. Father was very definite about that. Now, we'd best go back to speaking English so as not to alarm the American travelers further."

Masood sighed. "Somehow, the baboons of Badu Tanar seem farther away than ever."

Maggie sat in the living room alone, rolling the old scroll between her hands. What exactly had happened here? Had she picked it up from the seat of the car before stumbling out? She tried and couldn't remember the exact sequence of events. She'd fallen to the floor in the crash, the car had come to a stop.

Then everything went black and jumbled, and somehow, she was sprinting through Berry Hill at night.

None of it made any sense. Her head still ached, and she reached a hand around to massage it.

The doorbell rang at two sharp. Darla Maclain was a short, muscular black woman with the longest nails Maggie had ever seen. Maggie invited her in and showed her to the couch, then picked up a notepad and sat next to her.

"Could you tell me a little bit more about Beth? What she likes to do?" Darla said with a wide, bright smile.

"Beth is a very bright kid. She's into languages. She loves her computer. She reads a lot. And she's a chatterbox." Maggie grinned back.

"Does she like games? Board games, cards?"

"She sure does. She plays a mean game of Spades. Listen, can I get you something to drink or munch on?"

"No. I just ate me a burger. I'm fine."

"Let me get some information from you before I forget," Maggie said, pen poised over her paper. Quickly, she wrote down Darla's references. Then she said, "Tell me, how do you work with nails that length?"

"They ain't real, and they're hard as rocks. You get used to 'em."

Maggie sat back with a small sigh. She knew Anna would be home soon, and she wanted to alert Darla to the issues Anna presented. "Darla, I suppose I should tell you that there is a little problem here. My mother, Anna, well, she drinks. She's not a mean drunk or anything like that, but she's forgetful, and she oversleeps, and that kind of thing." Maggie felt her cheeks burn.

"Don't you worry about a thing. I've handled far worse in my time. I got stories I could tell!" Darla laughed.

"That's a relief. I just didn't want you to come into this, not knowing. Tell you what. Let's go see if Beth's awake. She had chemo the other day, and she was just in the ER last night because she passed out. The doctor said it was a low-grade infection and gave her some pills. She seems better, but she's still sort of a bit wonky from it." She stood and led Darla down the short hall.

Maggie opened Beth's room a crack, and at the sight of the girl typing away at her laptop, knocked lightly. "Beth, I have someone who wants to meet you."

"Hey! You're back! Come on in." Beth ran her hands through the remaining wisps of her long blond hair, then pulled them over her head to cover the baldness. "Lord I'm not fit to meet anybody."

"You always look great. Beth Purcell, meet Darla Maclain."

Darla walked straight to the bed, leaned over, and gave the girl a gentle hug. "Hey there. I hear you like cards. Me,

I like my bingo. We're going to have us a time!"

Surprised, Beth hugged her back with a little laugh. "Wow. Zata and Zaddie are dancing all around you, Darla."

"And who are Zata and Zaddie?"

"My fairy friends. And they have great taste. You must be a really good person."

Maggie grinned. "Oh yes, I forgot to mention the fairies. You're bound to think you've fallen in with a bunch of lunatics by now."

"No such thing! I got relatives who seen angels. Not that much different, is it, Beth?" Darla reached over and smoothed Beth's bed, then pulled the desk chair close and sat.

"Angels? Really?"

"Blessed Lord, yes. Why, my cousin Judy …"

Maggie quietly backed out of the room and went into the living room. She sat on the couch and finally felt able to relax. Darla would work out well with Beth, she thought. What a relief that would be. She leaned her head back against the cushion and closed her eyes for just a moment.

She jolted awake when Anna flung the door open and rushed in unsteadily. "We won! Sarah and I won our doubles match. We're twelfth seed now, Maggie."

"Congratulations. Hey, our new girl is in talking with Beth."

Maggie took Anna back to meet Darla and watched, bemused, as Anna charmed Darla with light southern wit and grace. They made arrangements for Darla to be at the house from seven to six daily, and be on call at other times. As Darla finally left, calling out that she'd see them in the morning, the sun began to set.

Maggie made her way back to the guest bedroom and picked up her cell phone with a frown. She hated to have to call work and tell Todd that she would, once again, miss the Monday meeting, but there was no other way. Beth was sick, and Maggie didn't feel right about having Darla on her own in the house for her first day. She couldn't plan on Anna being helpful in her place.

She dialed Xcorp, New York and left an apologetic message, informing her boss that she'd call him Monday afternoon. She hung up, then sank back on the bed. Todd could very well explode. His Monday morning meetings were almost religious to him. He felt Maggie had already missed too many onsite meetings and had threatened her with working full time there in the office.

Maggie stared at the pale cream ceiling and thought. If Todd insisted she work full time in New York, she'd be forced to find another job. She had to have a certain amount of freedom to deal with Beth. Working from home enabled her to travel as needed.

Somewhere nearby, a neighbor was mowing his grass, taking advantage of the coolness brought by the setting sun. The sound of the lawnmower ebbed and flowed. Maggie reached a hand to her neck and massaged the tight muscles, listening to the familiar roar. She could almost smell the greenness of the cut grass.

Then the sound seemed to merge into a low growl. Alarmed, she tried to sit up but found herself unable to move. Afraid that she was having a nightmare, she struggled to move and wake herself up.

The growl deepened. The air grew chill and dank around her, and the light in the room somehow brightened. Terrified, she moaned and fought to bring herself to her feet.

Then she was standing, looking into the depths of a black cave. Cool air breathed on her, and chills ran up her spine as once again the growl sounded, roaring just behind her.

As she slowly turned, a pair of slitted golden eyes looked into hers. A great wolf gathered itself, then leaped ...

With a scream that turned to a whimper, Maggie jerked

upright on her bed.

The familiar room with its rose damask wallpaper closed in around her. She wiped beads of sweat off her forehead. This was worse than the chanting. Something otherworldly was actively stalking her. And it was definitely getting closer.

She shivered as the air flowed from the vent above the bed. Even if singularly terrifying, it was only a dream. Or was it? She thought back to the chanting, the drums. All of it so unfamiliar. Goosebumps rose on her skin. What if she was ill? Deathly ill, to be seeing such things? And the scroll. What was it about this scroll? How had it really gotten back into her purse?

I've got to see a doctor. That's all there is to it. Maggie promised herself she'd make an appointment as soon as she got back to New York. There was nothing natural or normal about this. Nothing.

Just then Anna called from the kitchen, "Dinner and Spades! Who's up for a licking?"

Maggie felt herself shaking. What was happening to her? Hearing music, a suddenly appearing scroll, and now seeing wolves? Was it tension, exhaustion? It had to be. She drew in a deep, soothing breath and made her way to the kitchen.

Anna was chopping vegetables into a sizzling pan of oil, joking as the knife flashed up and down. Sitting at the table, Beth watched her and smiled.

"Mom, need any help?" Maggie offered.

"You and your black thumb with cooking? You just sit next to Beth and behave. Actually, you can go scrounge up the cards. They're somewhere in the desk in the living room, last I checked."

"I'll go!" Beth said, jumping up.

Maggie sank into a kitchen chair and rubbed her head, inhaling the scent of sizzling garlic. "Lord, that smells good,

Mom. So, what'd you think of Darla?"

"She seemed wonderful, I have to admit. And it'll be such a relief to have someone else here. I worry so much, even when I step out the door to go to the store."

Impulsively, Maggie stood, walked to her, and hugged her from behind. "I know. I feel the same way when I travel. I should have thought of this a while ago."

"Oh go sit back down," Anna groused with a small smile. "You'll make me chop my fingers off."

After dinner, Maggie cleared away the plates and Beth began to expertly shuffle the cards. Midway through the game, Anna was up by more than fifty points and both her daughters were razzing her.

"I haven't made a bid all night," Beth said. "It's all Maggie's fault."

"Me! Go ahead, blame me. Have you seen my score? It's your mother who stacked the deck before I got here."

Beth laid her cards down flat and leaned forward. "Mom, tell me again how Dad managed to black your eye while you guys were playing Spades."

Maggie saw a muscle under Anna's left eye tense briefly.

Anna took a deep breath and smiled. "You would want to hear about that. So I was winning, as usual. Then your dad got himself the best hand of the night. He bet double nil, and he made it. He stood up to go to the kitchen, did a little dance, and his shoe came off and got me right under my eye."

"Yeah! It was black for a few days, then it turned all sorts of gross colors." Beth laughed, never noticing Maggie's stillness next to her.

Anna looked keenly at Maggie, then made a small brushing hand motion to quiet her. Maggie looked down and remained silent. She remembered many occasions when Anna had had black eyes and bruises on her face.

Anna stood. "Well, with all this winning I'm sure thirsty. Anyone want something to drink?"

Anxiously clenching her cards, Beth looked at Maggie. Maggie winked at her. "Sure, Mom. Could I have a Coke?"

"Coming right up." Anna reached up for the glasses, and Maggie had a moment of déjà vu.

She'd been six or seven, and was dawdling over getting dressed for school. She heard the front door slam and her father yell something. So he was home. She hurried to pull on her dress and grab her bookbag to go into the kitchen.

Just as she came down the hall, she heard a loud crash and stopped short of the kitchen door.

"You bitch. Why do you think I don't bother coming home when this is what I come home to? This place is a fucking mess!" Tom Purcell bellowed.

Anna responded in a low voice, then came the slap and a gasp—almost a moan. Maggie ran into the kitchen.

A thin stream of blood ran from Anna's left nostril, around her mouth, and dripped off her chin. Maggie stood, shocked. "Momma, are you hurt?"

"It's just an owie, Maggie. Now sit down while I get you your juice." She turned, reaching up in the cupboard for a glass.

Maggie's father glared at her. Then, without saying anything, he turned and stamped back out of the house.

Maggie's breath caught in her throat at the memory. It had been one of the defining moments of her life. Every time she thought of it, she had the same unreasoned dread she'd felt as a child. And every time she considered getting serious with a man, the memory played in her head. Men weren't to be trusted.

Now Anna turned, a large bottle of Coke in one hand. "We might as well have popcorn with it. What's Spades without good hot buttered popcorn?"

Beth smiled, a bright smile of relief, and Maggie felt the tension in her own back release.

Early the next morning, Maggie awakened to the sounds of gagging coming from the bathroom. Groggily, she threw on her robe and made her way to the bathroom. Beth was sitting on the floor staring into the toilet, head held in both hands.

"Oh Mags, I'm sorry. Did I wake you up?"

"Sweetie, that's what I'm here for. Here, let me get you a cold rag. Oh no, there you go again." Maggie jumped forward as the small body lurched toward the toilet. She held Beth's head as she convulsed, then Beth slumped back against her legs.

"Okay, I think I'm done." Beth said, her voice cracking. "It kind of comes in waves."

Maggie got a towel, dampened it with warm water, and cleaned up Beth's too-pale face. Then she picked up the thin form and carried her to her room. "Don't move. I'm just going to get some ginger ale."

The house was dark and silent as she moved to the familiar kitchen and fumbled a glass from the cupboard. Tears blurred her vision. She set the glass on the counter and splashed water on her face before walking slowly back to Beth's room.

"Here you go. Think you could sleep a couple of hours? Darla'll be here at seven."

"I don't think so. I'm probably up for the day. You should go back to bed, though. I'm fine now—I'll just read."

Maggie sat in the desk chair, cocked it backwards and put her feet on Beth's bed. "Not so fast. I want to see if you can actually throw up your toenails next time."

Beth's laugh turned into a gagging cough. Maggie leaned forward, but Beth waved her away. "You make one more crack like that, you might get your wish."

They spoke softly until well after the sun was up. Anna looked in, dressed in her tennis whites. Maggie assured her that Beth was alright and, relieved, she left for her game.

Beth was reading and Maggie had just turned on her laptop when Darla arrived with a paper bag.

"Hey there! Look what I have. Where's Beth this morning?"

"She was really sick earlier. She's in bed reading now. What's all that?"

"I ran by my mom's house and picked us up a few old games. We don't have as many as I thought we did, though."

"Maggie? Is that Darla?" came Beth's voice from the bedroom.

"You bet it's me, and just you wait!" She winked at Maggie, then walked down the hall.

Maggie heard laughter, then Beth's squeals of delight.

Darla was certainly a relief, but Maggie realized that the new addition might cause her further problems at work. She didn't want to leave Darla alone so soon, not knowing her way around the house. Thinking she'd do better to talk to him in person, she picked up the phone to call Todd and request another day off.

"Maggie, I got your message. I understand you've got family problems, but you've got to see this from my point of view." Todd's voice was brusque, and Maggie could see him leaning back in his chair, twisting the phone cord. "We need you here. You've missed more meetings this year than you've made."

"I don't know what else I can do. She's only twelve …"

"I'm sorry, but that's not my problem. My problem is a team that consistently is without its lead troubleshooter. My problem is that without you, Brainstorm Theory just doesn't work. Everyone else is here, spinning our wheels."

"If you'd just let me use a webcam—"

"You'd see the diagrams and notes, but how's your team supposed to be motivated? By ESP? No Maggie, this really isn't working out. We're going to need to come up with a better solution. Brainstorming has solved many an issue, but without our lead troubleshooter, it just falls apart. You're back when, Wednesday?" At her assent, he continued, "I'm going to need to see your smiling face in the office every day for a while. Then we'll discuss your working out of the house."

"Wait," Maggie said, fighting desperation. "I'll be there Monday. I'll fly out tomorrow afternoon."

"That's a move in the right direction. Okay. Busy now." He hung up.

Upset, Maggie put in a call to Reeve. His line went to voice mail, so she left a short message, then picked up her purse and drove to the store for fresh fruit. She'd make a smoothie for Beth's lunch.

Faint thunder sounded as Maggie, bags in hand, walked out of the Apple Market. It sounded like a storm was brewing. She shifted the three bags to one hand and felt for her car keys with the other, one eye on the humped black clouds and hissing lightning just beyond the hills.

A drop of rain spattered on her bare arm as she inserted the key into the car door. Startled, she jerked. Then a hand closed on her shoulder. She dropped the bags, shrieked, and sprang sideways.

"Jumpy lady," Sherrie said, trying not to laugh. She looked casual in tight jeans and a 'Don't feed the cops' tee-shirt.

"Jesus, you almost gave me a stroke. I just picked up a bunch of fruit for Beth, for a smoothie."

"How's she doing?" Sherrie leaned back against a silver Ford Taurus.

"Not so great. She was really sick this morning. I'm hoping

to get an apple and banana smoothie down her."

"Sorry about that," Sherrie said. "Poor kid. She shouldn't be going through this at her age. What's she, thirteen?"

"Twelve. I know—she should be out playing." Maggie looked at Sherrie, wondering. *How had the woman found her?*

"I called your house and talked to Beth," Sherrie said, reading her mind. "Your cell phone is off. She said she thought you headed to the Apple Market."

"Oh hell," said Maggie. She picked up the spilled apples and placed them in the bag, then checked her phone. "Battery's dead. Just my luck."

"Could be worse. You could have been scared to death in the parking lot by a crazed police woman."

Maggie laughed.

"Got a couple minutes? I got something to tell you. Want a cup of coffee at IHOP?"

"Sure. I can't stay long, though, so I'll follow you."

After a short drive, they were seated in a booth watching the now-steady rain falling onto Hillsboro Road. The Nashville landmark restaurant was full, as was common on a Saturday morning.

They ordered coffee, and Sherrie threw her arms over the back of the booth and relaxed. "Got to love Saturdays. They're my day off."

"I don't know how you do what you do, though it must be interesting," Maggie said, stirring a pile of sugar into her black coffee.

"It's got its moments," Sherrie said with her snaggle-toothed grin. She took a sip of coffee and looked at Maggie over the rim of her mug. "Well, I got some news for you. I reckon I shouldn't be discussing this out of the office, so I have to ask you to keep it quiet."

"My lips are sealed," Maggie said, curious.

"I've got a buddy at Interpol. We went to school together.

He's living in London now, but we worked on a thing or two in the past. He knows about this business in Paris." She stopped, looked down at her coffee, indecisiveness written on her face.

"And?" prompted Maggie. Nervous, she put her coffee down and leaned forward.

"And he says they may try to get you back to France after all."

— CHAPTER EIGHT —

Maggie went white.

"They might try to charge you with 'leaving the scene of a crime,'" Sherrie went on, "but their real intent is to bring in members of the Paris cell, and have you look at them. I think the whole thing stinks."

"Oh God," Maggie gasped. "I'll lose my damn job if I have to go back there and waste more time. Can they force me to go?" She picked up her cup and looked into it as if the answer was written in the bottom.

"They can sure make life miserable for you if you don't," Sherrie said gently. At the stricken look on Maggie's face, she quickly added, "But we're doing all we can on this end so that won't have to happen."

"What can I do?" Maggie asked, panic welling up in her throat.

"Nothing … But we can ensure they got all the data they need on that end. Hey now," she said, noticing Maggie's look. "I said might try to get you back. It ain't written in stone."

"I can't believe how stressed out I am. It's an absolutely horrible time for this. I have a boss who's bitching I'm not in the office enough, Beth who's really sick, terrorists after this scroll and maybe me—"

"I'm sorry, I really am. It's not definite that they're going to get in touch with you, but I figured you'd want to know."

"Thank you. Forewarned is forearmed. Hey, maybe I should just make a run for it."

Sherrie, laughing at that, said they'd still find her. Maggie stared again into the depths of her coffee. She swirled the cup, thinking its blackness looked a lot like the sinkhole her life was becoming.

If she went to Paris, Todd would surely fire her. It wouldn't be a fast trip, and it might be complicated. She could even wind up in jail. She shuddered, and her coffee spilled out onto the table. Taking a napkin from the dispenser, she distractedly mopped it up.

How had things ever gotten so complicated? It was bad enough living with the threat of Beth's illness over her head. But this mess with the scroll ... Sole witness to the murder of a perfectly nice man. Getting snatched in front of her own house. And now, maybe being forced to go back to France at the worse possible time for her professionally.

She felt sick inside, like there was a darkness around her. Her heart ached for Beth most of all. Maggie had to somehow keep Beth safe from whatever influence she had brought into her life.

"Penny for them." Sherrie had stopped talking and was watching Maggie, concern in her eyes.

"Not worth that much. I think it boils down to Beth. Her safety's the most important thing to me in all this."

Sherrie flagged a waiter and ordered some blueberry waffles, but Maggie declined any food. After the waiter left, Sherrie rearranged herself in the bench seat and stretched her legs out. "Did I tell you Beth reminds me of my daughter Carol?"

Maggie looked up. "You had mentioned you had a child."

"She's only five, but she has long blond hair and blue eyes like your Beth. Curly hair, just like mine. But on her it's gorgeous." She unzipped her fanny pack, withdrew a fat wallet, and flipped through photos. Then she passed one over to Maggie.

"Oh, she's totally adorable! She does sort of look like Beth, right down to that solemn, intelligent look."

"She gets that from her father," Sherrie said, and went silent.

"I'm almost afraid to ask," Maggie said, seeing the shuttered look on Sherrie's face.

"No, it's fine. Especially after all you've told me." For a moment, the women shared a look of understanding.

"He's back in Alabama. He had a bad habit of stepping out on me, so I decided to step the hell out of Alabama, for good. Bastard."

"Oh, I'm really sorry to hear that. So that's why you moved to Nashville?"

"That, and there was an opening for a detective here. It sure wasn't because I knew a lot of people."

"Well, you know one more now," Maggie said with a grin. "I really live in New York, but I visit often to see Beth."

"Speaking of," Sherrie said as she loaded on butter and syrup to her freshly arrived waffles. "I'll run by the house while you're gone, on my own time. And you've seen my official car—it's unmarked. Your mom won't have a clue a cop's been by."

"That would be great," Maggie said. "What a relief!"

They chatted for another half-hour before Maggie regretfully said that she should try to get back and make the smoothie for Beth. Sherrie got her satellite phone number, amazed that Maggie could be found anywhere in the world, and they parted with a hug.

Back at the house, Maggie was putting sliced apples into the blender when she recalled Darla should be back from lunch soon. She sighed. This had to work out. It would ease her constant worry that Beth was alone. She'd know someone was there to keep her company. And of course, Sherrie had now promised to stop by as well.

She added a banana to the blender and drew in the sweetness. Then she frowned, puzzled. Where had she smelled that sweet, fruity odor? Then it came back to her, the shirt wrapped around her head. That nasty perfume had had definite overtones of banana in it. She shuddered and pulled the blender from its stand.

The smoothie finished and in the fridge, Maggie sank back on the couch and laid her head back for a moment. Then she picked up a pad of paper and began a list for Darla.

She was intently chewing on the end of the pen when Darla walked in carrying a large paper bag. Maggie smiled.

"I just was making a list for you. What's in the bag?"

"I bought a bunch more games, girl. Made good use of my lunch break—we got Trivial Pursuit, Monopoly, Life, Clue. I found a sale at Wal-Mart," Darla grinned.

"You know, I really feel good about this," Maggie said. "But you let me know how much you spent and I'll reimburse you. You're going to spoil Beth rotten."

"Seems to me she could use some spoiling," said Darla, pulling a long straight black wig from the bag. "This one's mine, but if she likes it we can get her a blond one."

"Wow! I don't know how she'll look in black, but that's a

great idea. Let's run over this list before Beth figures out you're here."

"Every day, Beth should have a bath. Hair, what's left of it, washed every other day. Oh I forgot to ask, do you cook?"

"I sure do. I cooked all my last family's meals. For a while, the old man wouldn't eat anything but my fried chicken."

"Oh yeah, this will really work out. Beth adores fried chicken. So, at least lunch and dinner, if you don't see Mom cooking." She folded her arms across her chest.

"Should I do her laundry too?" Darla asked. "I noticed the basket next to the door."

"I hadn't thought of that, but yes, that'd be great. I think the most important thing is to keep up with her calendar and her chemo, and make sure she's there on time. It should be another week and a half before her next one. She's on a biweekly schedule for now."

"Poor child."

"I know. It'll break your heart. She's incredibly brave."

"Who's incredibly brave?" Beth asked, rounding the corner.

"Mom, for daring to beat you at Spades last night," Maggie replied with a wink at Darla.

"Yeah, right. Hey Darla, you're back!"

"Hi, Beth. Are you hungry? It's getting right close to lunchtime."

"Not really. I was sort of sick this morning. I'd rather play those games you've got sticking out of that bag," she said, smiling.

"I'm one step ahead of you, monster," Maggie said. "I made you a killer smoothie with apples and bananas and a little cinnamon. You can down that, at least, can't you?"

"That's not real food! Bring it on."

As Maggie walked into the kitchen, she heard several cars

drive up. She looked out the window, and saw Anna followed by four other women, all dressed in tennis whites. She hesitated, looked back at Beth and Darla, then continued to the refrigerator.

Anna and her friends bustled into the house, sleek hair-styles with elegantly tanned skin. Beth greeted the women while Darla stepped out of the way.

"Beth, honey. Are you feeling better? She was a mite sick this morning," Anna told her friends.

"Yes, Mom, I'm fine now. And Maggie made me a smooth-ie for lunch," Beth said as Maggie crossed to her and handed her the drink.

"That certainly looks good. Darla, sugar, would you mind getting us all some sweet tea?" Anna said, dropping into an easy chair.

Darla went still and looked uncertainly at Maggie, who flushed to the roots of her hair.

"Mom, I'm already up, I'll do it." Maggie moved to the center of the room.

"You just sit down and visit with us for a moment," Anna drawled with a too-wide smile. "Let Darla fetch the drinks. That's what she's here for, right?"

Maggie knew that smile and felt her stomach sink. The other women began chattering brightly about their tennis game. Maggie opened her mouth to reply and Darla cut her off.

"I'd be happy to fix y'all some tea. Is it already made?"

"There's a pitcher in the fridge," Anna said.

Maggie threw a glance at Anna, who refused to look at her. Beth uneasily turned and went back to her room. After a moment, Maggie followed.

"You don't think Darla'll quit, do you?" Beth asked. "Mom didn't mean any harm."

"I hope not, but she couldn't have expected Mom to act

like that. Sometimes I wonder what she thinks—if she thinks—before she opens that mouth." Maggie began to pace back and forth across Beth's room.

"Maybe she doesn't think. Maybe it just comes out." Beth crossed to her bed, put her drink on the table, then flopped down.

"Never mind for now. You just concentrate on that smoothie. I went all the way to Apple Market for that fruit. It has no preservatives. It's free-range ..."

Beth laughed, sat up, and reached for the drink as Darla walked in.

"Darla, I'm so sorry about Mother. I'll have a talk with her later ..."

"Don't you worry about it. I was raised down South. I've heard a lot worse. Women her age, they just get used to acting a certain way," Darla said.

"Don't ever let her hear the bit about 'a certain age,'" Beth said with a giggle.

Maggie shook her head. "It was wrong, Beth. That was an insult to Darla, and really, an insult to us also."

"Ain't no big thing, Maggie," Darla responded, her face serious. "But I appreciate your words."

"I don't see what all the fuss is about," Beth said. "I don't get Mom's attitude at all. There are black kids, Asian kids, Hispanic kids at my school. What's the big deal? Even the cops last night, one was white, one Hispanic."

Maggie froze. Damn, she hadn't meant to inform Darla of the whole scroll affair. She had quite enough to handle with Mom and her drinking.

"Cops?" Darla asked, looking from Maggie to Beth. Beth blushed.

"Beth, you've got a big mouth. Did I ever tell you that?" Maggie said. "Darla, maybe it's best you know." Maggie explained the whole incident, including the fact that they were probably still after her. "Let me give you Sherrie's—the police woman's—phone number," she said. Sitting in Beth's chair, she went through her purse, found the number, and wrote it on a pad.

"Them bastards. They better not come near my girl, hear! After what just happened, I might give 'em Anna, though," she said with a big grin.

"I might just help you." Maggie ripped the number off and handed it to Darla. "Here, if you need to call her, just tell her you work for us. Listen, I'm sorry about all this. You sure didn't know what you were getting yourself into when you agreed to work for us!"

"Hey, life ain't easy. It could be a lot worse. If you knew some of the patients I've took care of, this girl, she's like a little blond gift." Maggie looked at Darla, who slowly smiled back. "Beth, I'm thinking you could do with a washing. Look at your hair! Maggie, you run along and relax. Beth and I, we got work to do."

"Then I'll leave you to it," Maggie said as she walked out.

Once Maggie was gone, Darla closed the door behind her. "Any of that bother you—what happened last night?"

"It scared me, but I'm mostly just scared for Maggie. I hate thinking something bad could happen to her," Beth said, eyes filling.

"Ain't nothing gonna happen to that girl. She's strong. You know that! Now, how about washing that hair?"

Beth looked up and frowned. "How bad do I look? And I saw the Afternoon Annies like this!"

"As if they'd notice, as pretty as you are. But, Afternoon Annies?"

"Yeah, Maggie named them that. Maybe 'cause you're here they're not doing it, but usually they have a bunch of drinks after they play. Real ones, you know."

"I can imagine. Listen, come on into the bathroom and stick your head in the sink. This won't take a minute."

Beth followed her in. This was a treat. Normally, she would have had to wait at least another day before she'd find the energy to wash her hair, even as little of it as there was. She sighed softly. Darla was such a relief. It was hard to ask Mom all the time to be doing things. Mom had enough to worry about.

Darla handled her hair like a professional, and it felt so good, Beth found herself moaning. Back in her bedroom, though, she was content to lie on the bed while Darla patted her hair dry with a towel.

"So tell me. What's this about fairies?" Darla asked.

"There are two who visit me sometimes. I named them Zata and Zaddie. They are so pretty! Sometimes they dance. Sometimes they just kind of hover and look at me. When I'm really sick, though, I swear they sing. I can't really tell what the words are—it just kind of sounds like humming. Oh, you must think I'm nuts."

Darla chuckled. "Girl, you don't know crazy. I started to tell you before about my aunt who saw an angel once? She used to threaten us kids that whatever we were doing, an angel was watching and we'd best behave."

"When did she see it?"

"Well, my aunt was married to a real no-good. He didn't have him a job. Didn't want one either. He liked to drink a whole lot more than he should, and when he did, he liked to get in that car and drive. No matter what my aunt did, she just couldn't stop him. She'd hide the keys—he'd have another set made. She'd tell him she'd leave him—he'd say 'go.' He was impossible.

"My aunt figured that if she went and sat down in the passenger seat, he'd never take off. But she found herself with a thoroughly drunk and upset husband cruising right fast down

I-65 at nearly midnight … Oh let me get a comb, this is almost dry." She paused, picked up Beth's wide-tooth comb, and began to run it through the long wisps of remaining hair. "I ain't hurting you, am I?"

"It feels wonderful. Please tell me more about the angel!"

"So they were going far too fast down the interstate, and good thing there weren't too many people out, mostly just truckers. My aunt was scared stiff, kept begging him to stop or slow down, but he didn't listen.

"He went to get off to get some gas, and some poor man was broke down right at the off-ramp. His little girl had done got out and crossed the road—I don't know why. But just as my uncle came around the big corner, going like a bat out of hell, there she was. My aunt said it was like slow motion. The child's face was so scared. She had long black pigtails and big blue eyes, round as saucers. And she stood in the middle of the ramp, just stood there with a teddy bear clamped in her arms. The car got closer, my aunt screamed, and then it happened.

"All of a sudden, a beautiful woman in a long white robe just appeared out of nowhere and snatched that child up in the air. My aunt swears that the woman held that child so high that they drove right under her! *Under her,* she said. Well, my uncle done hit the brakes and they like to slid right into her father's truck before they finally got under control, but my aunt didn't care. Her eyes were glued on that rear window.

"She saw the lady carry that child to the side of the road and set her down. She swears she then saw her look directly at my uncle, frown, and shake her head. Then she vanished— just like that." Darla snapped her fingers.

Beth sat silent for a moment, awed. "Wow. That's amazing. She took her up over the car? She flew!"

"Yeah, she did. And you know what else? Beth, that angel's

face ... was black."

"Of course she was. Angels and fairies come in all colors, just like we do. I think we see angels who look like we do."

"Kid, you're a wise soul. Has anyone ever told you that?"

"Mostly, I get treated like someone with no brains, because I'm sick. Sick people get treated like they're mental defects. Everyone's forever speaking slow and loud to us."

"Then they sure don't know you, do they? They sure don't know you." Darla hugged her tightly for a moment, then straightened. "Lord, I nearly forgot. Look what I brought you to try." She reached into the bag and withdrew the long black wig.

"Oh, I have to see how I look in that!" Excited, Beth stood. Darla twined Beth's thin blond hair onto her head, pulling the black wig over the strands. She smoothed it down, then presented Beth to her mirror.

Beth went speechless. In the mirror was an older, more mature Beth. *I look at least twenty! Goodness, when I'm twenty, I'll be driving a car, staying up as late as I want to. Maggie and I will go to R-movies every night! I'll live in New York ...*

Or would she? She looked at herself closely in the mirror, the blackness of the wig reflected in the smudges under her blue eyes. She usually refused to let herself think that way, but seeing herself as she could be ...

Would she, really? Live to learn to drive a car?

"You look like Morticia Addams, you do! Well I reckon we know you ain't good in black at all. Guess I'd do better finding you blond hair."

In her room next to Beth's, Maggie prepared to call Reeve on her cell. Clearing her throat, she felt tears threatening. As he always did, Reeve responded on the second ring. His deep, sexy voice made her grin briefly with relief. "Hey girl! How's the sprout?"

"Not so great. She was really sick this morning. But good news: I found the perfect girl to take care of her. She's here now ... She really is wonderful. They're in there right now giggling."

"And after you worried so much. From now on, you're going to be a more mellow soul, aren't you?"

"I don't think so. Reeve ... something really awful happened Friday night. I don't want you to worry—it's over with. But I was kind of kidnapped briefly. It was that damn scroll. They wanted it."

"Kidnapped? Okay, that's enough. I'm coming down there immediately." His voice grew rough with concern.

"No," Maggie broke in. "It's under control—they weren't the brightest. They wrecked the car, and I jumped out of the back and ran. I've been to the police. Nice detective named Sherrie found out from Interpol that they're terrorists. Why on earth would terrorists want a stupid scroll?"

"Have you ever thought that it might be a whole lot more than just a scroll? It might be worth a fortune. Wait, so the guys who kidnapped you were terrorists? Who are they?"

"Remember I told you the shop owner's daughter, in the French flea market, did all the artwork? Well, she was engaged to this guy, Faod, Sherrie told me. He's associated with Al Qaeda."

"Well, terrorists need money."

"Not Al Qaeda. They sure don't."

Reeve's voice deepened. "I'm sure Al Qaeda's not after you. I don't know exactly what's happening around you, but I think you'd be better off back here in New York."

"I agree, mainly so that Beth and Mom won't be exposed to this insanity. I'll be out of here tomorrow."

Before then, she'd have more information on the scroll. Surely Royce had looked at her email by now. She'd call him the minute she got back to New York, if he hadn't emailed her by then. The man had taught ancient languages for more than twenty years—he *had* to know something.

"Oh, I nearly forgot, Reeve. Now I've got another problem. Todd was a creep on the phone. He's threatening to take away my work-at-home privileges. Then what'll I do? I'll have to quit. No choice." Her voice broke.

"Oh, hell, Maggie. Let me talk to him. I bet I can work something out—"

"No. Don't. He is the way he is. It's just because I keep missing his precious Monday brainstorm meetings."

"Listen. It's like I've said a thousand times, girl. You can turn contractor and easily make twice what you're making now, and have better benefits, if you find the right company. I'm serious, Maggie."

Maggie sniffled and blew her nose. What if no one would hire her? How could Reeve understand? Xcorp had hired him three years after Maggie, and he'd already had several other offers from headhunters. It was simply different for men—they fared better in the corporate world.

"Beth and Mom depend on me completely," she said, "except that small check Mom receives from Dad's death. And you know that doesn't go far at all. I'm really worried."

"Mags, I might have an idea. I don't want to talk about it now—might jinx it. But I'm going to make a few phone calls. You hang in there. There's no use you freaking out until we know something for sure. You hang in there!" Reeve's voice was strong and determined.

"What choice do I have?" Maggie straightened her shoulders, then ended the call.

That night, as she washed her face in the bathroom, Maggie noticed her green eyes were bloodshot with fatigue. *But at least now Beth would be taken care of,* she thought as she changed into the oversized tee-shirt she used for pajamas.

The scroll. What was so special about that damn scroll?

Wondering, she sat cross-legged on her bed, gently unrolled it, and squinted at it uneasily. Something had changed. Were the symbols more visible than she'd seen the first time? Surely that was impossible. The symbols couldn't have darkened since she'd seen them last, but that's exactly what she thought she was seeing.

Again something nagged at her, like a memory just out of reach.

It's exhaustion, it has to be. Determined to try to sleep, she put the scroll back in her purse and turned off the light. Just before she fell asleep, she wondered why she didn't just get rid of the scroll. The trouble would be over then, wouldn't it? But what if Reeve was right and the scroll was worth a lot of money?

The next morning, Maggie awoke early and phoned the airlines. The best she could do for Beth would be to leave and take her troubles with her. She was in luck: there was a flight leaving for New York in several hours. She packed, said goodbye to Beth and Mom, and returned the rental car.

The flight to New York was rough. As the plane pitched just after takeoff, Maggie's damp hands clamped onto the armrests. At least she wouldn't have another waking nightmare, not if being relaxed had anything to do with it. The plane leveled out, and she nibbled a nail.

Finally back in her own apartment that evening, Maggie checked her email. To her relief, Royce had sent a detailed letter about the scroll. She scanned the letter and smiled, imagining the slight professor closely examining the scroll.

Royce was so intense about his chosen field. Whenever he became fully engaged in a lecture, a muscle above his mouth would pull his lips up in a sort of sneer, an unfortunate tic over which he had no power. The ruder students in his class called him Rolls Royce since his bared teeth resembled the grill on a car.

She shook her head and smiled. Royce wrote:

From: Royce Stevens [mailto: royce.stevens@columbia.edu]

Sent: Sunday, June 19th, 2005 4:12 PM

To: Purcell, Maggie (mpurcell@xcorpmail.net)

Subject: Re: Hello from an old friend

Maggie,

The scroll is indeed written in Aramaic. If you were here, I'd show you the difference in the vowels between ancient and current day Aramaic. However, the scan you sent is less than desirable. Parts are smudged or totally missing.

The scroll certainly appears ancient. I can see where it has crumbled away. And of course you only sent me a small portion of the whole, if I understand the situation correctly. At any rate, I was able to pick out the following phrases:

turn his face from thee ... other gods ... cities of gold.

I would be most interested in seeing the rest.

Royce

Maggie stared. *City of gold?* She leaned back in her desk chair and propped herself by one foot. Wasn't there a lost city of gold in South America? Pushing her foot against her desk, she rocked. *That couldn't be it. How could an Aramaic scroll discuss a city in South America?*

She stood and walked to her window, then stared at the steady stream of people on the sidewalk. Her small apartment was a sublet in trendy Brooklyn Heights.

She turned away, walked to her low couch, and sat. There in front of her, her latest artwork lay spread across the oddly shaped piece of old marble that functioned as both easel and coffee table.

The plaster lay clean and dry across her carefully crafted wire mesh base, ready for paint. She reached out a hand and ran it over the smooth medium. Near the top, the wire had been shaped underneath in boiling, heaped mounds of thunderheads riven by an inset path that would become a stream of light. The light would pour down onto the uplifted face of a blond girl, surrounded by droplets of rain.

Each drop would have a tiny fairy dancing, leaping, and in the case of one special drop near the child's right eye, reaching its arms out in prayer. Maggie could see all this clearly before she ever put paint to plaster.

A knock on the door interrupted her thoughts. She got up and let Reeve in.

"Hey girl, what's up? Wow, is that your latest?" He walked to the couch and stood, looking down.

"Sure enough. It's nearly ready to paint. What do you think?" Maggie asked, curious. Without paint, she could imagine that the plaster looked like a series of bumps and ridges to other people.

"That our Beth looking up? I'd know those eyes anywhere. But what's that all around her? Looks like a hundred fingertips sticking up next to her face."

Maggie laughed. "Nope. And I'm not saying yet. You're just going to have to wait until I get it painted. That is Beth, though." She was pleased that he'd seen that much.

"It's a gorgeous evening out there. Feel like a walk to the French place?"

"Sure."

On summer nights like this, New York itself could be considered a city of gold, Maggie mused. They took the elevator to the ground floor. Reeve stepped ahead of her to the outer door, and held it open. She started to pass him and stumbled—he caught her close to him. She froze for a moment and heard him exhale sharply. Then she hurriedly pushed by him and out the building. The city breathed in the early evening, its lights bright.

"By the way, I heard from Royce. He says the letter's in ancient Aramaic," Maggie said and went on to explain the brief translation.

"'Other gods' and 'cities of gold.' Curiouser and curiouser ... What have you gotten yourself into?" Reeve raised a brow.

"As if I did it on purpose! The shopkeeper just put it on top of the Napoleon letter and rolled it right up."

"Easy girl. Just tweaking you." He looked at her with concern. She had dark circles around her green eyes, and her usually bright complexion was sallow. "Maybe I didn't choose the best time. Listen, I never did find out. How were the Sprout's latest tests?"

"Not good. Her blood count is elevated again. If this keeps up, they'll want to treat more aggressively. She'll have to have chemo maybe twice a week instead of every other week."

Reeve felt his throat close with fear. Reaching down, he grabbed Maggie with one arm, and hugged her head to him as they walked. "I'm so sorry. When's the next test?"

"Next week. She has one just before every chemo treatment."

"Then I'll just have to redouble my prayers." He held her close to him briefly, then released her with carefully masked regret. "Prayers work, you know."

"A fat lot of good they've done so far," Maggie retorted.

"She'll get better. You'll see. You got to have faith. And look, now you have a wonderful girl to help care for her. What's that if not the answer to a prayer?"

"That was me calling a health agency and requesting a girl. That's what that was," Maggie said.

Reeve suppressed a smile. She was beginning to sound somewhat less depressed. They stood at the corner and waited for the light to change, the noisy crowds moving around them. He looked down at her black hair, gleaming in the street light, and repressed the urge to smooth the lock that hung almost over her left eye.

"Hey, did that professor of yours give you any idea how old that scroll might be?" Reeve asked.

"He only said it's ancient Aramaic."

"We need to get that thing carbon dated," Reeve said. "These people are after it for a reason. The more we know, the better prepared we'll be."

"It isn't old. The daughter did it, remember?" Maggie said. "I feel like just dumping it in the nearest trashcan, then putting up a big sign, 'Scroll here! Take it and leave me the hell alone.'"

"And what if they still come after you, because of the scroll's contents? Besides, I get the feeling it's a very valuable piece of writing. You can't afford to just throw it away, not when it's potentially valuable."

"I suppose not. Well, the least I can do is get a good copy of the whole thing to Royce. You'd really like him, Reeve. He was the greatest teacher. He made ancient civilizations come to life, and you know how I hate history. I can even remember what a Pharaoh's cartouche, of all things, looks like!"

Walking across the busy corner, Reeve stopped and let the crowd surge by him. "Dear God, I didn't know Egyptian males were into such bodily cleansing. That's actually scary."

Maggie, surprised, barked with laughter. "*Cartouche*, Reeve! It's like a symbol that's carved to show the person is a pharaoh."

Reeve tightened his lips over a grin. "Go ahead, laugh. So I'm not an expert on Egyptian hieroglyphics. Listen, I'm starving. Can we step it up a little?"

"Sure. And wait till I tell Professor Royce about your definition of cartouche."

— CHAPTER NINE —

MONDAY, JULY 20

After a rather boring Monday filled with meetings, Maggie and Reeve took the subway, then speed-walked through a drizzling rain to Royce's office in Columbia's Center for Anthropology.

Maggie knocked lightly on his door. Reeve watched as a small, extremely thin man in a well-worn plaid jacket came to greet them. He clasped Maggie's hand with a warm smile before leading them into his tiny, cluttered office.

"Good to see you again, Royce!" Maggie said. "Professor Royce, meet Reeve Hawkins." The two men shook hands. "Thanks for taking the time to help us out. A number of strange things have happened to us since I got this scroll. You think you'll be able to translate more of it?"

"Certainly," Royce said with a wide smile. "Why don't you let me have it for a few days and I'll examine it thoroughly."

He looked at the scroll in Maggie's hands and took a deep breath.

"That's a really bad idea," Reeve said. "There's a lot of trouble surrounding this scroll. Best it stays with Maggie." He watched the professor with care and saw the twitch and resulting sneer before the man answered.

"I only meant that I could study it much better if I had it, itself, on hand, rather than a copy. However, I'll make a thorough scan of it, if you can bear to be separated from it for a few minutes?"

"Really, we didn't mean it like that, Royce," Maggie said with haste, glaring at Reeve. "Believe me, you don't want this scroll. I've been attacked over it. Here, and thank you for helping. Oh, let me ask you: is there any way of figuring out how old it is, just in case it's *not* a forgery?"

Royce took the scroll and leaned against his desk. Slowly he unrolled it into his hand. He brought it close to his face, his eyes squinting behind the thick lenses of his glasses. Then he held it at arm's length and began muttering to himself. Maggie watched and smiled at Reeve.

"It is most definitely ancient Aramaic," he finally said to her. "See the way this character here is formed? And this one?" He indicated several places.

Obediently, Maggie looked where instructed.

"But Maggie, that means nothing. As I taught you, anyone can draw ancient Aramaic or Egyptian hieroglyphics. The actual proof of the pudding, so to speak, will be the Carbon-14C dating procedure. You're both somewhat familiar with the process?"

Maggie nodded and Reeve shook his head. Royce finally relaxed, grinned, and set one hip on his desk.

"C-14C dating is the most precise dating process available today. It's simple, really. All life—plants, animals—is comprised of carbon, and while you're alive, the carbon inside you is equal to that in the atmosphere. When you die, the metabolic function of carbon uptake ceases; there is no more radioactive carbon going in, only decay. The decay occurs at a constant rate, which is measurable. In 5,568 years, half the original sample is gone, you see.

"By measuring the C-14 concentration or radioactivity of a sample, we can find the number of decay events per gram of carbon. Comparing this with modern levels of activity and using the measured half-life, bingo, you have the date of death. Because I'm relatively certain this scroll is made of animal skin, which was once living, we'll be able to use the procedure."

"Radioactivity—isn't that sort of dangerous?" Reeve asked.

"These are minute levels we're testing. An Accelerator Mass Spectrometer machine does the actual testing. Unfortunately, it's a very expensive piece of equipment. We don't have one here at Columbia. But Maggie, I'll overnight a tiny sample to Oxford, to a colleague who owes me a favor or two. Not only do they have an AMS, but they have tested actual Dead Sea Scrolls, so they have a control for the test, so to speak." In his enthusiasm, the muscle under Royce's nose leaped and pulled his mouth into his habitual sneer.

"You think this might be a Dead Sea Scroll?" said Maggie, her voice rising in tension.

"I think it's an excellent fabrication," he said, "but in science, we test to make sure. And this is fascinating, your little mystery. Now if you'll excuse me, I'll just take a minute portion of your scroll for testing, then I have a class." He took a single-edged razor blade from his desk and scraped off a tiny flake of the scroll near where the scroll had crumbled away from age, adroitly including some of the faded ink in the process.

"I don't know how to thank you," Maggie said. "How long

should this testing take, do you think?"

"The setup of the sample takes a few days—the preparation of the chemicals and so on. Actual testing only takes a few hours. Call me next Monday, and I should have answers for you. And you can always visit the Israel Museum's Shrine of the Book in Jerusalem, as well. They have an extensive collection of Dead Sea Scrolls, and have done research on them. You could compare what you have there."

Maggie and Reeve both shook Royce's hand and walked back into the hall. For a moment Royce stood and watched as they reached the stairs and began to descend. Then he sat down behind his desk. He placed the sample of the scroll in a small glassine envelope, then held it flat in one hand, as if weighing it. He turned it one way then another. Finally, he laid it on his desk next to a framed photo.

In the photo, his wife MaryAnn, in all her bulk, stood in front of a large column. Though the house was tiny, it sported two enormous columns which were the major reason MaryAnn had insisted they buy the house—that, plus the location on Long Island Sound, where most other houses seemed to sprout foreign luxury cars from their crushed stone driveways. His own salary as a tenured professor permitted only the purchase of an aged Japanese compact.

Most other professors at Columbia lived well, he thought, and his muscle twitched lightly. But no professor lived on Long Island Sound; it was usually reserved for the Hollywood or old-moneyed set.

Stevens picked up the photo. As always, MaryAnn was solemn, the wrinkles in her forehead matching the deep indentations that scored each cheek. She was dressed well though, in a deep blue silk jacket over a white skirt, cut cleverly to hide her weight. If he squinted, Stevens could still see the laughing girl he'd married.

His two children stood stiffly in front of the other column, favoring their heavy mother with her dark coloring. Behind the house, Long Island Sound gleamed in the bright sun.

The facial muscle twitched, and his mouth lifted upwards. He knew he was over his head with that house, had been since they'd bought it three years ago. He'd been forced to rely on credit cards for staples such as groceries, and now his debt was steadily mounting with no end in sight. But MaryAnn had insisted.

The house wasn't nearly as large as her original family home in Virginia, but the fancy location and wealthy neighbors were a comfort to her.

Sometimes, when he was going over the ever mounting pile of bills, he wondered why she'd married a professor. But then, the state of their dismal finances never stopped her from buying designer clothing for herself and the children, but not for him—he stood adamant about his own simple needs. For the most part, her needs were paramount, and that was as it should be. He was a lucky man, that a girl from such a distinguished old family had married him. She never let him forget it, either.

He snapped the framed photo down. As much as he cared about Maggie, with her impressive, curious mind, he needed to look toward the future.

He pulled up his address book on his monitor, paged through it, then highlighted a number. For a moment, he stared at the small envelope, muscle leaping under his nose. At length, he sighed and picked up the phone.

"Samuel Greene, please … This is Professor Royce Stevens from Columbia University, calling about the speech he made here last year."

After several moments, a deep voice came on the line. "Samuel Greene. This is a surprise, Professor."

"Life is a process of change, Mr. Greene. Tell me, would you be interested in the acquisition of the material you so passionately discussed in your speech?"

There was a brief, tense silence. "I'd need certain guarantees, but I believe you can rest assured of my deepest interest—as well as my ability to indulge it."

"It goes without saying that any such item would be well-documented."

There was a pause, then Greene said, "Might I inquire as to your rather drastic change of heart? You were adamant about such things and how they belonged to humanity, not to mention the 'sacred rights of your ancestors.' Isn't that correct?"

Royce nervously cleared his throat once, then again. "*Your* ancestors, not mine. It's a private matter. Suffice to say, there comes a time when a man must fight for what is dearest to him. Surely you understand that. In any case, I might have news for you next week, should you be available." Royce picked up the small envelope and turned it between his fingers.

"Must it wait so long," Greene nearly purred.

Royce coughed. "Certain tests must be run. I'm sure you understand. Proper methodology must be followed. And, of course, we'll need to agree on adequate compensation."

"I'm prepared to offer seven figures, on receipt of documentation verifiable by my team of experts."

"One assumes Oxford would be satisfactory, for testing the scroll?"

"How could it not? They *are* the ultimate authority. Well then, contact me as soon as possible." He hung up.

Royce slowly placed the receiver back in its cradle. One last time, he stared at the morsel of scroll in its envelope, then dialed the number for Federal Express.

"He's sure an odd one," Reeve remarked over a drink that evening.

"He's truly brilliant," Maggie said. "You shouldn't have been so short with him."

"He wanted to get his hands on the scroll. Didn't you see that?"

"He *wanted* to help me out. He's a good guy."

"And how do you know that?"

"Well, I don't, really. But I've never even heard him raise his voice." Maggie shook her head. "Never mind Royce for now. That scroll has caused me enough trouble."

"Anyway, tell me what the Todd God said to you in his office earlier," Reeve said.

Maggie sipped her wine. "Well, he's not happy, that's for sure. He said again that I've missed too many meetings. The team is suffering because of it, and he can't have that. Reeve, he said outright that he wants me onsite every day until the end of the month, and then 'we'll discuss it.'"

"That's not good, girl. Tell me again why you won't at least consider looking for another gig?"

"The benefits here are killer—you know that. Full hospitalization, dental, and even prescriptions for my family. The pay might be low, but Xcorp has the best benefit package of any of the others I was offered. Believe me I went through all of them. I'm not sure what would happen if I ever tried to transfer Beth's insurance," she continued. "I doubt anyone else would insure her. And right now, that's the priority."

"We need to look into that. I'm not sure you're right, or if it's even legal for the new company to drop her. Plus, with your experience and expertise, I just know you'd rake in the big bucks at another company. What they pay us just isn't scale in these parts."

"Listen, ninety-K is probably more than most people make in the city. And I need every cent. Benefits aside, Mom's check doesn't cover even half their bills. Not to mention the huge debt I have from Beth's hospitalization."

Reeve watched her, his mouth half-open. "Ninety? They're only paying you ninety? You *know* that's not right. I've been there three years less than you, and they offered me one-ten when they brought me on."

Maggie began to slowly tear a cocktail napkin to shreds as she looked down, trying to fight the tears. "That takes the cake. That really just takes the damn cake."

"Oh damn it, now, don't cry. Me and my big mouth. Every time—"

"No, it's better that I know. I just can't win, I really can't." She plucked Reeve's napkin from under his martini and dabbed her eyes.

Reeve reached out and held her thin shoulders. "Sweetie, we're going to clear all this up—you know we will. And just think, you might have an honest-to-God Dead Sea Scroll in your possession."

"Oh yes, that'll clear everything up. Not that I think it's real for a second, but how could that man have given me such a thing?"

"He obviously didn't want others to get their hands on it."

"I just don't know. It doesn't make any sense. Nothing makes sense. I cannot believe all this is even happening," Maggie said on a rising sob. "I want rid of this scroll!"

"I don't think it's that easy," Reeve said quietly.

"It's simple enough to just stuff it in a trash can."

"And then when someone attacks you again, you just say you threw it away? No, there's got to be a better solution. We just haven't thought of it yet."

"One thing's for sure, I'm not going to sit and bawl in public anymore. I can't believe I'm doing this." Maggie sniffed back tears and raised her head.

"No crying." He reached out to her face, hesitated, and put his hand back on the table. "Anyway, I do have a little good news. We have a new client—a company in New Jersey wanting to set up high security for their new online financial product. Todd was going to give the gig to Alana and Steven, but now that we're in town, it's ours. So for a few days, anyway, you won't be in the office."

"You devil. You should have told me that earlier. That's great! When do we leave?" She straightened in her seat and ran her hands through her hair.

"Sooner the better. Maybe toward the end of the week. We'll see how it goes."

"Great. I think I'll feel better outside New York. I have this awful feeling I'm being watched. They know where Mom lives in Nashville, they probably know where I live here, and they might even know where you are."

"We can't just spend our time worrying about it, Mags, at least until we know for sure what we got. Probably, they're not even interested in it anymore, now that you've been to the police."

Looking out over the twinkling lights of the La Jolla, California marina, the view from Samuel Greene's cliffside house was superb. Even his large ketch in its slip was adorned with its own little stars of light.

Heart still pounding from the earlier conversation with Royce, he stood and walked from his desk to the small display room off his office. There, he kept his most valued possessions, which he rarely displayed to others.

In the center of the room, in its own softly lit case, lay his pride and joy, part of an actual Dead Sea scroll—the Josiah scroll. He ran a finger over the glass. The scroll detailed the life of a man named Josiah, his wives, and his household accounting.

The Dead Sea scrolls had held a fascination for him since he was young. He'd seen a documentary on them and how most had yet to be translated. He especially longed to see, hold, and touch any scroll that referred to the life of Jesus Christ. While such a thing had yet to be found, Samuel was certain it existed. All historic data pointed to it.

He exhaled heavily and looked down at the scroll, remembering Becca, his beloved wife. A Christian, she had prayed devoutly and tried to bring Samuel into her faith—right up until the moment breast cancer took her life. Tears filled Samuel's eyes as he recalled her holding his hand and praying in her breathless voice.

During that last stay in the hospital, new scrolls had been discovered at Qumran. She'd said she'd do almost anything to see one of the scrolls. But she never left her bed again.

After she died, it had become somewhat of an obsession for Samuel to possess a scroll: it was a way for him to keep her closer.

Ten years ago, he'd been invited to join a very private auction website, *Lost in Time*. Rare paintings, jewelry, and other valuables were requested there, at a price very few could afford. Samuel had bid on and lost a Picasso just the year before.

The process was interesting, considering the Picasso had never legally been for sale. One placed a bid on a desired item, which was then illegally wrested from its rightful owner. The website, of course, never addressed this.

But when the Josiah scroll had come up for bid eight years ago, he hadn't lost. He'd bid for forty-eight straight hours to acquire the old parchment, he recalled with a rare grin. And then it had only taken a month to be "acquired."

Now, he allowed himself an atypical moment with the Josiah scroll. From his pocket he took his key ring and found the small silver key to the case. The air hissed into the climatized case, custom-built by the same company that built the display for the scrolls in the Israel Museum's Shrine of the Book in Jerusalem. He'd told them he had documents dating to the American Revolution and wanted to ensure their perfect care.

Gently, he took the brittle parchment in his hands. Only a six-inch fragment of a scroll, it was still the possession he prized above all others. He ran a finger over the aged black ink. Most scrolls described the lives and times of those living within a hundred years of Christ, and Samuel was determined to own as many more of the elusive, highly-controlled documents as he could.

Suddenly, he replaced the scroll in its case, turned, and went back to his desk. With a few keystrokes, he accessed the *Lost in Time* auction site and went to a long-running ad he'd placed for information leading to "valuable writings." He added a zero to the end of the amount offered and stared until the screen saver came on.

— CHAPTER TEN —

TUESDAY, JULY 21 – FRIDAY, JULY 24

Early Tuesday morning, Maggie was at her desk. She was apprehensive about seeing Todd, who'd been out of town the day before. As if the devil himself could hear her thoughts, he stalked by, cup of coffee in hand. He didn't so much as nod at her.

She suppressed a sigh and opened the documents describing the network for Elmore Corporation in Morristown, New Jersey. If she were to help them enhance security for their new web-based financial product, she'd need to know specifics of the setup there.

A few hours later, she was so engrossed in the technical specifications for the password database that she was startled when Reeve poked his head over the dividing partition between their cubicles.

"Hey, girl, I just got a call from the Todd God. Our main server just harked up a hairball."

"Oh no. I'm right in the middle of this," Maggie groaned. "Well, it's my turn. I guess I'll go check it out."

As she walked to the server room, she could hear the other employees grumbling about the files lost when the server suddenly died. She made a face. Would they never learn to save their work as they went, or at least leave the auto-save option enabled?

Twenty minutes later, she rebooted the server for a final time, and watched closely as it came back to life. Delighted to have fixed the problem so quickly, she trotted out of the small, windowless room and ran straight into Todd.

"Oh, I'm sorry. Are you alright?" she said.

"Fine. Good job with the server. I have a potential client coming in half an hour and I was really beginning to sweat."

"Could I talk to you for a moment?" Maggie had spent a sleepless night thinking about the difference in salaries Reeve had told her about, and while she didn't want to cause Reeve any trouble, she was determined to raise the matter with Todd.

"Sure. I need another cup of coffee. I'll meet you in my office in five."

Maggie walked nervously back past her own cubicle and into Todd's small office, which sported a window that looked out over lower Manhattan. Weak sunlight filtered through gray clouds that surrounded skyscrapers like sullen blankets. She sat in one of the two chairs facing his desk, crossed her legs, and waited.

Todd came in and closed his door with his usual, "What can I do you for?"

"Todd, we need to talk about my salary. I feel it's time for an increase," she said, hoping her nervousness didn't show. She hated discussing money.

"Oh you do, do you? This from the one team member never here—"

"The meetings aside, I am your top troubleshooter. Your biggest clients call and request me by name."

"Not meetings aside. They're part of why the team functions as it does, and those clients request us," he retorted as he leaned back in his executive chair and rocked. "Maggie, I just don't know how much of a team player you've been lately."

"I always get the job done, Todd," she said in an even tone. "Moreover, I happened to find out that all members of your team aren't compensated equally."

He straightened in his chair, his feet hitting the floor with a bang. "Who've you been talking to? You know it's against policy to discuss remuneration."

"Just scuttlebutt I heard in the break room. I've been here for almost five years, you know."

"We took you right out of college, as I recall." He punched a few keys, then waited. "Offered you ninety as a starting rate. That was unheard of for a—for someone with no experience."

"And in five years I've only gotten two small raises. The last one was more than a year ago. If you look at my evaluations—"

"I keep track of your evaluations. Hell, Maggie, for the past two years I headed up the evaluation team. Your work is excellent, for the most part. But you know you don't play well with others. You're blunt with your coworkers. Five years and you're still just a security engineer? I can't move you to Team Leader, Maggie. People couldn't come to you. I'll look into to it, but I have to say it doesn't look good. Now, I've got these people due shortly, and I need to look over my pitch."

Wordlessly, Maggie got up and walked back to her desk past a curious Reeve. As she reached her desk her cell phone rang. She grabbed it and sat, taking deep breaths to calm herself. "Maggie Purcell."

"Maggie? This is Alan from PetSmart on Lexington. We have good news. Thanks to the North American Bird Show, we received your bird nearly two weeks early. He's here and ready to be picked up."

"Cocktail! You have my bird." Maggie said, surprised. "I had totally forgotten. Wow. Listen, can you put together for me the supplies he'll need, as well as a book on cockatoo care? Did he arrive okay?"

"We'd be delighted. And he's fine. Extremely vocal, but fine."

"Great. I'll be there near six, if that's alright?"

She got directions to the store and hung up, then walked into Reeve's cubicle. "I totally forgot to tell you, but when we were separated in Paris, I bought Beth the coolest bird."

"You mentioned it briefly. What kind of bird?" Maggie saw him noticing her legs under her short black skirt. "Always did like short skirts," he muttered to himself with a grin.

"Anyway, he's a cockatoo. You know, the large white ones with the crest, that speak?" She said rapidly, blushing.

"A 'Baretta' bird! How very cool. Can I come with you to get her?"

"Him, and sure. For now, I'm going to get back to the tech spec for Elmore Corp."

The rest of the day passed rapidly for Maggie, and she was certain she'd located a few weak spots in the Elmore network configuration by the time she and Reeve left for PetSmart. She told Reeve this, and he was glad for her. The faster and better they dealt with the new client, the happier the client would be. It was too bad that had no bearing on Todd.

They arrived at PetSmart just after six. Maggie walked to the back counter, where Cocktail greeted her with a happy shriek.

"Awww. Reeve, look at this fellow. Now do you see why I couldn't resist him?"

"A giant beak is what I see," Reeve said, keeping a safe distance from the cage.

"Come here, you big baby, and meet him. He's a pussycat. Aren't you, cutie?" She cooed at the bird. He cocked his head at her, then purred as she remembered, and stuck his head through the wire for a scratch. Delighted, Maggie rubbed his soft head with one finger.

"Well, would you look at that," said a male salesclerk, coming up to them. "I'm Alan. You must be Maggie Purcell. That bird most definitely hasn't been that nice since we've had him!" The man smiled at Maggie, who continued talking softly to the bird. Reeve looked at Alan and rolled his eyes.

"Don't listen to them, Cocktail. You're a dear. Alan, can you tell me the basics of cockatoo care?"

Alan handed her a brief computer printout, as well as a book and a variety of toys and supplies. "Got this all ready for you," he said. "Will this do?

"Wow," Maggie said. "You saved my life. I had no idea how to care for one of these fellows. Actually, he's going to live with my sister. She'll worship the ground he walks on. I can't thank you enough!"

Maggie paid for her new bird accessories and signed what seemed to be stacks of papers, then walked out of the store carrying several plastic bags. Reeve held the large cage, through which Cocktail was trying to bite off one of his buttons. "You're a devil. You're a pretty devil, though, just like your new mama."

"Thanks ... I think," Maggie laughed. "How are we going to get this big boy home? Do you think he'll fit in a taxi?"

"We could always take the train, but I think the noise and stench might terrify him. I'm not sure we could take him on a bus. Yeah, let's try for a taxi." Reeve gave a sharp whistle.

Cocktail tried to imitate him as a taxi swerved to their side. The driver was fascinated by the beautiful white bird and even broke rules to let Maggie sit up front, while Cocktail rode in style next to Reeve in the back.

Once at her apartment, Maggie decided to put Cocktail in her bedroom. Reeve hung the Fascination Ball—a toy Alan recommended that was hung with different colored objects, tempting to a bright, inquisitive beak. Cocktail gently hooted in delight before attacking it with his curved beak. Maggie grinned and flopped on the bed, exhausted.

"You think Beth will appreciate all this?" she said.

"I know she's going to adore that bird. It's your mama I'm worried about," Reeve replied.

"Mom will just have to accept him. Beth has wanted a pet for years, and Mom has always had some excuse. You never know—Mom might like him too." But Maggie didn't have much hope.

Later that night, she began to have serious doubts about her impulse purchase. She heard a loud clanging noise, but when she sleepily crawled out of bed and looked around, nothing seemed to be out of place. Cocktail must have banged into something, she thought.

Then he started yelling. "Java below," it sounded like. He repeated it a bit louder. Puzzled, she strained to understand. "Java below." It meant nothing to her. She looked at the clock—2:35 a.m. "Java below!"

Coffee? Her exhausted brain struggled to process the bird's squawks. Then she heard a sharp banging on the wall. Evidently, her neighbors didn't appreciate the raucous cries.

Slowly, it dawned on her: it had to be French. Without a second thought she picked up the phone and called Reeve.

"Maggie, have you lost your mind? Do you have any idea what time ... What is that racket?"

"That's why I'm calling, I don't know what to do, and my

neighbor is banging on the wall. Can you hear Cocktail? Does this make any sense to you?" She held the receiver toward the bird, who obliged with another shout.

"Maggie! Maggie, he's yelling *'Je veux de l'eau.'* He's thirsty."

"But I gave him—" she stopped and looked into the cage. The metal pan was upended and the newspapers were soaked.

"Oh, Reeve, I'm sorry. He kicked over his water. Go back to sleep. Thanks."

She hung up, made her way into the kitchen, and refilled his water bowl. As she approached his cage with the full bowl, he looked at her, purred, and cocked his head. Unable to resist, she offered her fist. He gracefully stepped on. She sank onto her bed in exhaustion, talking lowly to him. He muttered back, then snuggled his head up under her chin. Maggie giggled and stroked his white belly.

For a moment, she thought of Reeve's voice on the phone, rough and sexy with sleep. Cocktail murmured under her chin, and Maggie drifted to sleep imagining strong arms wrapped around her.

It was also late for Beth, who was searching the web for Aramaic translations. She found one site that assumed a far greater knowledge of the language than she possessed. Heartened, she leaned back against her pillows and drew her laptop closer to her. The screen glowed behind the clear picture of the scroll.

The characters were evenly spaced across the leather, from left to right. At the bottom right of the scroll were three closely grouped characters. A signature? she wondered. She leaned forward and studied them, then went back to Google and her search for Aramaic translations.

Nearly an hour passed and more by luck than anything else, she'd translated the phrase, "I shall stay with thee." By now, she was deep in the search results, where the pages sometimes didn't have much bearing on her original search.

Then, she pulled up a striking site with an elegant revolving logo in one corner. She skimmed the contents, not certain they had any bearing on her quest. But as she delved further into the site, something nagged at her. She kept seeing that spinning logo.

Suddenly, she stiffened in disbelief. She clicked on the window containing the scroll scan and looked at the last grouping of characters.

It was a match. In her bed, Beth stared at the screen, unable to believe what she was seeing. Tears flowing freely, she smiled in wonder. Her fairies materialized in front of her and reached out gently to her face. Ignoring them for once, she ran her fingers across the bottom of the screen.

This was knowledge she didn't dare keep to herself—no matter the hour. She picked up her phone and dialed, but Maggie didn't answer. She left an urgent message to call home in the morning. At the last moment, she added that everything was okay.

One more time she compared the logo to the scroll—no doubt at all.

Slowly, her smile faded. The people who had kidnapped Maggie probably knew what she had. Beth frowned. There probably wasn't another one like it, anywhere.

Maggie was in terrible danger.

When Maggie awoke that morning, she had a vague memory of the phone ringing. Groggily, she checked her voice mail while her morning coffee was brewing. At the sound of Beth's tearful voice, she stiffened and sank onto the couch. She waited until the end of the message, then relaxed only a fraction before picking up the phone to call her sister.

The conversation was short and bizarre. Evidently, Beth was fine and so was Mom. Having worked on the scroll all night, she had discovered something of such importance that she refused to go into detail on the phone, for fear of being overheard. But she did try to show off her new knowledge of Aramaic.

It's not as if she's prone to exaggeration, Maggie thought. Beth was extremely level-headed and incredibly intelligent. Too intelligent, Maggie now worried. What could she possibly have discovered about the scroll to worry her so?

Behind the Purcell house in Nashville, a conversation was raging in a small blue Toyota. Two Arabs equipped with a parabolic mike had been sitting in front of the ball park since 1:00 a.m., and had been forced to leave twice when the police drove by.

"This is it, I tell you. Did you hear what that girl said?" The passenger addressed the driver in fluent Arabic.

The driver responded in the same language. "Yes, and it is typical of the infidels for them to think things are urgent. How can you think this is what our leader wanted us to learn?"

"Uqbah, I tell you, call him at once. Let him decide."

"I should make you call him, you are so certain," the driver grumbled. With a grunt he picked up a cell phone and dialed an overseas number.

After the ritualistic greetings, he said, "We have news. The sister thinks she has translated part of the scroll. She made a call and said her news is urgent."

He listened for a moment, then said, "We shall obey, as in all things. *In sh'allah.*" He hung up and grinned at the passenger.

"We should be ready to take possession of the package soon, he says. And he also says it doesn't matter what shape the package is in."

"What did he say about the translation?"

"He didn't say anything. He wasn't surprised that the sister knew something. Odd, but it isn't for us to understand."

— CHAPTER ELEVEN —

FRIDAY, JULY 24

Reeve picked up Maggie and the excited Cocktail outside her apartment. Maggie was relieved to be getting out of the city, even though she felt she'd traveled an inordinate amount in recent weeks. She felt confident she could put a good system in place for the Elmore Corporation in New Jersey—she'd done her homework.

In a buoyant mood as he always was when traveling, Reeve said, "So! Next stop—Elmore."

"And Hilda's looking good," Maggie remarked, running a hand across the soft leather of Reeve's beloved Jeep.

"Running like a top, too. Just had her detailed. I swear she knows it. Listen, you back there," he said over his shoulder to Cocktail. "You just keep your crap inside the cage."

"He's a good boy, as long as there aren't buttons within reach. Oh, just as I open my mouth." Cocktail let a shriek of terror, then started gibbering worriedly.

"It's okay, fella," Reeve said. "It's just the Lincoln Tunnel. Mags, put your window up, will you? I think the noise is scaring him."

Maggie obliged. "I'm not sure how well he likes being in the car. How long should this take?"

"It's just over thirty-two miles. Shouldn't take that long—it's an easy trip. And then we're off to Nashville!"

Once they emerged into the sunny day on the other side of the Lincoln Tunnel, Reeve reached down and put some Coltrane into his CD player. He hummed along happily.

The smooth jazz blended into the sound of the wheels on the road. Closing her eyes, Maggie leaned her head back. She concentrated on the music to clear her mind.

Not a jazz fan, the music seemed overly repetitive to her. In particular, a light saxophone melody was repeated several times, accompanied by a low drum. As she relaxed into her seat, the drum became louder, more rhythmic. Her breathing slowed in time with it.

Then she became aware of chanting, almost in the background. Not again. She struggled to wake, but as always, she couldn't move. The chanting swelled over the music. Soon Maggie could almost pick out individual voices. Heart pounding with nerves, she tried to understand what they were saying, but it was as if they were at a distance. She simply couldn't distinguish words.

She was roused with a jerk forward when Reeve stomped on the brake. "Sorry, Maggie. This turkey has been on our tail since we got on the Turnpike. Drives an Expedition and thinks he owns the road!"

Disoriented, Maggie reached up a hand and rubbed the back of her neck. "I was totally out. Wow, that's not like me at all. You know I usually can't sleep in cars." She considered telling him of the strange, dream-like drums she kept hearing, then decided against it. There would be time enough after she visited a doctor. The moment she returned from Nashville, she'd make the appointment, but it wasn't for another couple of days. What if I'm losing my mind, she thought with a shudder.

"I sure didn't mean to disturb you, either. But at least the jerk is staying back now." Reeve glanced into the rear view mirror. "Oh, there's the 95 split. I'm going to get off at the next exit and get some gas. You need anything?"

"Sure. Would you grab me a Coke?"

"No problem. Here we go," he said as he braked and took the ramp. "Looks like my buddy in the Expedition needs off also."

Uneasily, Maggie turned in her seat. The windshield of the large SUV was tinted and she couldn't make out either the driver or the passenger. Then Reeve pulled into a gas station and the larger vehicle passed them. Maggie reached into her bag. "I think I'll cut up an apple for you-know-who. It'll keep him busy while we're in Elmore."

She took out an apple and a knife, then started cutting it into pieces.

Reeve handed her a Coke, then filled the tank. Maggie talked softly to Cocktail.

"We have to leave you in here for a bit while we check out Elmore. This was supposed to be a surprise. Alright, here's one piece to last you until we get there." She passed it back over the seat. His curved beak gently took it from her fingers. "You are such a love. I don't know how I'm ever going to give you up."

"Give who up?" Reeve said, flinging his long form back in the seat.

"Cocktail. I'm already getting attached. Unlike this scroll, which I'd give up in the proverbial New York minute." She put the apple core into a waste bag, then tucked the knife into a baggie and back in her purse. Reeve started the car and headed for the on ramp.

"I think that scroll is something pretty special. You know Aramaic was Jesus' language," Reeve said.

"Yep, but look at the crap this scroll has caused. I have to watch behind me everywhere I go—"

"If it's a real Dead Sea Scroll, though, can you imagine? They were all written around the time Jesus lived," Reeve said, his voice low with awe.

"It can't possibly be real. No doubt Achmed Kiyat's daughter did the work."

As he drove the short distance from the train to his house in Long Island, Royce Stevens was wondering if he'd been right, if the scroll was as ancient as it seemed. Maybe today he'd hear from Randolph Granger, his long-time associate who taught at Oxford.

No one was around when he unlocked the door and called. The small, extremely expensive house was empty and silent as he made his way toward his study with guilty pleasure.

The only room in the house not "decorated" by MaryAnn, the study was filled with warm furniture from their original apartment. The deep tweed couch, spotted and sagging with age now, reminded him of their first years when MaryAnn was a student in his Ancient Civ class. He remembered wistfully how she'd thought him so elegant in those days.

Now, her idea of decorative elegance was evidently emptiness. Both living and dining rooms were nearly devoid of furniture or decoration. The cost of the house had precluded any unnecessary spending on decor.

Sinking into his old desk chair with its sprung, comfortable seat, he grunted with satisfaction. The light was blinking on his answering machine. Randolph Granger had left a message, his English voice slightly high with excitement.

Hunched in his chair, Royce dialed the overseas number, and Randolph informed him that initial tests proved an age of roughly two thousand years for the scroll. Final test results on composition and a more precise age were several days away.

Royce hung up with mixed feelings. Immense satisfaction and excitement: the scroll was indeed a valuable artifact. But a bit of guilt stung. He was betraying his friendship with Maggie.

But his bills. He studied the pile of envelopes neatly stacked in their bin. They were so far behind on bills, he didn't see how they'd ever catch up. The house payment alone ate most of his salary. The clothes MaryAnn insisted on buying chomped through the rest, and more. Agitated, he bared his teeth repeatedly.

They'd been living on credit cards for the last three years, since he'd let MaryAnn talk him into buying this house. He looked into the early evening darkness outside his window and sighed.

"Royyyce? Royce!" MaryAnn's voice floated back to him.

"I'm in my study," he called back.

"Well, come out of that shabby hole for a minute. I need to talk to you!"

He gave a longing glance around the comfort of his study, then stood and turned out the light. He passed through the small dining room and was almost run over by Sarah and Winston as they charged up the stairs.

"Royce, I have the most wonderful news," MaryAnn said. She stood in the kitchen, unloading several paper bags.

"So do I, potentially," Royce said, watching her.

MaryAnn held up a sack-like blue silk dress. "Look at this! Bloomie's had a sale. Isn't this just perfect?"

"MaryAnn, you know we can't afford ..." Involuntarily he

sneered, and he held his hand over his mouth, embarrassed.

"Of course we can. I saved you so much money. And just look at the darling track suit I got for Sarah!"

He'd never seen the overweight Sarah so much as run and play, he thought miserably. Then he brightened.

"MaryAnn, it could be that we're going to come into a considerable sum of money."

She turned from the counter and faced him. "Oh really? How considerable?"

"We'd be able to pay off this house, and have a little extra to settle some of our other bills."

"Royce! That's wonderful! We can actually get out of this small place and get a fabulous house at Sag Harbor. Anyone who's anyone has a house there. And …"

He ignored the rest of her droning. It would never be enough—he saw that now.

Suddenly Maggie remembered. She pawed through her purse and extracted the scroll, shaking a little with dread.

"Maggie?" Out of the corner of his eye, Reeve noted her excitement.

"This has bothered me for a week. It's something Achmed Kiyat told me about his daughter's art. She signs the bottom of everything she does!" At his puzzled glance, she added, "The scroll. Her initials should be on it somewhere."

The sun was streaming in through her side window. She turned slightly toward Reeve and held the scroll up until the sunlight fell directly on it, passing through it in the places it was worn away from age. She studied it closely.

"It's not there. No initialed signature. Whatever this scroll is, it isn't artwork done by Fatima Kiyat. Of course! It's probably someone's souvenir directly from Israel."

"No one would be trying so desperately to get that thing from you if it didn't have some kind of value," Reeve insisted. "Maggie, I have a feeling about that scroll. I can't tell you exactly why, but something about it calls to me on a level—well, at a depth I haven't felt since I was a little kid in Sunday school."

"I simply don't believe it could be a Dead Sea scroll. What on earth would it have been doing in France?"

"France is a hotbed of smuggling artwork. Someone could have brought it in to sell. I don't know. Point is, it could well be real."

To Maggie's amazement, Reeve's eyes were glassy as he stared, unseeing, at the highway.

"So what are you trying to say? That somehow this scroll is holy, this thing given to me by a total stranger in Paris? Come on, Reeve. And if it is real? All the more reason to get rid of it. Isn't it against the law, taking something like this out of Israel?"

"Girl, you didn't take anything. That poor man gave it to you. When I think that it could have been written around the time of Christ, I get goosebumps. It's a wonder."

"I didn't know you were so religious," Maggie said.

"My dad always made sure we went to Mass. I guess he was afraid we'd turn out like Grandmère Amelie if we didn't." He rolled his shoulders to release the tension and laughed. "After all the summers I spent with her, I sure used to sound like her, *eh bien?*"

"You still break into that accent when you're upset. I think it's neat. Your Grandmère Amelie sounds like quite the character." Maggie stared at his profile as he drove—the beautiful straight nose, and the deep, startling blue of his eyes against his coffee-colored skin. Mass? She'd had no idea. Religion wasn't something she thought about often, if at all. And a God who let a young girl get cancer wasn't a God she wanted to believe in. Besides, when she'd heard the resounding crack of hand against skin, and her mother's despairing wail, she'd lost any faith she might have had.

Reeve went silent himself, remembering. His fingers tapped on the Jeep's wheel.

"Grandmère Amelie really is something else. You don't know how pissed Mom and Dad get when she shows up in all those colorful caftans, not to mention the fresh crawfish and crab she brings with her. Dad had this large university party for Christmas one year. You know how stuffy those university types are. Well, about a week before the party, Grandmère Amelie called and said she was coming in for Christmas. Mom and Dad had one of the worst fights they'd ever had."

"Your mom doesn't like her?"

"They don't see eye to eye. I love Mom, but she's not real accepting of anybody different. She takes the lawyer ethic way too far. At least Dad knows when to kick back."

Reeve's mother and father both taught law at Georgetown University, where the professors considered themselves head and shoulders above everyone else. And Lord knew his mom had reason for her high self opinion, with her proven publication track record. The competition between professors was fierce—to be published or to gain tenure.

Reeve's mother well knew how to play campus politics. His father, a more relaxed black man originally from New Orleans, believed in working to live, not the reverse.

"What happened at the Christmas party?" Maggie prompted him.

"Oh, lord. Grandmère Amelie brought several bushels of fresh crawfish. I thought Mom would have a stroke when she went to the baggage claim and there they were, all those little antennas waving out of the holes in the basket. Mom was horrified thinking of all those snotty professors faced with mudbugs. You have to eat them with your hands, you know.

Crack the shells and pull the tails off. Mmmm, mmm, mmm! And the spices are so hot, you have to wash your hands after.

"Anyway, imagine this stodgy group of law professors in their button-down suits faced with platters of boiled crawfish. My sisters and I were watching from the hall, waiting our chance to snag some. Dad walked right up to the table and shelled the first one, then handed it to Dean Grigson. Never saw a white man eat anything that fast." He grinned at the memory. "Next thing you knew, Dad was showing them all how to crack the shells. They talked about that party for years as the best Christmas party the law school ever had."

Reeve's cell phone rang. He answered, then his body language changed. He cleared his throat and turned his head sideways before saying "Can I call you back?" He shot Maggie an uncomfortable glance. "Now's really not a good time ... Yes, I'm really sorry I missed you. Couldn't be helped ... No, I'm not seeing anyone ... only a few days ... I'm looking forward to it!" He disconnected, then put his phone in his pocket without a word to Maggie.

Maggie's face burned and she carefully looked out the window, reluctant to have Reeve notice. She took a deep breath, surprised at how upset she felt.

She knew full well he dated—had even seen girls meet him in the lobby at work.

"I missed you?" A pang of pain shot up through her heart. And here she'd thought—what really? He'd never so much as touched her. Any attraction she'd imagined on his part was all in her mind. Just his automatic flirting with any female.

Tears pricked and she surreptitiously brushed them away. *I have far too active an imagination. That's what it is. Better late than never I find out he's seeing someone else.*

"Hey, here we are. You ready?" Reeve pulled into a wide

lane leading to a three-story glass building. A low brick wall in front proclaimed *Elmore Corporation: Elegance in Finance.*

"Let me get my briefcase and give Cocktail the rest of his apple. I'd better leave the window down for him. Good thing it's not roaringly hot today. Still, I don't want to leave him more than an hour, so let's get in and out of there." She reached into the backseat and retrieved her leather brief-case.

"It won't even take that long—with all the work you've done. I'm going to upload the backdoor while you talk to Alan Sherman, and then we're out of there."

For the first time in weeks, Maggie felt great as they came back out of the office building. She knew there had been a strong element of luck involved, but she'd located a large hole in the web server credit card application, and was able to show the client its location and how it could have been exploited. With a few lines of code, she adroitly slammed the door on any hacking activity. Then she tested and proved her patch by running a fake credit application, which was rejected. The client, Alan Sherman, was grateful and de-lighted that Maggie had found the flaw and corrected it so quickly. But when she thought of Todd and his refusal to consider her raise, Maggie deflated a bit.

Perhaps the man had a point, she thought as she climbed back in the car. She really had been absent a great many days to deal with Beth. It still seemed unfair that Reeve, though well-qualified, had been hired at such a higher salary. She groaned softly. No use dwelling on it.

"Hey. What was that groan? Girl, you just worked a miracle. I never saw anyone find and patch a hole that fast—ever."

"It was pretty fast, wasn't it?" Maggie said, pleased. "And we didn't have to leave His Winged Highness back there alone but for thirty minutes."

"I've got to call Todd," Reeve said, taking his phone out of his pocket and dialing as he steered out of the parking lot.

Maggie relaxed against her seat and listened as Reeve told Todd about the speed of the visit. Unfortunately, she heard his response as he retorted that it was about time Maggie pulled her own weight, sick sister or no.

Red spots blooming on each cheekbone, Maggie jerked erect in her seat. Hastily Reeve reached out and put a cautionary hand on her shoulder. He got Todd off the phone, then slapped it shut and thrust it back into his pocket with a sideways glance at Maggie.

"That bastard," she seethed. "How dare he? 'Sick sister or no!' I feel like just calling him up and telling him to stuff the job. I'd do it in a heartbeat if I didn't need the security so badly for Beth. Maybe soon I won't," she said darkly.

Reeve rubbed her shoulder. "Girl, I'm sorry you had to hear that. He's just blowing off steam. You know how he is. What did you do, hit him up for more money?"

Shocked, Maggie stared at him, then burst into laughter. "How did you guess? That's exactly what I tried, yesterday. Of course, he said no."

"Keep in mind that I have another idea but I'm not going to say anything about it until I know more. But you just hang in there. As talented as you are, he should be willing to jump through hoops to keep you. By the time he figures that out, with a little luck you'll be gone."

"I wish. Now every time I see him I'm going to hear in my head what he just said about Beth. What a total jerk." Cocktail let out a squawk from the backseat and Maggie grinned. "And Cocktail agrees."

After several hours, Reeve pleaded exhaustion and Maggie took the wheel while he put his head against the window and fell fast asleep. She put some of her favorite Eric Clapton on, and thumped her fingers on the wheel to the driving southern beat.

The miles seemed to pass slowly under the wheels of the Jeep. She rolled her neck from side to side, checked her rear view mirror, and frowned. Could that be the same Expedition that had been behind them earlier? This one was dark blue. Exasperated, she shook her head and mumbled, "Now I'm seeing people behind me. My life sure used to be a lot less complicated." *How did all this ever happen?*

A soft snore answered her and she looked at Reeve, long curled lashes laying against his dark chocolate skin. He was one fine-looking man. And it had been so long. But he was such a player.

Several years before, she'd dated Arne Ross, a slightly stodgy investment banker with bright blue eyes. The relationship had started fast. They met in a bar on the East side, and had spent the next several months dating. Arne was an incredible lover. He was also solid and dependable. She didn't feel the overwhelming attraction for him that she had for Bruce, but to her, that was a good thing.

Then Beth had a bad reaction to medication, and Maggie broke several dates with Arne to fly to Nashville. She explained about Beth, how much she meant, and how sick she was. She thought Arne understood, his face serious under his bright red hair.

The last time she'd flown back from Nashville, she found a note on her door: "Sorry. You just have too much baggage. It's my fault—I can't handle it. Best, Arne."

"Best?" they'd been so close, and he signed the note "Best?"

It reinforced the idea that men couldn't be trusted. Again, she flashed onto that slap, when her dad had whacked her mom because of a dirty kitchen. And Reeve's sly phone call, earlier—he could have told that woman he'd call her back.

Enough of those thoughts. As attractive and sweet as Reeve was, he was dangerous, and she needed to concentrate all her energy on Beth. And everyone knew the trouble inherent in an office relationship. It was best to keep such a friendship just as it was, considering they worked together. And of course he was already dating someone else. Whom he specifically told he wasn't seeing anybody. While sitting next to her in the car, no less.

Still, the loneliness is overwhelming sometimes. The need to simply be close to a man, just be in his arms, at peace. She reached over and inserted another CD.

The bright sun was intermittent between large clouds of deep gray and black over the Pennsylvania fields. Grateful they'd made an early start by leaving New Jersey just after lunch, Maggie yawned and checked on Cocktail, who was amusing himself by playing with his hanging ball. She noted that the blue Expedition was still in sight, although now it was behind a smaller vehicle. She was beginning to get seriously worried. Should she disturb Reeve? No, he had driven all the way to New Jersey, starting with the awful New York traffic. He deserved his sleep. Anyway, they'd be fools to try anything in broad daylight, she told herself.

A particularly loud clap of thunder overhead made her start. Reeve, as usual, didn't stir. The cars coming toward her were dripping with rain, headlights on. Nervous, she peered into the darkening afternoon. Heavy blue thunderheads boiled upward into a black sky cracked by strikes of lightning.

Then the rain started with the typical suddenness of a summer storm. Instantly the windshield was flooded with sheets of water. Maggie, alarmed, pumped the brake lightly.

Reeve woke with a start. "Whaa?"

"A nasty storm just blew in. Don't suppose you want to drive your baby, do you? It's a little more intense than what I'm used to."

"Sure. Pull off and we'll swap," he said through a yawn.

Maggie pulled to the side, near a heavily forested area. Gallantly, Reeve got out of his side and ran to the driver's, allowing Maggie to scoot across into the passenger's seat. Relieved, she saw the Expedition drive slowly past, brake lights flashing. As the sound of rain intensified on the roof, Cocktail warbled and hooted from the backseat.

Reeve accelerated smoothly back onto I-81. "Hey, where are we?"

"We just crossed into Virginia a while back. You slept a good couple of hours. Feel better?"

"I sure do, and I appreciate you letting me nod off like that. You go ahead and do the same. Pass me the map first, though."

Maggie folded the map and slid it into his waiting hand. In the near darkness of the storm, he turned on the inside light briefly to check his location. "Hey, we're making good time. I'm thinking we should be in Nashville by eleven or so."

"That's about what I guessed." Maggie reached into her large purse and withdrew a bottle of water and an apple. "I'm going to give Cocktail a treat and top off his water. He's been such a good boy, hasn't he?"

"I never knew a neater bird. Beth'll really love him."

Maggie began carefully slicing the apple. "I'm really worried about her next test."

"Oh no, don't even think that. The sprout's going to improve—I have a tingle on it."

"This tingle better be right. But I do have to admit that your tingles are right more often than not," she said as she leaned over the seat and opened Cocktail's cage enough to insert her arm without letting the large bird free. He purred at her as she poured water into his bowl and hand-fed him an apple slice before putting the rest in his dish.

She resettled her purse on the floor, then twisted until her back was against the window and flipped her bare feet into Reeve's lap. Daylight was waning, and the storm had diminished into intermittent drops above their heads. The headlights of cars coming toward them were limned in a dense gray fog.

Maggie moaned. "Reeve, what would I ever do if I lost her? How could I even go on living?"

"It's not going to happen. I mean it. You can't let yourself think like that, sweetie. She could catch that attitude, and she needs all her strength to fight this—and yours, too."

Swiftly Maggie leaned forward and kissed Reeve's cheek. "I know you're right. What would I ever do without you?"

"You'd be totally lost, girl. Absolutely and totally lost!" He grinned, blue eyes crinkling.

The hours passed in friendly bickering, comfortable silences, and a long nap for Maggie. When she awoke, it was pitch black and there was almost no traffic on the interstate.

"Wow, I feel like I slept for hours. Where are we?" She yawned and stretched like a cat.

"About forty miles from the Tennessee state line," Reeve said with a matching yawn.

"Want me to drive now that the rain has stopped?"

"Sure. Let me pull into the next market. I could use a cup of coffee about now."

"You and me both. Plus I'd like to let Cocktail—carefully—out to stretch his wings before we get there. Maybe then he'll be calmer when he meets Beth and Mom." She looked over her shoulder at the bird, his eyes shining in the dim light.

"You beautiful fellow, I'm sure going to miss you. Reeve, I forgot to tell you. He slept with me last night. How adorable is that?"

Reeve hit his turn signal. "Lordy, we just passed a market sign and I didn't even note how many miles off the interstate it was. Did you?"

"No, I'm sorry, I was looking at Cocktail. It can't be that far, though," she said, straining to see as he took the off ramp to the right. Thick black woods pressed against the narrow road, summer-heavy branches straining against a starless, overcast sky. Maggie rolled her window down and inhaled deeply. The night was muggy and thick, like warm molasses. She looked into her mirror and, satisfied, pulled on her Adidas.

"We're in the middle of nowhere," Reeve noted as the road narrowed and wound its way around a low hill. The ride became rougher as the Jeep bounced over several large potholes. Cocktail's cage bounced on the seat and he squawked in protest. "Sorry, fellow. Mags, I'm thinking we should turn around. We have no idea how far the store is."

"Might as well keep going, now. It can't be much farther." As Reeve slowed the vehicle, the night sounds filtered through the cracked window. Cricket chirps waxed and waned, a cow lowed nearby, and several dogs barked in concert.

The road narrowed yet again. By the light of the head lamps Maggie could see that it hadn't been repaved in years. Reeve tried to avoid great ruts worn into the old tar and large potholes filled with rainwater that shone in the headlights.

They came around a steep, hairpin corner and saw a light ahead. "Aha! At last! Can it finally be?" Reeve said, and accelerated slightly. The Jeep responded with a roar, then hit a particularly deep pothole and went briefly airborne. Maggie shrieked and Cocktail hit his head on the top of his cage, then moaned like a child.

"Reeve! You trying to kill us?"

"Sorry, I just got excited. Civilization at last!"

As they grew closer and the lights became brighter, Maggie had her doubts. The store had to have been a barn in a previous incarnation. Several graying, aged boards hung free from a pointed roof. A crooked sign flashed "Open 24 hours." When Reeve got out, Maggie joined him to stretch her legs.

"My leg is asleep," she said as she jumped up and down. An older man in overalls watched from the doorway as they approached.

"How y'all doing tonight?" he asked.

"Little sore from travel, but fine," Maggie responded. "And you?"

They chatted a bit as they entered the old store past shelves of fresh tomatoes, beans, and peppers of all kinds. Bins of fruit caught Maggie's eye and she bought a bag of strawberries, their size and scent too tantalizing to pass up.

She stood at the cash register and chatted while Reeve poured coffee into two large styrofoam cups, adding milk and heaps of sugar to hers. A sudden screech of brakes made her whip her head toward the door.

"Don't pay them no mind. Young'uns in this neck of the woods ain't got much else to do," said the man behind the counter with a smile.

Maggie squinted at the bright tail lights of the vehicle, which had slowed opposite the store. As she watched, the lights went dim, and it took off with a squeal. "I'm from Nashville," she said. "We used to drag race all the time. Got to love the country."

"Couldn't imagine livin' nowhere else," the man said, handing her the strawberries.

"Cocktail will love these," she said as they walked out.

"Cocktail, hell!" laughed Reeve. "You better save some for me and your family. They're almost the size of peaches."

Maggie placed the large paper bag of strawberries at a good distance from the large eager beak in the back seat, then gave him a few before taking her place behind the steering wheel. After she adjusted the seat forward, she pulled out of the small parking lot.

With the store lights receding in the mirror, she carefully crossed the deep grooves in the road. Just as she came up on the first steep curve, a light misting rain began to fall. "It waited for me to drive again, didn't it?"

"You want me to drive?" Reeve offered. "It's only a few hours more, I can make that easily."

"No, I don't mind the rain except when I can't see past the windshield. This is nothing. You just sit back and relax and—"

With a roar, another vehicle was on them, bright lights glaring in the rearview mirror. Maggie, alarmed, sat up straight in her seat. "Hey, it's that Expedition. Where'd he come from?"

"I don't know. He has to be nuts coming up that fast on this road. Be careful, Mags."

She didn't answer. The other vehicle pulled out and was next to her, and to her horror, she saw a familiar robed shape in the passenger seat. The man scowled at her and motioned her to pull over.

"The hell I will," Maggie cried out and hit the accelerator hard. The Jeep leaped ahead of the larger Expedition, then hit a small pothole. The back end whipped off to the right. Cornered, Maggie steered into the Expedition to regain traction. The driver instantly steered into her.

The two vehicles hit with a screech of metal, but the Jeep was now running smoothly forward. Reeve yelled, "Watch out!" as the other driver jerked his wheel to ram them once again.

Maggie slammed the accelerator down and whipped the

wheel to the left. The back end of the Jeep shot to the right. The Expedition just missed them as the Jeep pulled ahead and into a sharp curve.

Maggie downshifted into second. The gear screamed, but the Jeep slowed into the curve. She quickly upshifted as she shot out of the curve.

"Dammit, Maggie! This isn't a Porsche," Reeve yelled over the howling engine.

Maggie couldn't respond as the Jeep jerked viciously to the left, caught in the deep ruts carved into the old road.

She adjusted quickly and hit the gas just as the Expedition once again paralleled them. They were on a short straight-away. She dared a fast look to her left. The white of the robe gleamed softly as something darker was raised out the window.

"Gun! He's got a gun!" Maggie yelped. She leaned forward as if to impel the car faster, and the Expedition surged ahead also, ready this time.

But then she stomped on the brakes. The Jeep's tires shrieked but bit and held. But the Expedition had antici-pated her move and also had applied the brakes.

Cornered again, Maggie stomped on the gas and prepared to swerve to the right of the larger vehicle.

But once more, he anticipated her move and the much more powerful Expedition surged ahead, in front of the Jeep.

Maggie frantically jerked the wheel to the right, but it was too late. They slammed with force into the long nose of the Expedition, rebounded off the other side of the rutted road, slammed through a fence, and crashed into a tree.

Maggie's head whiplashed onto the steering wheel and her world went black.

— CHAPTER TWELVE —

LATE FRIDAY, JULY 24 – SATURDAY, JULY 25

When she awoke, Maggie thought she was still dreaming. Why did her head hurt so ferociously? And why was Reeve in her bedroom, fighting with ... Who was that? At once she came totally and painfully awake.

Reeve was backlit in the harsh wash of the Jeep headlights, delivering an expert kick to the head of a white-robed figure. The sight was enough to cause her vision to gray around the edges. Determinedly, she kept herself upright in the seat. Something on her face was wet, and Cocktail screamed repeatedly in the back seat, terror in his high voice.

She reached an unsteady hand to her forehead and it came away gleaming darkly. A thump rocked the Jeep, as another man came up behind Reeve and knocked him onto its hood.

Frantic, Maggie fumbled with the Jeep's door. It creaked open and she fell face-forward into the damp field. Now the grunts and slaps were loud in her ears as she pulled herself to her knees and began to make her way toward Reeve.

She was stunned as Reeve leaped off the hood, spun, and kicked one of the men directly in the ear. The man fell as if axed.

Then, with amazing smoothness, Reeve turned and shot the side of his hand into the second man's face. Maggie just had time to recognize the man's squint, before he too fell and Reeve was running, tripping over a stump to where she knelt crying.

"Get up. We need to get out of here, now," he said and pulled her to her feet.

"I … can't … see …" Maggie gasped as she lurched forward, the blood now running down into both of her eyes.

Reeve pulled her hair away from her face and looked at her. "Oh God, no. Baby, you'll be alright, but we have to move. Now!"

In one motion he picked her up and ran to the other side of the Jeep. He reached in through the window and opened the door, balancing Maggie on his hip, then gently placed her on the seat. She slumped against the window, heart pounding, unsure whether to faint or get sick. Cocktail shrieked until Reeve shouted, "Shut up!"

Reeve slipped the key into the ignition, and to Maggie's relief, the car roared to life. Reeve accelerated into a sliding circle and aimed for the smashed section of fence, the Jeep bouncing heavily across rows of corn that whipped by Maggie's window.

She bit her lip hard to keep from crying out as the Jeep jolted over the worn rim of the road. Reeve shot a hand out to press her into her seat. "Hang on, sweetie. Let me get back to the Interstate and we'll check you out. Are you alright?"

"I have a cut and a bad bump on my forehead. I'll live. But you! What were you doing?"

"Takin' care of business," he said, his accent turning faintly Cajun. "Hilda here ain't bad either. Takes a lickin' and keeps on tickin'. Beat the crap out of her front bumper, though."

"Oh God, I'm sorry I wrecked your baby, Reeve. We should call the police, shouldn't we?" Maggie pulled a packet of tissues out of her purse and dabbed her forehead, using the Jeep's lit passenger mirror.

"I don't think so, girl. For one thing, my insurance would rocket. It's bad enough in the city. And for another—" He fell silent and shot her an uneasy glance.

"And for another?" she prompted him, pressing on the painful lump to stop the bleeding.

"For another, I'm a black man and this is the South. We call the police, and with you looking like you do, I'm going to jail, sure as hell."

"Reeve, you know that isn't—" She stopped. She didn't know for sure that he wasn't right. A burning shame rose in her cheeks. "That's just, well, that's bullshit," she spat.

Surprised, Reeve grinned. "Listen to you. No, it's true and you know it. They'll hassle me if nothing else. Tell you what, though, I have a decent first aid kit in the glove compartment. Pull it out, will you? I'm stopping briefly right under that sign." He motioned ahead to a well-lit interstate sign advertising a Nashville bar.

Maggie located the kit as Reeve pulled off the road. He took the kit from her, turned on the Jeep's interior lights, and exclaimed, "Lordy, but you're gonna have one hell of a shiner. Come here." He ripped open an alcohol wipe and quickly rubbed it over the swelling. Maggie yelped and pulled back.

"Hold still, sweetie. Got to get this clean." He dabbed, then opened a package of surgical tape.

She shuddered. "I can't believe this is happening. I should just give up the scroll."

"I'm afraid that's not all they want."

"What else is there?"

"Your blood," he said without thought. Then he focused. Her face was pale white in the dim light, and her lip was quivering. "Oh, hell. Well, you know what I mean. They might not stop with just the scroll." He reached over and expertly taped the split closed.

"I can't think about it anymore. Hey, another of your secrets? You went to med school?" She wasn't sure why, but her feelings were hurt.

"Another what? I got no secrets. But I sure do get banged up on occasion from class." At her questioning look, he added, "Tae kwan do."

"I didn't know you were into tae kwan do. I suppose now you'll tell me you're a black belt."

"Third degree," he said. putting the first aid kit away.

Maggie was silent, the hurt increasing. The sport must be a large part of his life and he'd never so much as mentioned it. She glanced at him, now intent on pulling back onto the interstate. What else didn't she know? Secret phone calls. And did she even have the right to feel insulted? Her eye ached and throbbed. Better to think of this than the horror of those robed figures in the headlights, although she knew that, sooner or later, she'd have to face these thoughts.

Reeve tightened his lips as he cautiously brought the Jeep up to speed. He hadn't meant to keep the tai kwan do a secret, but he hadn't gone out of his way to tell Maggie about it, either. Its roots were based on something private he had shared with only one other person. Then again, it would be a good thing to get her mind off the horror. Even if he had to bare himself to do it.

The silence stretched. He risked a quick look at Maggie:

her lower lip protruded in a slight pout, while the angle of her head, held high, indicated her hurt.

He sighed. "Look, there's the Welcome to Tennessee sign. We're almost there."

She didn't respond. He snuck another glance, and to his dismay saw tears shining on her face in the faint glow from the dashboard. "Oh, hell. Don't do that."

She angled her face away from him to face the darkness.

He sighed again. "Girl, you just don't understand. Listen, I told you that when I grew up, I spent every summer with Grandmère Amelie, didn't I?"

The back of her head dipped in a nod but she didn't turn.

"Grandmère Amelie lived in this tiny town, Grand Coteau, a few hours north of New Orleans. Real Cajun country. Amelie didn't speak English, and you know my mom. She's thinking, 'My son isn't going to turn into some wild Cajun. I won't have it!'

"So Amelie and I went to the night school there, along with many of the other old folks who only spoke Cajun. The school offered night classes to teach them English, and she refused to go alone." He smiled. "Lord, that was one small town, Grand Coteau."

Maggie relaxed a bit in her seat but continued staring out into the night.

"Girl, we had just the one cop, this little old black man named André. He was sheriff, too. Grand Coteau had one, and only one, traffic light. André got so bored that he'd turn the light off and direct traffic himself." Reeve laughed at the memory. "André knew I was plenty spooked, too, those nights when Amelie and me went to that school. The town's only funeral parlor was right next to it. André would see me coming and say, 'Hey sha! Time for Amelie to speak the English, her.'

"Anyway, I got quite the Cajun accent. I was in high school in DC, and God, you have to know they picked on my ass unmercifully about that accent. I was different. The coolest guys at school were this bunch of black guys who ran the streets. Do-rags, the whole nine. They called me 'that inbred Southern nigga.'" His voice tightened and Maggie turned slightly to face him. He straightened his shoulders and continued.

"One beautiful spring day after school—I remember all the cherry blossoms—they surrounded me behind the track. The guys must have been stoned on something, but they got on me and took turns beating the living shit out of me. Broke my nose in three places. I had to have it broke again and reset. That's why it looks so straight now.

"Afterward, I was lying half-propped up against a cherry tree. There were fallen blossoms everywhere, a bunch on my lap."

He took a deep breath and eased his foot off the accelerator; the Jeep had been inching up to ninety as he spoke.

"I was stunned, I reckon. I looked up and here's this Japanese kid, Hiro. His dad was the political attaché for the Japanese or something. Hiro spoke great English, but his accent and looks made him a target more than me. They called him Hiroshima, said his mom must have been radiated from the bomb, and that's why Hiro was so retarded.

"Anyway, Hiro, he just stood there and looked down. After a minute, he said, 'Want to learn how not to get bloody next time?' It was the 'next time' that got me.

"After that, Hiro took me three times a week to tae kwan do classes. Mom hated that, but the sight of my face that day did a lot to convince her I needed help. I got pretty good at it, too. Hiro and me—he's about the closest thing I've got to a brother. He's back in Japan now. Found himself a great wife.

"And there you have it. I was on the college tai kwan do team, and we made the national finals my senior year. Didn't win, but we done good. I still run katas at a place near my apartment several days a week, when I can."

Maggie reached out a hand and touched his cheek. "I'm sorry they hurt you, but I'm really glad you learned tai kwan do. Did those high school guys ever come after you again?"

"As a matter of fact, that summer Hiro and I'd been out playing pinball—Hiro was the world's best. We were on our way back to his house in Georgetown, but we had to go through a rough area to get there.

"As we walked past this abandoned house they used as a sort of clubhouse, same group of jerks jumped us and dragged us behind the house. It was all kinds of nasty back there. Needles and condoms and old used tires. I think Hiro and me were afraid to even hit the ground for fear of some kind of infection … Anyway, there were seven of them. They circled us, they moved in, and then we took them apart." He fell silent.

"That's it? What happened to them?"

"Who knows? I do know we broke a few arms. Couldn't be helped. We aren't trained to hurt people, only to stop them from hurting us." He didn't add that he began to consciously mimic the northern accents he heard at school. Nor did he mention the pain Amelie had felt the year he refused to visit New Orleans.

"Well, you saved my life back there. I owe you thanks."

"No thanks necessary," he replied. "I was really protecting Hilda." His straight face evoked a chuckle from Maggie. He stole a sidelong glance at her and inwardly ached. How he longed to pull over right then, sweep her into his arms, and kiss away her fears and hurts. The sight of her crumpled on the ground next to the car had caused him to go weak, and he knew he had a lot of thinking to do later. Not now though.

He steeled himself. "Hilda's front bumper is going to need some work, I'll bet. We're lucky she didn't break a headlight."

Several hours later, Maggie quietly fit the key into the door at her mother's house. Behind her, Reeve whispered to be sure and tell Anna that they'd only had a fender bender. Maggie nodded in the dark, then pushed the door open.

The house was dim as they quietly walked in, leaving Cocktail asleep in his cage in the backseat. A yellow line glowed under Beth's door. Maggie tapped softly on it and Beth told her to come in.

Beth struggled to push away her laptop, then she noticed the bandage on Maggie's forehead. "Mags, what happened? You got blood all over you!"

Maggie crossed to her and gently hugged her. "Hi, cutie. Good to see you, too. We had a fender bender while I was driving, and I cracked my head on the steering wheel."

"You're okay, then?" Beth wondered.

"Yep. Just too bad the car is pre-airbag." She grinned.

Dressed in her over-large shirt from Columbia that Maggie had given her, Beth shook her head. "I'm glad you're okay. You guys won't believe what I found out about the scroll. Maggie, can I see it?"

"Sure you can, but first I have someone who really wants to meet you. You have to promise to keep quiet, though, He's kind of excitable," Maggie said with a straight face. "Reeve, would you do the honors?"

Beth's eyes grew wide. "Excitable? What on earth ..."

Reeve went back out to the Jeep, noting ruefully the crumpled front fender under the street light. He opened the back door and extracted a sleeping Cocktail, who roused enough to murmur at him.

Back at Beth's door, Reeve stopped and slipped the cage behind him, talking to the bird softly. "Just another minute. Keep the beak shut or you'll wake the Wicked Witch. Trust me, you don't want to do that."

With his other hand, he opened the door and walked in.

On her bed seated cross-legged, Beth looked at him. "Reeve, what is it?"

Roused by the light, Cocktail let out a questioning squawk. Beth's eyes grew large. Maggie giggled.

Reeve pulled the cage from behind his back with a flourish. "Meet Cocktail the Cockatoo. Imported from Paris, no less."

"Oh my gosh!" Beth shrieked. "Is he for me? Mine? Maggie, I love you love him love you!" She threw herself off the bed and ran to the cage, which Reeve placed on the floor.

"Be careful, sweetie," Maggie cautioned her. "He doesn't know you yet."

Beth knelt in front of the cage, and murmured "Who's a beautiful boy? What a pretty boy. You wouldn't hurt me, would you?"

In response, the large white bird twittered and did a long, deep purring trill, sticking his head through the bars of the cage. Beth extended her finger and rubbed his soft head. His low purr grew into a shriek of contentment and the door burst open.

"What the hell is all this noise? What is *that*?" Anna screamed, eyes narrowed as she took in the cage on the floor. Cocktail hurriedly brought his head back in and shrieked again with a note of alarm.

"Mom," Beth said excitedly, "his name is Cocktail. Maggie and Reeve brought him for me. Please say I can have him? Please?" She looked appealingly at Anna.

Just out of bed in her blue silk nightgown, her hair

squashed flat on one side, Anna Purcell put her hands on her hips. "Certainly not. Maggie, you should know better. Filthy creature. Can't you shut him up? Get him the hell out of here this instant!" Enraged, her thin lips pressed together under her long nose. To Maggie, she looked bird-like herself for a moment.

A vulture, Maggie thought. "He's certainly not dirty," she replied softly. "He loves nothing better than a bath in his bowl."

"Well, I won't have it. This is still my house, and I damned well won't have a filthy, stinking—"

"You will or the monthly checks stop coming." Maggie's face had gone white under her bandage.

"How dare you! Your father's rolling in his grave. If he knew the way you treat me, things you say ... you really are the most ungrateful—"

"Mom, it's late. Why don't you go to bed and we'll discuss this in the morning." Maggie didn't like Anna's color—a dull, ugly red crept up her face like a slow rash.

"I can't sleep with all this racket, knowing that filthy creature is spreading germs throughout my beautiful house."

"If you go to bed and we turn out the lights, Cocktail will sleep, too. It's been a long day for all of us," Maggie said, her head pounding.

Anna stopped and really looked at her for the first time. "What happened to you? Did that damn bird do that to you? And now you want to get rid of him here."

"Cocktail had nothing to do with it. We had a fender bender a while ago and I cracked my head on the wheel."

Anna shot Reeve a poisonous look. "And why wasn't he driving?"

"He drove all day. Listen, it is really late. Why don't we all have a drink and then go to bed? Reeve can stay on the couch, if you don't mind."

"Now that's the best idea I've heard yet," Anna said, brightening as Maggie had hoped she would. "But I'll have mine in my own room at peace. You three figure out how to get rid of that damn bird first thing in the morning. I mean it: I won't have it, and that's final." She turned on her heels and went through the door, slamming it with a resounding bang.

Cocktail yelped in fear, and to Maggie's horror, fluffed all his feathers out and scuttled to the bottom of his cage, where he visibly trembled under his food dish.

Before Maggie could stop her, Beth slid the door of the cage open and gently took the large bird in both hands. Crooning to him softly, she backed up and slumped on her bed. Still trembling, Cocktail uttered little cries of distress but snuggled up to the girl and put his white head under her chin.

Reassured, Maggie said, "He sure loves you already. Don't worry, he's not going anywhere, and for once, I'll have the final say. I meant it about her allowance. All it does is pay for her country club fees, liquor, and new clothes. When's the last time she got you anything nice and new? No, don't bother to answer. All I've got to do is this," she growled.

In rage, Maggie whipped open the door to Beth's closet. The selection of clothes was pitiably thin, and everything was well-worn. "Just look at this. You know, things are going to change around here. Starting with me."

Reeve shot Beth a calming look. She was crying soundlessly, her hands gently stroking Cocktail. Maggie closed the closet door, took a deep breath and sank to her knees in front of the bed. "Sweetie, I'm so sorry. I didn't mean to scare you. I love you and I've put up with too much around here. The clothes are probably the least of it, but thankfully we have Darla to look after you now."

Beth wound one arm around her neck and hugged her,

cupping Cocktail protectively in the other. "You didn't scare me. You couldn't. Don't worry about silly old clothes. I sure don't. Maggie, this is the neatest thing I've ever seen, Cocktail is. Look how sweet he is."

Restive, Cocktail squirmed out of her grasp and hopped to one shoulder, where he was gently tasting Beth's tears with his tongue. "Promise me you won't take him away. I don't think I could stand it. But I don't want to make Mom mad." Suddenly very pale, Beth moved her legs onto the bed and sighed. Then her eyes flew open. "Wait. I nearly forgot. Maggie, here, take Cocktail and pass me the scroll for a minute. I have some pretty neat news."

Maggie retrieved Cocktail and put him in his cage, where he tiredly pecked at his food. "Cocktail's going nowhere. I got him in Paris, and who else speaks French around here? Not me. We'll work it out with Mom. Don't you worry. Listen, sweetie, it's late and you're beat. Can't it wait till morning?"

"No, it really can't. I'm very serious, Maggie. This is big."

"Everything to do with this scroll is bad news, I'm not sure I can take much more of it," Maggie said under her breath.

"What do you mean? It's the coolest thing ever!" Beth's eyes were shining.

Maggie raised her eyebrows at Reeve. He shook his head.

Beth didn't miss the exchange. "Hey, what's going on?"

"Nothing. Now, didn't you have something to tell me about the scroll?"

"It can wait a second. What aren't you telling me?" Beth's blue eyes were clear and direct, and Maggie groaned.

"Well, I'll tell you what happened in Paris, but don't tell Mom I did—don't forget, okay?"

Beth nodded.

"I went into this really neat writing shop in the Paris flea market. Oh, Beth, it was great. They had calligraphy, handmade books—just about anything you can imagine. And this nice Arab guy, Achmed, who ran it ..." She stopped and teared up.

"Maggie! What on earth?" Beth leaned forward from her bed.

"I'm okay. It's just awful. He was telling me about his daughter, who was visiting New York, and how she initialed the Napoleon letter so everyone would know it wasn't real. I was paying him when the door opened. I had my back to it. But I kind of turned, and there was this other Arab in full white robes, staring right at me. I started to say something to the owner and BAM. He was shot. I ran out the back of the store. Worst thing I ever saw, ever. Reeve and I decided the smartest thing to do was to get out of Paris, so we flew directly home."

For several minutes, Beth stared at her, mouth open. "You've got to be kidding, Mags. You could have been killed!"

Maggie forced a laugh. "You didn't see how fast I moved. Nothing on two legs could have caught me."

"Mags, you think we should try to find his daughter in New York?"

Maggie frowned. "I don't know why we should. There's nothing I can do to help him now. I think it's best we forget the entire thing happened."

"You're probably right. But, I don't know if I can forget it. It's so scary." She shivered. "I do have some neat news about the scroll, though. Pass it over, will you?"

Curious, Maggie fished the scroll out of her purse and handed it to Beth. "Here you go."

Shaking a bit from excitement and nerves, Beth reached for the scroll. As her fingers curled around it, a low peal of thunder rumbled the windows.

Beth looked briefly at Maggie, then coughed once and gagged, dropping the scroll on the floor. Maggie leaned in to catch her.

"Beth! Are you alright, sweetie? Beth?"

But Beth couldn't speak. Struggling to draw in another breath, her entire body turned a delicate pink.

"Reeve! Call 911!" Maggie cried in horror.

Reeve didn't move for a moment. He stared at the scroll on the floor, then bent to pick it up. Immediately he dropped it. "Oh my God, it's hot."

"Of course she's hot. She's burning up. Call 911 now!" Maggie said, cradling Beth in her arms.

"No, don't bother," Beth said suddenly. "I'm good, Maggie. I feel—I don't know—better somehow. Wow, did you hear that thunder? That's the first time I ever touched that scroll. It's intense, Mags."

Maggie took a closer look. The pink still suffused her pale cheeks but was slowly fading from the rest of her body. Beth's eyes were clearer than Maggie had seen them in months. The whites were no longer crisscrossed with angry red striations. Puzzled, she carefully put Beth back on the bed, then slid to her haunches and plucked the scroll off the floor.

Reeve's eyebrows went up when she didn't flinch.

"Are you sure you're alright? I really think we should run you by the ER just to check things out," Maggie said.

"I'm serious. I don't need to go. I've had enough of hospitals, and for right now anyway, I feel great!" Beth said. "Maggie, look at the bottom of the scroll. This is serious. It explains a lot."

Maggie sighed but obediently unrolled the scroll. Beth swung her laptop into place and rapidly typed at the keyboard. After a moment, she said, "Ah, here it is. Okay, hold up the scroll. See those three characters at the bottom?"

Maggie and Reeve both nodded, mystified.

"Okay, then. Check this out." She triumphantly spun the laptop to face them.

In the upper corner of the web page, a beautiful gold symbol revolved—the three distinct characters from the bottom of the scroll.

Three words were italicized under the revolving symbols. *"Son of Man."*

— CHAPTER THIRTEEN —

SATURDAY, JULY 25

Reeve sucked air through his teeth and leaned over to scrutinize the scroll. The characters were identical and unmistakable. "Son of Man," in Ancient Aramaic, was carefully lettered at the bottom of the scroll with a flourish. Eyes swimming in sudden tears, he reached a shaking hand out to the scroll. Her attention still fully on Beth, Maggie snapped the scroll into his hand.

"From what I remember in college, no Dead Sea Scroll so much as mentioned Jesus Christ," she noted.

"This one was written by him!" Beth said with a huge smile.

"Jesus probably couldn't even write," Maggie responded.

"He wrote in the sand, John 8:5–7," came Reeve's quiet voice from behind her. "He most assuredly could write." Tears fell down his face unnoticed as he ran his hands gently over the scroll.

Was it possible he was touching the same scroll that his

Lord and Savior had once held and written upon? The thought was nearly too much for him and he struggled to get his emotions under control, only half-listening to Maggie and Beth as they clicked through more of the website.

"See, Maggie. Right here, on their 'About' page. 'These three characters translate directly to 'Son of Man,' as Jesus of Nazareth commonly called himself.'"

"All that means is that some biblically knowledgeable art forgers exist out there somewhere," Maggie said dryly.

"But Mags, that would sure explain why those Arabs want it back so badly. It's worth more than a fortune. It's priceless," Beth said.

"Such a thing would hose their entire religion," said Reeve. "They say Jesus is only a prophet, not anyone to be worshipped. I'd think they'd really want to lay their hands on it to destroy it. Also, how could they possibly know what it says?"

"Mags, I don't think ancient Aramaic is that different from modern day Aramaic. Maybe somebody knew Aramaic and simply read the signature themselves before you got it. And it's not like they couldn't have found this website, too."

"First, you think it's a Dead Sea Scroll, and now you have it written by Jesus himself. It's a nice fantasy, but it's impossible, sweetie. I do think maybe it's old and valuable. I don't know why else those people would be so determined to lay their hands on it.

"Reeve and I have plans to take it to the Shrine of the Book in Israel. They'll be able to tell us exactly what it is, and better yet, maybe I could sell it to them. After all, if it really is a Dead Sea Scroll, that's where it belongs—not with some unreligious heathen like me." Then she saw Reeve furtively mopping his face. "Reeve? Are you alright?"

"Yeah, I'm just totally exhausted, girl. That was one long drive."

"Look at the time. It's nearly two a.m. Time for bed. Reeve, let's get you settled on the couch."

Reeve sighed inwardly but nodded and smiled. He longed to go to a hotel, any hotel, grab a room, and sleep for the whole of Saturday. Somehow, he knew at Anna's house, he'd be up early, and it wouldn't be a pleasant awakening.

Maggie tossed and turned under her comforter, eyes wide open in the darkness. The fight between Reeve and the Arabs was on instant replay in her head, and sleep was distant.

When she'd first become conscious, she thought Reeve was being badly hurt. And the emotion that burst into flame was a mixture of frantic worry and something else.

Reeve's track record with women was spotty at best, from what little she knew of it. To Reeve, women were of the Flavor of the Month variety. And she didn't intend to become Miss July, especially since that spot was most likely already taken by the mystery woman of the phone call.

His last girlfriend had been a stunning redhead, big hair and long thin legs. Maybe that's who was on the phone earlier, in the car. Maggie crumpled the comforter between her fingers.

But his laughter ... and his gentleness as he'd picked her off the ground as easily as plucking a flower, before putting her in the car ...

Her heart leaped, remembering the feel of his arms around her, until she frowned in the darkness. *No. and that's all there is to it. He's got a girlfriend. He works where I work, and that's a dangerous thing. That job is my lifeblood. I can't endanger it. I won't put it at risk.*

But still ...

Finally, she fell into a restless sleep, and Reeve's face danced through her dreams. His smile topped the tree in her favorite painting, but behind him a redhead tossed her hair and glared.

Buried under a comforter and two pillows to escape the bright morning sunshine, Reeve awakened to muffled shouts from the nearby kitchen.

"I tell you, I won't have a damn bird. They're full of *filth*. You can get a dread disease from their caca. I've heard about it. It gets down into your lungs and turns them to pure cement!"

"That's *chicken* crap you're thinking of, Mom. When we all went to France that year, Sally Anne came back with histoplasmosis from a *chicken* farm. There's nothing unclean about Cocktail. He's always been just an indoor pet." Maggie's voice was strained.

"How do you know where he's been! You didn't even get him here at home. Oh no, you brought him from some foreign country with God knows what kind of diseases. I will not have it, do you hear me? Period. Your sister's health is delicate as it is. Do you want to make her sicker?"

Maggie finally snapped. "As if I'd do *anything* to hurt Beth. The bird is healthy. He's had all his shots and he has an international passport to travel. He's probably in better shape than you are. He'll be great company for Beth, for all the times she's alone in this damn house!"

"He won't be any such thing. He'll be out of this house and so will you and your damn boyfriend!"

Reeve struggled, still exhausted, to put his pants on under the comforter. From his spot on the couch, he could see Beth's door open a crack. One teary blue eye looked directly at him. He shook his head at her and motioned her back into her room, but the eye only shifted focus and looked down the hall.

Though bare-chested, Reeve was now overly hot from his struggles with the jeans. He threw back the comforter and stood to meet Maggie's eyes, amused through her anger, and

Anna's enraged, reddened ones.

"I'm fixing to change things around here, Mother." Maggie's voice was suddenly soft and Reeve felt a prickle over the back of his neck. Hurriedly, he slipped into his tee-shirt. "It's my fault for not keeping a better eye," she said, "but I finally did take a close look at a few things last night, including Beth's closet."

The older woman had the grace to flush and turn away, filling the coffee pot with a rush of water.

"That money I send every month is for *Beth* and the *house*. You have Dad's check, too. Yet, what do I see in Beth's closet? Hardly anything, and what's there is old and worn. How could you?"

"How dare you!" Anna slammed the pot onto the heating element. "Where are you when she forever more needs to be sick, needs to go to the hospital, always needs! And where the hell are you—"

"That's enough," Maggie said in a voice so soft Reeve had to strain to hear. "I've hired Darla to take care of Beth now." Quietly enraged, Maggie looked her mother right in the eye and saw an odd, almost confused expression, then dismissed it. "I had no idea things had gotten this bad. From now on, I'm going to send half that check to Darla every month, to take Beth shopping. If I hear one more word from you about the goddamn bird or anything else, I'll go to Child Protection Services and have you declared an unfit mother. *Then*, I'll take Beth back with me to New York and you won't ever have to worry about her needs again."

The silence echoed with her final words. Reeve froze with one foot half-sneakered, then the phone rang and all three adults jumped.

Anna noisily exhaled and shot Maggie a venomous look before picking up the receiver with a cheery hello. She listened for a moment, then without a word, shoved the phone at Maggie. Sobbing as she went, she stalked down the hall to her bedroom. Maggie spoke a few words and listened as Reeve went into the bathroom with his kit.

He hastily brushed his teeth and didn't bother shaving, just ran a washcloth over his stubble. He emerged from the bathroom to see Maggie sitting at the kitchen table, head propped on hands, gazing out the kitchen window.

Without looking up, she said, "You won't believe it."

"I heard the whole thing." He raised a brow.

"Not that. The phone call. It was Todd. Mohammad Ishtara called. Said it's urgent. Someone hacked into their database last night and got their entire client list, passwords, all of it. They've just turned off their servers, but he insists we get there 'yesterday,' as Todd put it."

"Cairo? We're going to Cairo? Cool." Reeve shook his head and went to the bubbling coffee maker.

"Todd already made the arrangements. Same flight as last time—leaves JFK at nine tonight. He found us a flight from Nashville to JFK at three."

"Wow. That isn't much time. It's nearly eleven now. Will you be able to ..." and he gestured toward Anna's room.

"I'll just have to, won't I?"

They sat in silence, hearing only Anna's sobs coming down the hall. Beth's door opened and she crept silently into the kitchen, thin shoulders hunched.

"Come here, love," Maggie said, holding her arms out. "I'm so sorry if you heard any of that." Beth ran into Maggie's embrace and crawled onto her lap, burying her face in her sister's neck. Maggie felt the warmth of tears and her heart twisted. "Shhh now. It's going to be alright. It'll blow over. It always does."

"Maybe you should just ... just take Cocktail back to New York," Beth said between sobs. "I never meant to cause all this trouble."

"You haven't caused anything. Mom is a drama queen. That's all there is to it. And she doesn't usually think of anyone but herself." Maggie heard the bitterness in her own voice and fell silent.

"That's not always true, Mags. She sat with me for hours during those treatments and held my head while I ralphed for days after."

"I know she has," Maggie said with effort. "Okay, I'm going to talk to her now. You sit right here until I get back."

She picked up Beth and deposited her on Reeve's lap. He wrapped an arm around her waist and gave her a gentle hug. "Maggie will fix it, sprout. Just give her a moment."

As she walked down the hall, Maggie wondered if she *could* fix it. They'd had their quarrels, she and her mom, but it had never gone as far as it had this time. She looked down at her feet in great sadness.

Anna was seated on the edge of her canopied bed, her blue silk housedress matching her silk comforter. Her back erect, she lifted her head and stared Maggie in the eye as she entered.

"I'm not a bad mother, you know. I did well enough by you as you were growing up, didn't I?"

An unbidden thought came to Maggie. She was five years old and learning to ride her first bike in front of the house. Anna was walking alongside, calling out encouragement. As usual, her father wasn't there. And when finally Maggie had succeeded in riding unaccompanied to the end of the street, Anna hooted and shouted her glee.

She leaned over and hugged the older woman. "Of course, you're not a bad mother. I'm sorry I said that. But I do feel firmly about Cocktail. I got him to keep Beth company. He's a little noisy, but I have the feeling he'll really cheer her up."

Anna hugged her back. "She has full responsibility for that critter. I expect that cage to be immaculate. No stench, no mess. It stays in her room and doesn't go anywhere else."

"You won't regret this, Mom. She's a responsible kid."

Maggie turned to leave the room and Anna reached out a hand. "Wait. There's something more I need to say. Something you need to know about your father."

Maggie stiffened. "What else is there to know?"

"He didn't … take the easy way out, as you always put it." Nervously Anna picked a tissue from the ornamental box near her bed and began to shred it.

"What else would you call it? He couldn't handle the stress of having a sick child, so he called it quits."

"Is that what you think?" Anna took a deep breath. "Your father was a lot of things, but he worshipped you and Beth. He worked his fingers to the bone so we'd have this house. So you'd have a permanent place to grow up."

Maggie's eyes filled and she slumped on the bed next to her mother. Anna stiffened and moved a bit away from her, then continued. "He worked so much that he was almost never here. But he did take you and Beth to Nashville Shores at least once a month. I know you remember that."

Maggie did. Beth had been small at the time. Tom Purcell had delighted in mounting the highest ladders at the water park, then with his tiny daughter screaming between his legs, plummeting to the pool below. She smiled through tears at the memory, then shook her head. *But if it hadn't been the pressure of taking care of a deathly ill child, what had caused Tom Purcell to drive into a tree at nearly a hundred miles per hour?*

"… and you he loved more than life. You look just like him, you know—that dark hair and green eyes." Anna reached for another tissue.

She went silent for a bit, dabbing at her eyes and drawing in great sobbing breaths. Maggie wanted to reach out to her, but something about Anna's thin, stiff back encouraged her to keep her distance.

"Did you know I wasn't your dad's first love?"

Maggie's blank look prompted Anna to continue. "His first love was a girl called Serena. And she was just like her name: beautiful, calm, and loving. They were supposed to get married. Their families had been friends since before Tom was born. It was all perfect," Anna said with bitterness.

Maggie was spellbound. Dad had been in love before? Somehow the knowledge made him more of a person to her, more real.

"They set the wedding for June one year. But in January, Serena had some kind of stomach bug. It wouldn't go away, and then they found she had pancreatic cancer. It's not something you recover from. She was way past the point of walking down the aisle in June, and from what Tom said, she refused to marry him though he begged. She was dead by July."

Maggie sat still, tears spilling.

"I met him a year later. And I tell you this—he was a broken man. When we found out our Bethie had leukemia, well … Tom decided he was cursed." She reached for Kleenex and blew her nose. "He used to get so drunk, he'd sit in the bathroom and scream out for Serena."

Then Maggie did remember. At the time, she hadn't known that "Serena" was a name, but she well recalled the drunken, plaintive wails.

"And Maggie, that night he did it again. It'd been years since he'd called out for her. I thought we were over that. To hear him yell her name, with such longing—even though I knew he was so, so drunk, it just cut me to the bone. I went and banged on that bathroom door and told him to get the hell out." She sobbed, took a breath, and continued.

"It was my fault, Mags. I told him to leave. He did, and he never came back." She folded herself forward at the waist and wailed into her lap.

Maggie pulled her mother into her arms. "Don't ever think that. It was him, his choice. I had no idea."

"I know you didn't. It still hurts me to this day to talk about Serena. Isn't that silly? To be jealous of a ghost? Two of them, now."

Maggie bent her dark head over her mother's and the two women cried together. Then Maggie gave her one last hug and went to pack.

— CHAPTER FOURTEEN —

SATURDAY, JULY 25 – MONDAY, JULY 27

Late that night, on the red-eye to Cairo, Reeve's little snores lulled Maggie further toward sleep herself. She was fighting the urge to doze, dreading the chanting and voices that frightened her more each time.

She took a walk up the aisle of the large plane. Most of the other passengers were relaxed or asleep in their seats, mouths agape. Jealous, she returned to her own seat, located at the front of the tourist section, where there was plenty of room for Reeve's long legs.

She settled back in between him and the wall of the plane, pressing her face to the cool window. Fighting to stay awake to avoid hearing the voices, she thought about the system they'd installed a year earlier for Mohammed Ishtara. She'd thought it was hacker-proof, she remembered drowsily. *How had someone managed to get access to the client database and pull all the passwords?*

The plane's huge engines thrummed and roared through her body, further relaxing the tension residing in her neck and shoulders. Just audible over the arrhythmic beat came low voices, chanting. Alarmed, she tried to sit back up, but it was as if tons of water pressed her deeply into her seat.

The chanting grew louder and she became aware of individual male voices, speaking in some unknown language. Whatever they were saying rang with passion and conviction. And, slowly, she realized she was outside in a beautiful, sunny day, suspended in the air over a peaceful countryside that looked totally untouched by man. No roads, no cars, no planes.

The sensation of flying was pleasant and she moved through the air at will, vaguely aware she had no body. Cresting a low hill, she encountered a man in a short belted robe walking along the ground.

She swooped in for a better look and found herself hovering just above his dark, bronzed left shoulder. She was so close that she could see individual black hairs on his wrist blowing in the breeze as he swung a stout walking stick.

Looking down, she noted his rough leather sandals over dusty feet. It looked as though he'd been traveling for miles. She smelled the pungent leather of the bag he'd thrown over one shoulder.

She angled herself so she could see the face of this bearded man as he strode confidently along.

And then she couldn't breathe. All thoughts were blown out of her head along with the last breath she'd taken, as she found she was looking directly into the angular face of Jesus Christ. He looked just like most pictures she'd seen, the warm brown eyes looking through her down the path he intended to take, a small smile cracking his curly brown beard. His wavy brown hair bounced and shone in the sunlight with every step, and he was humming a little tune as he went.

Maggie was overcome by a wonder and awe so profound that it closed her throat both in and out of the dream, and she felt herself fly upwards. For one timeless moment, she became a part of the very time through which she'd just flown. Then she was gasping for breath back in the plane.

But she wasn't in her seat. Still in deep ecstasy, she found herself hovering above her and Reeve's seats.

She could see the individual tight curls on the top of Reeve's head, some squashed against the back of the seat as he slept. It was the sight of the top of her own smooth dark hair that caused terror to override her other emotions. With an almost audible snap, she was back in her body, face still pressed against the window.

She gasped for air. *No way. Not happening. Didn't happen. I don't know what's going on with me. It was just a dream.* This was more up Beth's alley for dreams—odd and pleasant. Even Reeve would be more comfortable with the vision she'd just had, if that's what it was.

She found herself sobbing softly, there in the darkness, feeling terribly alone on a plane full of people, Reeve not six inches away. As if he'd heard her thoughts, he opened one eye and said, "Not the bad dream?"

"I don't want to talk about it. I don't think I can." Her sobs built until she was again gasping for breath.

Completely alarmed, Reeve shook himself awake and sat up, crushing her to him with one long arm. "What is it, girl? Come on, talk to me."

"Can't. It's too much," she whimpered. She pulled away from him and curled up against the window. And then it all came out. "Reeve, I'm going crazy. Seriously nuts. I keep hearing chanting ... and drums. It's like I'm asleep, but I'm not. I'm terrified." She took a deep shuddering breath.

"This time I dreamed I saw *Him*, just walking along like an average Joe—I even saw his beat-up sandals. The left one was flapping as he walked."

Reeve went still. "Saw *who*?"

"I don't want to talk about it …" She buried her face in her hands.

Reeve said, "I'm not sure what's going on with you, either, but I got a strong tingle it's going to be alright. All of it."

"How can it ever be alright when somehow I'm dreaming of things that happened thousands of years ago? I'm not even religious. Or I didn't think I was. I haven't been to church in ages." She drew a deep ragged breath. "I'm just terrified I'm losing it."

"I don't think you are," Reeve said carefully. "I believe all things happen for a reason, and while it's not clear yet, we'll find out why this is happening."

"I'm going to pretend none of this is happening. Because it really isn't. My imagination is working overtime. That's all this is."

"You're probably right," Reeve said as he reached over and kneaded her shoulders. "Girl, you're getting bony. You know that?"

"Gee thanks," she said sleepily. It felt so good, his hands massaging the tight muscles of her shoulders. So good … and she was asleep.

Ishtara International looked as it had a year ago—a long, dusty low warehouse in the south of Cairo, with offices that Mohammad's father had built in the back. Maggie and Reeve walked into the same mayhem she remembered. Several robed men were wrapping soapstone busts of Nefertiti in bubble wrap. A woman was carefully polishing a lovely brass ashtray that resembled a swimming pool, a naked woman's hip providing a cigarette rest. Mohammad Ishtara's business was doing well, although the back of the warehouse was stacked high with unsent boxes.

A short man in a denim shirt and tan slacks approached them and Mohammad introduced him. "This is Zeb, our new, how you say, person for computers. I hope you can show him how to stop this problem."

Maggie eyed the short man skeptically. With his smooth olive skin and long-lashed eyes, he looked just out of school. "Hi, Zeb. Why don't we go back to the server room and take a look?"

As she brought the four large servers back online, Maggie found it was going to take much more than a look. A Trojan horse, a small program that infiltrated a computer, then sat silent until its master called it, had permitted access to all of Mohammed's files, not just the database. Worse, the Trojan horse contained a malicious piece of code that, once the desired information was delivered, would scramble all the remaining data. At least Zeb or Mohammad had stopped the process before the hard drive was totally eradicated.

Wearily, Maggie explained the effects of the virus to Mohammad, then paused. Reeve looked at her with his left eyebrow cocked. She gave him a little nod, then said, "We will need at least five of your best people to repopulate the database. That won't be a problem, will it?"

"No, there's a company I will hire for data entry. But Maggie, have you any idea how this happened?"

Maggie tapped the keyboard and a small window appeared on the screen. For several moments, she scrolled through the contents, then leaned back in her chair with a little moan. "There it is. Mohammed, good news and bad. The good is that I beefed up your firewall last time I was here, and we left a port sniffer running to ensure nothing got in or out that we wouldn't know about.

"Here—" she pointed to the screen—"this shows activity on the port that the Trojan horse was using, so we know where it was going to send the data from. The bad news: that port was enabled inside the firewall. It should have been disabled with all the rest, so it had to have been enabled through *this* server." She felt the young Zeb stiffen beside her. Reeve stayed silent, looking around the office. A girl and two men were rapidly typing at computers and hadn't stopped when Maggie booted the servers.

"You mean someone from *here* did this? But I know and trust everyone here. Zeb is the only new one, and his father attended school with me. It's not possible," Mohammad said, anguished.

"Perhaps someone broke in," Reeve suggested.

"Also not possible," Mohammad said. "We have a great alarm system. I would know."

Maggie leaned back in her chair and rubbed her eyes. The jet lag and stress were combining to give her a wicked, pounding headache. She looked up and noticed Zeb's eyes on her, calculating. Quickly, she looked away. "For now that's all we can do," she said. "Let me get a good night's sleep, and you place the call to the data entry company. We'll see you back here in the morning."

After a solid sixteen hours of dreamless sleep, Maggie felt sharp, alert, and ready to go. She removed the bandage on her head before leaving the hotel, glad to see the wound had scabbed over and nearly healed.

She and Reeve found the office hopping, a person typing busily at each of the twenty machines. "Wow, Mohammad. It shouldn't take but a few days at this rate."

"Time is money," he said, eyes reddened and drooping. "We are here since six last night. I tell them they get bonus for overtime."

"Well, Reeve and I should also get to it." Maggie went to

the server rack in the corner and sat. Along with Zeb, they worked steadily until nearly 10:00 p.m.

By Monday afternoon, Maggie was feeling nearly back to normal. At Ishtara International, the work was progressing smoothly, if very slowly. She had just reworked the firewall ports and was ready to test when her cell phone rang. To her surprise, it was Royce with news.

"Maggie, the test results are in. Oxford is very excited and wants to see the scan I made of the entire scroll. Maggie, the scroll tests to nearly two thousand years old, give or take a few years. The ink is comprised of lampblack and gum, which tested to the exact same date. The scroll is validated."

— CHAPTER FIFTEEN —

MONDAY, JULY 27

Maggie's mouth went dry. She picked up her mug and sipped the lukewarm coffee. Professor Royce's voice became a murmur, and she suddenly saw Beth in her mind's eye.

What did this mean for her, for Beth? She had a terrible, sinking feeling the danger would escalate. Validated as being a real Dead Sea Scroll, the thing would surely mean trouble. Big trouble.

"I'm sorry, what did you just say? Are you sure it's real?"

Royce had fallen silent. Then he said, "It's very real. Even the ink components test to usual Dead Sea Scroll materials." He paused.

"Royce? Are you still there?"

"Yes. Maggie ... we've known each other for a while. You know I'd never do anything to hurt you, correct?"

Puzzled, she concurred.

"I've had an offer for your scroll. They are willing to pay half a million dollars."

Outraged, Maggie said, "You discussed my business with someone else?" Now the news would get out that she had such a valuable object. Now—

"Only that you have a valuable artifact in which this individual holds considerable interest," he said hastily. "Would you at least consider the proposition before dismissing it out of hand?"

"I think you had no right whatso—half a million dollars? You can't be serious." Maggie's hand went limp on the phone and she nearly dropped it.

"Very serious. And it's important to him that he has an answer soon."

"Why? A sum like that, he must really want the scroll badly. How can I make a decision like this so fast?"

"What's to decide?" Royce's voice was soft and cajoling. "It's the opportunity of a lifetime."

Maggie told him she'd consider it and hung up abruptly.

"Reeve, we need to take a walk. Right now." Maggie was bloodlessly pale, her hands shaking as they walked the length of the busy warehouse and emerged into the dry, absolute heat of the Egyptian sun.

She took a deep breath, and dust from the street went into her lungs. She coughed explosively and Reeve patted her back with a gentle hand.

"Did I hear what I thought I heard? I presume the tests came out well," he said.

"Oxford verified both the scroll and the ink as being roughly two thousand years old, and the ink was made of lampblack, exactly what was used on the scrolls." At his raised brow, she continued. "Lampblack is made by burning pitch resin from trees, until right before it's total ash. It's very fine and coal black. Anyway, I definitely have a Dead Sea scroll, they think!" She walked to the corner, small cars creeping past and men on bicycles zigging in and out of the heavy late afternoon traffic. They stopped and waited for a break in the traffic.

"Did you hear about the half-million dollars? Royce called someone. God, Reeve, a half-million dollars!" Her eyes bright as the magnitude of the offer hit her, she continued, "I could pay off Beth's bills. I could put in a pool for her. She would just love that. I could even have it heated!"

Reeve's mouth straightened into a thin line. He looked across the heavy traffic to a butcher's shop on the opposite corner. Flies hung in furry blankets over slabs of meat strung above the sidewalk. A break in traffic prompted him to take Maggie by the elbow and steer her off the low curb. A passing cyclist hit his horn and spat as they quickly crossed the narrow street.

Reeve looked at Maggie, whose eyes were shining as she walked along, almost skipping. He sighed inwardly and began, "I know you don't want to hear this right now, but girl, you need to give a real thought to what you're doing. That scroll will change hundreds of thousands of lives, just by its very existence. It's unique. One of a kind. It was touched by the hand of Our Lord Jesus Christ himself," he said in complete awe, eyes filling. "If you sell it to some rich eccentric, he could put it away in a small room and no one would ever see it again."

"Why would anyone do that?" Maggie said idly. Not concentrating on Reeve's words, she was imagining Beth's and Anna's faces when she told them the news.

"They do that because they can, and because it gives them pleasure," Reeve said tightly. "What an incalculable loss to the world. Maggie, you just have to think this over, hard and long."

"What's to think about?" she said, quickening her step as

they passed the unpleasant-smelling butcher's shop. "You have no way of knowing who wrote that scroll, you know. It's just another Dead Sea Scroll. And the person who buys the scroll ... It could be a church, a museum, we don't know."

"But we don't *know* what they'll do with it. What if it winds up somewhere the world can't see and experience it?"

"And I suppose you expect me to simply donate it to a museum?" She was outraged.

"I'm sure a museum will pay you good money for it. I never knew money was so—"

"And why would you? Your parents are professors at Georgetown. You weren't raised to wonder where your next meal was coming from. Ideals are fine, but I have a sister with cancer, huge bills. She's the most important thing in my life. Everything I do is aimed at Beth's security. She has no one else to take care of her, and—"

"And you don't know anything about how I was raised," he said, stung.

"How you were raised has nothing to do with this. It's about Beth and Mom. And one more thing! I've had nothing but grief from that damn scroll! I got manhandled into the back of a car from my own home in Nashville. Then, I was run off the road by nuts in robes!"

She whirled on her heel, then stopped. "I've had enough. Whoever it was written by, that scroll is a menace, and not for one damn moment do I think Maggie Purcell owns a scroll written by Jesus Christ! Sooner or later, someone's going to get really hurt because of that damn thing, and I'd just as soon not have it be me or mine." Her jaw set, she stepped back past the butcher's shop with her head held high, eyes flashing in anger.

Reeve watched her go, unsure of what he was feeling. He knew what such a sum would mean to her family, but ...

He walked aimlessly and soon came across a small dusty

lot where laughing children were chasing each other. He made his way to a bench and sat, sickness rising up in his throat.

As stubborn as Maggie was, she *had* to be dissuaded from giving up the scroll. How was it she couldn't see what such a thing, such a magnificent symbol, would mean for the entire Christian faith? "Faith" was the operative word, he thought wearily.

For millennia, Christians had gone largely on faith, in regards to what Jesus had actually said during his life. And, of course, Jesus himself being the Son of God was the real leap. Head throbbing, Reeve drew a deep breath to try to calm himself.

Remember John 6:40, he told himself. *And this is the will of him that sent me, that every one which seeth the Son, and believeth in him, may have everlasting life: and I will raise him up at the last day.* And he believed. That was the rub.

Imagine what knowledge of this scroll would do for multitudes of Christians who had taken everything on faith their entire lives. No one truly knew if God exists nor if anything they'd been taught regarding their salvation was true. They'd had to have faith in what they'd been taught—faith that God *does* exist.

The existence of this scroll would increase the believer's faith. It would burn so brightly in the heart, not to mention the millions of nonbelievers who would be brought to Christ.

Faith had been, right up to now, an affair of the heart.

And now, words from His own hand existed. At the thought, Reeve felt a deep shiver run up his spine. In spite of his confusion, he experienced a desire to know exactly what the scroll said. It was, in every way, a miracle—a miracle that the scroll had lasted two thousand years, and certainly a miracle that it had been found and was now in Maggie's possession.

Even for so brief a time, he thought bitterly.

Only to be hidden away for the eyes of a greedy reclusive millionaire? He couldn't allow that to happen. He stood and made his way back to Ishtara. He and Maggie needed to talk, and perhaps his own priest could help him marshal his arguments.

Unable to resist telling them the incredible news, Maggie called Anna and Beth the night she received the offer from Professor Royce.

Anna had been, for once, completely speechless. Beth, however, had reacted oddly, Maggie thought. While she couldn't quite believe the offer, she showed a marked lack of enthusiasm. Maggie wrote it off to apprehension about her upcoming chemo treatment. Realistically, she knew that no sum of money could make Beth better, but it could certainly make her more comfortable.

The next few days passed in a blizzard of work and stiff interactions between Maggie and Reeve. Maggie treated Reeve with an unfailing politeness, and there was a high, happy color to her face. She alternated between jubilance at the thought of being debt-free, anxiety about Reeve, and a rising sense of stress over everything. As soon as they eradicated one part of the octopus-like virus, another tentacle would grab a port, and they'd be back where they started.

She and Reeve fell into a rhythm of work. They awoke every morning and poured cups of strong, muddy Egyptian coffee diluted with real cream. Their driver, Dave, an elderly Egyptian with a white beard, would drive them from the Cairo Hilton to Ishtara International and let them off in front. Zeb was a constant presence behind them. Reeve found him proficient and quick to learn, soaking up all he was taught.

By Thursday morning, a skeleton of the database was up

and running, and all the back orders were being shipped. When Mohammad suggested a free afternoon to see the pyramids "as they should be seen," Reeve jumped at the opportunity to smooth over the argument with Maggie.

Outside Ishtara International, though, Dave wasn't waiting with the car. To Maggie's dismay, Zeb was waiting for them in a four-door Toyota. He smiled and lowered his window. "Come on! Today is a treat on Mohammad."

After a nudge from Maggie, Reeve got into the front seat while Maggie found herself in the back next to a large picnic basket that smelled strongly of Egyptian sausage and fresh baked flat bread. She tried to relax.

The small car wove its way through Cairo's awful traffic, bicycles and cars racing along amidst a cacophony of blaring horns. The crowded streets of Cairo gave way to the much reduced traffic in the tiny village of Mena.

To Maggie's amused shock, a small group of camels grunted and groaned just to the left of the large parking lot. Shimmering in clouds of dust, the pyramids appeared enchanting, but Maggie doubted their transportation to the distant monuments would be quite so pleasant.

"I'm not sure about this," she said to Reeve as they approached the group of camels, several of whom were on their bellies, ridiculously long eyelashes blinking in the white morning sun.

"But this is a great honor," Zeb said. "Camels are no longer permitted around the pyramids—the hawkers bothered the tourists so much. Mohammad had these specially ordered to take you and Reeve properly."

"Wouldn't it be just as proper on foot?" she asked, as Reeve put a light elbow in her ribs. "Oh, alright."

"I'll be right there with you, and so will Zeb," Reeve said with a grin.

"Now *that's* reassuring," she muttered, walking gamely up

to the camels. Zeb had already reached the group, picnic basket under one arm, and was discussing something using great theatrical arm movements. Dickering, Maggie figured. She grinned, and finally relaxed, though she eyed the enormous beasts with trepidation.

There was a lull in the dickering, then money changed hands and was carefully counted. A short, very young boy in dusty jeans motioned her over to his charge, a giant beast of a camel resting peacefully on its belly with its eyes closed. Maggie stopped, terrified. She didn't even care for horses.

"Madame, come! Madame, come here," he shouted, then he beckoned her forward. She looked at Reeve, who was standing in front of a smaller camel. As she watched, the beast went to its knees, then lowered its pointed little rump with a deep groan. Reeve threw his leg over the hard boat-shaped saddle and let out a yip of surprise as the camel lurched forward and jerked to its feet.

Zeb was helping a boy tie the picnic basket onto a donkey. Maggie was wondering if she could perhaps ride that friendly *little* creature when her own boy took her by the arm.

"Madame, come!" he guided her to the side of the camel.

"Reeve, if I die here, I'm not leaving you your favorite painting," she said in a quavering voice.

"Get your ass on the camel, girl! It's great up here—but watch out, that first step is a doozey."

"Thanks for the encouragement." She cautiously put a leg over the camel. Flies buzzed around the beast's head, and its strong, gamey scent wasn't unpleasant as she sank into the saddle, then clung tightly to the rope.

"Lean back!" Reeve called, and as she did the camel lurched heavily upward. Remembering the other end came next, Maggie leaned forward as the beast scrambled to its feet, but she nearly rolled right off, to the boy's glee.

Reeve was already moving off at a good clip as Maggie's

camel simply stretched its neck, oblivious to the pleading and tugging of the boy at its head. Maggie grinned. *This wasn't so bad after all*. Her camel didn't have the inclination to move, much less run off into the desert, as she secretly feared.

Exasperated, the boy ran behind Maggie and cracked the camel on its bony rump with a stick. The camel lumbered forward into a trot and Maggie lost her balance, toppling backwards.

"Whoa! Stop! Reeve, help!" she cried out as camel and boy, little legs flying, rapidly gained on Reeve.

She heard Reeve burst into laughter and couldn't fire off a reply. Her torso was going in one direction and her behind in another as they ran right up to Reeve's camel.

"Go, girl, go. I didn't even know you could move that fast," he said between bellows of laughter.

"Go on, laugh," Maggie managed, bone jarring thumps echoing up her spine. Then she looked up and forgot her fear.

In person, the pyramids are a very different thing, she thought, amazed. No image she'd seen had done them justice. As he drew up next to her now walking and panting beast, Zeb informed her that each stone weighed more than two tons.

"I had no idea. They are so incredibly massive," Maggie said, breathless.

"Hate like hell to have one of those babies fall on your toe," said Reeve as he ambled up on his smaller camel. The three rode in silence, the only sounds being the creaking of the saddles and the wind roaring around the pyramids.

"Ebbi, I thought no more camels were allowed at the pyramids," Masood said. He and Ebbi were walking along with binoculars, once again playing tourists.

"They are not. It must be private matter. Mohammed Ishtara is powerful man."

Masood fell silent, looking at his feet and kicking a small rock along. Finally, he pouted and said, "Ebbi, we are so close to Badu Tanar, so very close. Cannot someone else watch this pain of an American so we could go home, just for the weekend?"

"No and no. We know her. We have been on them for weeks. It is better that we do the job for which we are here, especially now that we know what she has."

"But Ebbi, we know not for sure if she has *the* scroll. Do not you find it hard to believe that this scroll of legend, this scroll written by Jesus Christ himself, surfaces in Paris, France in the hands of a white American girl and a black American man?"

Ebbi blew his cheeks out. "I know not why such a thing has happened. We always thought the tribe would find and protect this priceless scroll, as it is written in legend: 'The scroll shall come to Badu Tanar when the day is long and the time is short.' That is what our legend says."

"'Day is long and time is short?' What does that mean?"

"Masood, I have always thought it means that we will find the scroll many long years from when Jesus wrote it. Now, I simply do not know."

They walked to a lone enormous block, pulled themselves up and sat. Enviously, they watched as the little group dismounted their camels at a smaller pyramid away from the majority of tourists and laid out an appetizing lunch, complete with iced drinks, evident from the beads of sweat running down the bottles.

"This air is so dry. Can I walk back to that kiosk and buy bottle of water, Ebbi?"

"By all means. Buy two. But hurry, their lunch will not take long."

Maggie wasn't looking forward to the short trip back on the camel, and when Reeve suggested they walk around the pyramids before returning, she quickly agreed to let the rented camels return on their own.

They spent the rest of the afternoon wandering among the imposing structures. Once or twice, the hair on Maggie's neck rose as she thought she saw a familiar face surrounded by robes, but here, most people wore robes. She told herself to stop projecting and just enjoy the day.

Close behind Maggie and Reeve were Faod and his partner, Uqbah. Faod couldn't believe his fortune that he was back in his native Egypt. Surely it was a good omen that he would finally acquire the scroll. Now that he knew what the scroll really was, he was yet more bent on retrieving it for sale to the highest bidder.

He was well aware that the rest of his small cell in Paris intended to destroy it. In a secret fatwa issued just yesterday, the mullah had proclaimed that it was of great harm to the Muslim nation. The heavily bearded religious leader had included in the fatwa that the scroll was to be located and destroyed at all cost. The contents of the scroll were so explosive, the mullah insisted, they should never be viewed by the public.

But what they didn't know wouldn't hurt them, Faod reasoned. He'd pretend, for Uqbah's sake, to destroy the scroll. Then he'd smuggle it directly back to Paris. *A shame I'd had to kill Achmed Kiyat*, he thought idly, his hands running over the prayer beads in his pocket. The old man had had wonderful contacts to sell the scroll, but his usefulness had come to an end the day Faod overheard him talking to his old friend in Badu Tanar. What kind of Muslim would turn over such a thing to the infidels? Fatima didn't understand, either, and had run off to New York when he'd shown her the scroll and told her excitedly of his plans to sell it. Let the silly woman stay there, he thought in disgust. Too much time in Europe had spoiled her—she wasn't a proper woman anymore.

But she was certainly better than the one he was following—the black-haired harlot with the green eyes. He'd like to crack this woman's legs backwards and use her like a horse for many hours. Perhaps he could arrange that, he thought with a small smile. A bonus.

Money and honor he would have, in the end. The clothes, the cars, and all the green-eyed harlots he wanted. His eye twitched, and he absently rubbed the large growth under it. He could maybe even see to having the growth removed, though Fatima had said the harmless mass gave him a manly, dangerous squint.

But first, he needed the scroll, and his time would come. It was certainly taking longer than he'd thought. He was very tired. But on the day of victory, no one is tired.

— CHAPTER SIXTEEN —

THURSDAY, JULY 30

Maggie awoke very early the next morning with severe stomach cramps. She had alternately vomited and had diarrhea for several hours. Mohammed called on a Dr. Hiad to look her over, who determined Maggie had a mild case of food poisoning.

By the afternoon, she felt totally spent and dry. She wondered if Zeb had done something to the food the previous day.

"Girl, you can't go thinking things like that," Reeve said. He'd come by to make sure she had what she needed to drink throughout the day. "He's been a pretty good guy. He's worked like a dog to fix the servers. Why would he want to make you sick, and not me?"

"I don't know," Maggie said weakly from her hotel bed. Reeve sat alongside in a chair, his stocking feet propped next to her, and a bucket at the ready.

"There's something not right about that guy. You really should have seen the look he gave me when I told Mohammed that someone inside Ishtara had enabled that port for the Trojan horse. If looks could kill, I'd be a dead woman."

"Thought we'd decided it was just jet lag. He hasn't done a thing since, has he?"

"Look at me now and tell me that. I feel like someone tried to rip my belly straight up through my throat and right out my ears," she moaned.

Reeve plucked the washrag off her head and dunked it into a bowl of ice water on the coffee table. He wrung it out then replaced it to a relieved groan.

"Thank you. You're saving my life. I'm sorry to be such a pain."

"Of course you're doing it all on purpose—this ralphing and carrying on. But we really can't blame …" He trailed off, seeing that Maggie was slipping into sleep.

Maggie awoke briefly that afternoon, called Royce, and insisted she needed just a few more days to make a decision on the disposition of the scroll. Royce, alarmed, told her that the client was eager and that the opportunity was too good to miss. Feeling obdurate and ill, she said she was having trouble staying awake and promptly hung up.

Royce awakened her half an hour later to report that the client understood, but that he needed a firm decision by Monday, especially in light of the fact that the scroll was now public knowledge. Horrified, she asked him how the news had gotten out. He replied that such a major find would always become public knowledge, and that initial reports had come from Paris, along with a partial translation. *Evidently I wasn't the only one to scan the old scroll*, she thought with a grimace.

She assured him she'd call on Monday and fell back into an agitated, fevered sleep.

Two days later, and none too soon for her liking, Maggie finally felt well enough to return to Ishtara International. Reeve had worked most of Sunday afternoon on a certain segment of code, and had seen it change right in front of his eyes.

The saboteur was still at work at Ishtara, and that meant they were no closer to leaving for home than they had been the first day. With an annoyed huff, Maggie donned an embroidered blue shirt over long khaki shorts. During the trip to the pyramids, she'd developed a decent tan. She blessed her skin for not burning as she picked up her briefcase, slid into a pair of sandals, and headed for the door.

Reeve was already in the back of the car, waiting, as she walked out to the front of the Hilton, but Dave, again, wasn't driving. He'd been replaced by a younger stranger.

"Where's Dave today?" Maggie asked as she climbed into the back next to Reeve.

"Dave, he sick," the man said briefly.

"Oh, that's too bad," Maggie said and settled back with a sigh.

"So, feeling better today?" Reeve looked at her closely.

"Yes, thanks mainly to you. Ever consider becoming a doctor?" For hours over the past two nights, he'd helped her to the bathroom, and once had even sponged her body after she'd had an accident. She blushed at the memory. They'd avoided the subject of the scroll carefully, but Maggie was well aware that the deadline was not far away.

"Hell, no. I can't stand the sight of blood," Reeve said, embarrassed. "Makes me queasy. I nearly pass out if I see a drop of blood when I get a shot."

She grinned. "Big guy like you? And with all you went through with me in the last few days? Who'd have thought?" As they fell silent, Maggie looked out the window. "Hey, this isn't the way to Ishtara."

"He's probably taking us another route," Reeve said.

"This is a really crappy part of town. Driver," she asked, worried, "do you know where Ishtara International is?"

"Dave, he sick," the man said softly, with a glance at them in his rearview mirror.

"It's okay, Mags. There's probably more than one way to get to Ishtara from the Hilton."

"But why go this way? Oh no, look at those children," she said sadly.

The area of Cairo they were driving through was bleak indeed. Houses were little more than tarps spread to protect residents from the sun, and open fires dotted the dry, littered ground. The children, dressed in ripped old shirts and shorts, were pathetically thin, running to the car as it slowed and swerved to miss a large pothole.

"This can't be right, Reeve," Maggie said, leaning forward.

"Driver, is this the way to Ishtara?" Reeve said, enunciating slowly and clearly.

The driver ducked his head and fumbled with something, then repeated, "Dave, he sick."

Before Maggie or Reeve could react, he spun in his seat and sprayed something directly in their faces. Maggie had just long enough to wonder why the driver was wearing a gas mask before she lost consciousness.

— CHAPTER SEVENTEEN —

SATURDAY, AUGUST 1

The driver hired by Faod immediately extended his arm out the window in a jubilant closed fist. Faod and Uqbah gave trilling yells of triumph and pulled their old Land Rover closely behind the Toyota, which stopped next to a water vendor.

Uqbah ran to the Toyota to help Faod shift Reeve's muscular form to the back of the Land Rover. After they tied his arms behind him, Uqbah pulled out a syringe and injected his hip. They returned for Maggie, loosely slinging her next to Reeve before giving her her own injection. Uqbah stood back and stretched.

"You are certain the injection will last until the camp?" Faod asked, unconsciously rubbing his nose, splinted from his last encounter with Reeve.

"It will last more than twelve hours. Even if you drive like a turtle, we'll be at the camp in ten," Uqbah said with a smile.

"Good. Then we have a moment to search," Faod said, eyes sparkling.

"You will not touch them, nor their belongings, until we get to camp. Do you understand?"

"But how do we know the woman has the scroll?"

"We know. Shut up and drive."

"This cannot be right," Masood said. Since Cairo, they'd kept their old rented Jeep at a discreet distance behind the Land Rover. The Land Rover threw up a cloud of dust as it traveled too fast down the neglected road.

Behind the wheel, Ebbi mopped his dripping forehead. "For one thing, we would be better off with air conditioning."

"I was not referring to the heat, brother."

"I am aware, but what would you have me do? We are only to follow and observe—you know that."

Masood frowned, troubled. "And I understand it less. We see the girl get thrown into the back of that vehicle. And again, we do nothing. She could be hurt, you know—"

"She is the Chosen. Nothing bad will happen to her. We must believe that."

They drove in silence, Ebbi concentrating on avoiding the deep potholes in the ill-kept road. Masood stared straight ahead, unblinking.

As Maggie slowly awakened to deep nausea once again, she heard an evening call to prayer somewhere close by. Dazed and disoriented, she struggled to blink through eyes crusted shut. Head rolling every time she moved, all she could do was take in great lungfuls of heated desert air. She stiffened with panic. Desert air? Fear overrode the nausea and she rolled onto her side.

For a moment, she froze, completely confused. She was on an army cot in a small tent, which was flapping loudly in the wind. Sand was everywhere, her skin was raw and her throat was dry and inflamed. She tried to swallow and was racked by coughing spasms, choking on the gritty particles. But worse was the fact that she was entirely alone—there was no sign of Reeve anywhere.

She heard harsh shouting in Arabic, followed by several bursts of gunfire. Then, the shouting came again, and another burst.

Heart pounding so hard she could feel it beat in her ears, Maggie rolled off the cot. Just outside the tent, she caught sight of a man draped in a bandolier, holding a large rifle. He stood with his back to her.

She gasped softly and backed up till her legs hit the cot, then sat. Where on earth was she? She remembered the poor section of Cairo, the poverty, the children ... and the gas mask on the driver. Then nothing. Where was Reeve?

Wherever he was, he had the scroll, though he didn't know it. While they were on the plane, she'd opened his briefcase and extracted his shaving kit, which he carried with him everywhere. She'd placed the rolled scroll at the bottom, under a flap of leather. He'd never know it was there.

Now, she had a bad feeling about him. It didn't bode well that he wasn't with her, and she had no doubt that it was because of that damnable scroll.

In the next tent, Reeve took a punch to the face. He groaned involuntarily, feeling something crunch under his eyes. He felt dampness spread on the right side of his face and feared it was part of his nose.

"Where is it? Tell me now! I am not enjoying this either."

Uqbah said, grinning. Uqbah winked at the muscular man behind Reeve who'd been systematically delivering well-aimed slaps and blows for the better part of an hour.

Tied to the tent pole with his hands above his head, Reeve didn't respond.

Uqbah looked over Reeve's shoulder and nodded. The torturer reached back and picked up a tire iron. He waited until Reeve's eyes were fixed on it, then he lashed out and cracked Reeve's left arm just below the shoulder.

It was so sudden and so fast that the arm went totally numb.

Uqbah repeated, "So where is the scroll?"

Reeve took a deep breath, lifted his head, and looked Uqbah in the eye. He remained defiantly wordless.

The man took a cigarette from his pocket and lit it. Reeve's eyes went to the cigarette.

"That is right, it is time for you to do some thinking. It has not been pleasant up to now, but now it will get worse. This is the start only."

Reeve closed his eyes and let his head hang forward, breathing shallowly through his mouth. The pain slammed up through every nerve ending and peaked in a massive headache so raw that his eyes watered. Blood ran warmly down his chin and dripped onto his bare chest.

Then he felt something burning just above his right eyelid. He jerked his head up with a cry, and the muscled man looked at him with no emotion. He was holding the business end of the cigarette inches from Reeve's eye. He gasped.

"That's right, man," Uqbah said. "Next time, it will be very close indeed. Now I think we will just have a word with your white girlfriend."

It was late in Nashville—very late. He was fully prepared.

Quietly he moved up the street from his inconspicuously parked car, relieved to see that the house was dark and silent. As he approached the gravel driveway, he pulled the ski mask down over his face and immediately began to sweat in the sweltering Nashville night.

Using a tiny spot flash, he pulled out his map of the house. There—last room at the far left. He moved to the bushes in front of the window and began to unload his backpack.

The glass cutter came first out, followed by the gas rig, whose parts he laid out on the carpet of leaves behind the bushes. He sparingly used the flashlight to assemble it.

This gig had better be worth the enormous added expense of the gas rig, he thought sourly.

When ready, he flashed the light briefly through the window. As expected, the girl was asleep. He didn't see a car in the drive, so she probably was alone in the house. He felt a fleeting disgust.

Who left a child alone at such an hour?

He used his tiny glass cutter and made his usual perfect oval in the glass, large enough for his fist.

Then, after satisfying himself that the gas line was closed, he fed it slowly into the room and over the body of the sleeping girl, who was directly under the window. She never moved as the plastic line slid silently up her body until it came to rest just under her chin.

Suddenly a raucous voice cried out in a strange language: *"Voleur! Éspèce de con!"*

Hurriedly, he unclipped the line and the amyl nitrate rushed into the house with a small whoosh.

He ran the flashlight over the room until it picked out a large cage. He inhaled in relief: only a bird. In the sudden light, the creature shrieked and beat its wings against the cage. Then, sluggishly the girl moved. She saw the figure in her window, moaned, and fumbled for something next to her bed.

Alarmed, he inserted his arm in the hole he'd made and unlatched the window. He swung it open and as he landed on her bed, he heard her mutter something into ... she had a phone. He hung it up just as she passed out from the gas, then he applied a clip to the line, lest he succumb himself. He moved out of her room to scout the rest of the house, giving the gas time to dissipate.

He moved faster than usual, though the house proved deserted. *Who had the kid called?*

Maggie was horrified by the shrieks and moans coming from somewhere nearby in the camp and was afraid to picture what could be happening to Reeve. She sat miserably on her cot and cried. As thirsty as she was, she wondered how she had enough moisture in her to produce tears.

She closed her eyes and said a rare prayer. *I know You haven't heard from me in a while, but please. Please let Reeve be safe. He's a good man. He doesn't deserve this. And oh Lord, let us get safely out of this. In Jesus' name, amen.*

Then the tent flap opened and in walked a man with a blood-soaked shirt. He noticed her eyes on the shirt and smiled.

"Hello, Maggie Purcell. I see you like my fashion state-ment. Myself, I thought it a bit much, such a bright red against the white, you know." He watched for a reaction, then took a deep drink from the mug he carried. She noted that his little finger was missing.

"Here, drink this and we will talk," he said and passed her the mug in which only a few sips of water remained.

She reached a hand out and drained the mug, gagging at the stale, rank taste of the water. When it hit her stomach, she gagged again more severely, then desperately choked the water back down.

"Not good enough, is it? Would we prefer Perrier? So sorry that the accommodations don't suit Madame. If you would like them to improve—plenty of water with a big dinner—you will tell me where is the scroll." His English had a distinct British flavor, she noticed.

Maggie relaxed fractionally. They hadn't found it. She looked up at "Finger," as she decided to call him, with a frown. All she could do was play for time and hope that Reeve would put his black belt to good use.

At her silence, he grinned and stepped out of the small tent. She heard a spate of Arabic and a laugh, then he strolled back in and stared at her with a cold smile.

She dropped her eyes uneasily. Then she heard a thud and a cry that was unmistakably Reeve's. She jumped off the cot and ran to the tent flap. Finger caught her by the shoulder, painfully.

"No, no, sit down. Now your friend will not enjoy the rest of his evening."

She said nothing. Finger grinned and said, "Why don't I leave you to think on these things? Perhaps at morning you'll feel more like talking. For a certainty, you will have great hunger and thirst.

"You do know that one can live with no food for two months, but in the desert, without water, you will die in three days? Interesting, no?" With an easy smile, he left her.

Horrified and frightened, Maggie stood by the tent flap. She swallowed and tasted the dry grit. Turning slowly, she took in the paltry accommodations of the tent. One small cot, a thin blanket with holes, and an empty bucket at the foot of the cot. She had a good idea what the bucket was for, and a twinge in her bladder alerted her that now was time to use it.

After, she curled into a tight ball on the cot. There was no more sunlight coming in through the flap, and the evening air had a distinct chill to it. Her tongue felt immense from desiccation. She sucked on a finger to try and induce moisture, then licked her cracked lips.

She thought about Mohammed, the extremely wealthy and well-connected Mohammed. He would definitely be in deep trouble without her and Reeve. This might be the thing that brought his business down, losing his two main contractors at such a time. Also he thought a lot of Maggie and Reeve. He would be absolutely desperate to find them, with his business in such shape. She nibbled a nail.

They couldn't be far from Cairo—at most, only a few hours. Mohammad will pull out all the stops and find them in the morning. And, of course, he would have contacted the Embassy.

Sherrie Adams heard the call come in over the intercom. The 911 operator's voice was, for once, worried. The call had come in from a child. She'd whispered "Help! Help, someone is—" then the phone had been dropped. Over the entire call, a bird had shrieked and squawked.

When Sherrie heard the address, she called to Brian and ran to their unmarked car. It was Maggie's address, and the caller was almost certainly Beth.

Eight minutes later, she extinguished the lights on the car and glided silently to the driveway on Barrywood Lane. The house was dark, and there was no car in the driveway. Anna wasn't home, Sherrie realized with disgust. Three a.m. and Beth was alone—except she wasn't.

In front of the living room window, she saw a dark figure flit—far too big to be the girl. She called out in a low voice, "They're still inside. I'm going in."

"We should wait for backup," Brian hissed back.

"No time," she returned. "There's a child in there."

He nodded and ran silently around the corner of the

house.

Sherrie tried the front door. Locked.

She moved to the living room—no entry there. She eased behind the bushes, and spotted the open window. Beth's form was still under the comforter, and Sherrie felt her heart leap with alarm.

She was through the window and at Beth's side in seconds, the bird cawing weakly when he spotted her. The air had a strange tang to it, and she realized through her whirling head that there must be gas in the room. She put her head outside, drew in a deep cleansing breath, then moved back into the room.

A footstep sounded and suddenly a dark form was standing in the doorway, something glinting in his hand. Sherrie stepped forward, drew her weapon, and yelled "Drop it! Police!" The figure raised his hand as if to shoot, just as Sherrie heard wood splintering at the back of the house—Brian gaining entry.

She got off one round, the figure whirled and fled. She heard a yelp, then Brian yelled "Stop! Police!" and the night went silent.

Lightheaded, she called out, "You get him?"

"Actually, you nailed him in the shoulder. He's down. Clear!"

Sherrie moved unsteadily to Beth's bed, picked up her still form and hoisted her out the window.

Hog-tied on his cot, Reeve tensed and released each group of muscles in his shoulders. He had to be ready to move when the opportunity arose. Cursing softly, he wondered where Maggie was and if she'd been tortured, too. The thought filled him with a blind rage that caused his heart to thunder in his chest and his bonds to tighten. He purposely slowed both breathing and heartbeat. Then, in the near blackness, he heard a slight rustle as someone entered the tent.

"Not a word," came a voice Reeve incredulously identified as Zeb. "I can't stay. You mustn't tell them anything about the scroll. They'll kill you, Maggie, and both your families once they have it. They know there are copies out there, and there's a fatwa on everything to do with that scroll."

"Why a fatwa? The Muslims believe Jesus Christ was a real prophet, and they honor him."

"The contents of the scroll. The scroll predicts no true prophet *after* Jesus. Do you see? Jesus was the Alpha and the Omega—the only true Son of God."

"How the hell do they know what the scroll means?"

"A translation was found in a terrorist's house in France. Reeve, it's all over the world now. Listen, I can't talk anymore. I'll be back if I can." He slipped out.

Astounded, Reeve admitted to himself that Maggie had been right, partially. Zeb was involved in this. But whose side was he on?

When she awoke, Maggie's tongue was so dry and swollen that she could only breathe through her nose. She stood, walked to the tent flap, and got her first good look at her surroundings.

Low plaster and mud buildings spread in front of her. There were five or six tents alongside her own. Reeve's voice had sounded so close last night—he had to be in one of them. Fires dotted the ground, and the smell of roasting mutton was rich in the air. Saliva filled her mouth and she swallowed, grateful. The man standing guard at her tent turned and looked at her from head to foot, then curled his lip and turned his back on her.

A sudden burst of gunfire split the air. To her left was a firing range, consisting of large plastic jugs with incongruous smiley faces painted on them. One group of men, on the ground laying in a perfect line, aimed and fired. Another group stood behind them, waiting. A man with a black beret called a command, and firing ceased.

She shivered, though the scorching sun was above the shimmering desert. The building just across from her tent was a large adobe structure with a wooden tower on top. As she watched, a man climbed up the tower and began the familiar Muslim call to prayer. The gunfire ceased. People—men, veiled women, and children—approached the mosque from all directions.

Maggie shook her head. *What kind of life was this for a child? Trapped in the desert with only target practice and prayers. Dismal prospects indeed*, she thought as she walked slowly back into her small tent.

Her thoughts turned to the scroll. Why on earth had Achmed ever put that scroll into her possession? Yes, she was a Christian—she believed in Jesus Christ. But aside from the occasional prayer, she didn't practice, and never went to church. With a cringe, she thought about her dead father, then about Beth, diagnosed with leukemia. *I lost my faith a long time ago*, she said to herself. *What kind of God allows a twelve-year-old, and such a wonderful kid, to suffer like that?*

Still, she recalled the peace at the church Dad had insisted they attend—how much fun she'd had in Sunday school, the projects she'd created from paper and glue ... the innocent belief in a benevolent and kind Jesus.

She shuddered and was silently crying when Finger entered her tent.

"Already up, I see. I thought you might like to know what your closed lips have done to your friend. Come with me." He pushed her out the tent ahead of him.

The sun was already strong and the smell of gunpowder floated to her nostrils as Finger lead her to a larger tent a few yards from her own. To Maggie's horror, Reeve was sitting on a chair, hands tied to the tent pole behind him. Both his eyes were swollen nearly shut, and blood oozed from his ruined nose. In front of him stood a shirtless man with well-defined muscles, black lashes curling over his dark, expressionless eyes.

Maggie cried out and, pushing Finger aside, ran to Reeve. "What have these bastards done to you?"

He lifted his head and looked her in the eyes. "Maggie. You're okay, thank God. Baby, don't tell them—"

Crack. His head whipped against the tent pole.

"Cut him loose and take care of him right now," Maggie blurted, tears flowing down her face, "and I'll tell you where it is." The sight of him in such condition turned her heart sideways. Nothing was worth the harm done to him.

"Maggie, no! They'll—" *Crack.*

"It's in his kit under a leather flap at the bottom."

For a moment, no one moved, then Finger barked an order, and the torturer trotted out of the tent. He came back moments later and nodded at Finger.

Finger unclipped a long knife from his belt and cut through the ropes that bound Reeve to the tent pole. Reeve pitched forward onto his hands and knees, and let out a barely suppressed groan.

When Maggie tried to leap forward, Finger casually brought a knee up into her gut. She bent forward and spewed a thin stream of bile.

Reeve lunged upwards, and the torturer kicked him hard in the ribs. Then he reached out and grabbed Reeve's foot, flipping him to the ground. Reeve was suddenly on his feet, but Finger had a revolver out and pressed to Maggie's ear.

"Watch your step, or your girlfriend will pay."

Reeve stood quietly and watched as Maggie was forced back to her tent.

— CHAPTER EIGHTEEN —

SUNDAY, AUGUST 2

"Maggie's gonna pay for this," Anna said darkly. She was in the kitchen with Sherrie, Brian, and Beth. Beth had suffered nothing more than a headache from the amyl nitrate.

"We're still talking to the suspect," Brian said. "We found a pillowcase full of goodies, including a laptop. It may well have nothing to do with Maggie."

"I don't believe that for a second," Anna said. "I've lived in this house for almost thirty years and we've *never* had a break-in, much less a burglary."

"If you'll allow it, we have a few questions for Beth," Sherrie said, getting out her notebook.

"Sure," Anna said, pressing her lips together.

"Beth, can you tell me exactly what happened? From the beginning?"

"I'll try ... oh my head hurts ... I was sound asleep. Then

Cocktail woke me up screaming something. He never does that—it scared me to death. Then, I looked up and there was this man coming through the …" She dissolved in tears.

"That's enough," Anna said sharply. "Leave her alone. She's going to bed." She moved to the table and took Beth into her arms. "She's had enough for one day."

"Beth, did you get a look at the man?" Sherrie quickly asked.

"No," the girl said, between sobs. "He had a mask on. It was dark and scary."

"Uncle Kevin and me, we're taking her to Florida," Anna said, moving with Beth down the hall. "We're getting the hell out of here."

"He's not my uncle," came Beth's small voice.

Uqbah, known only by Maggie as "Finger," used a jug of precious water to clean the blood off his skin before looking for Faod. He spotted the shorter man tinkering with the Land Rover's engine in the shade of the one large building, a mosque complete with minaret where the muezzin sang out his call to prayer five times daily.

"Did you find the problem?" Uqbah asked him.

"I believe so—the plugs were filthy. It's all this infernal sand. I will be glad to get back to civilization."

"You *have* gone soft, haven't you?" said Uqbah in an even tone. "I am thinking you have spent far too much time in that bordello of a city, Paris."

"No, no, I am glad to discover how the Army of God lives here. I am just not used to living in the middle of the desert. I was born in Cairo, you know. Hardship is not new to me." Nor would it be a lasting circumstance, now that he knew where the scroll was. It meant more money than a man could spend in one lifetime. He'd seen the offer himself. One million dollars! How could one man offer such an amount for an old scroll?

"You were born the son of a rich bookseller," Uqbah said with scorn. "What hardship did you ever endure? Deciding which robes to wear in the morning?"

"Hey, we were not rich. I had four brothers and a sister, and only my two oldest brothers had the opportunity to go to school. The others are still here," he said in disgust, "working in the marketplace."

"How did you come to work for the cause? It certainly was not for the money."

"All the most popular people did. In addition, I am a believer," Faod said honestly. "I remember one boy had a brother who had the honor to be a human bomb. He was treated like a king."

"All the most popular—" Uqbah sputtered. "When I was seven, my mother and father and I, we lived in the Gaza strip, in the poorest camps. There was never food in the camp, or water.

"My mother got pregnant. She was so thin, she cried every night for her baby, never for herself. Being little, I grew adept at stealing fruit, and one time I even stole a live chicken. We lived for a week on it. Then I got caught stealing bread." He extended his hand with its nub of a little finger. "So I would never forget, the vendor quoted the Quran: 'And the thief, male and female; cut off the hands of both, as a punishment exemplary from God.' He grabbed my finger, put it on his wood block, and chopped it off. I was lucky he did not take the entire hand."

Faod straightened up from the engine and rubbed his back with one greasy hand. "Then you *do* see. What is a piece of bread against the hunger of your pregnant mother, and of course, your finger? You did what needed to be done. Uqbah, we get that scroll, and I know about a man in

California who will pay—" He paused, then said,

"—hundreds of thousands of dollars for it. I have a replacement that I found in the Souk. Looks just like it if you don't look closely. We swap it with the real one and ... " he rubbed his hands. "... we are rich beyond our wildest dreams."

"The fatwa, it means nothing to you?"

Misunderstanding, Faod laughed. "Who cares what an old man says? They live in a world whose time is past. This is a modern world, and I mean to get by in it."

Uqbah turned an ugly, deep red. The tips of his ears glowed with rage as he snapped his knife free, grabbed the surprised Faod in one hand, and neatly slit his throat with the other. As the man's body fell in a wash of blood, Uqbah spat.

Who cares what our Imam says? Eyes burning, he spat again on the body. Such words he expected from the Great Satan, but from a fellow Muslim, they could not be borne.

Sherrie entered the room in Vanderbilt Hospital without knocking. William Wilcox was awake and sullen, shoulder bandaged.

"Up to a few questions?" Sherrie asked, pulling a chair to his bedside.

"No."

"Tough. Tell me why you chose that particular house."

Silence.

"Do yourself a favor. I might not mention a certain bag of pot I found in your van."

"Don't give a shit." He leaned over, awkwardly and in visible pain, and poured himself a glass of water with his free hand.

"Hurts, does it?"

"Yeah, I need something for pain real bad." He reached

up for the button and, moving fast, Sherrie blocked him.

"We'll have our talk first."

He moaned, face white and pasty under a thick growth of black stubble. "What do you need to know?"

"I'll ask you again. Why that house?"

"Had something I needed."

"Such as?"

He went silent again, moaned a little and tried to weakly reach for the pain button. Sherrie blocked him.

"Such as some old scroll. And that's all I'm gonna say."

"Oh, you'll say more, if you want your pain shot. How did you find out about the scroll?"

Sweat broke out on his forehead. "Can't say more. They'll kill me. You don't understand."

"Help me understand. I hate seeing anyone in this much pain. *Who'll* kill you? Tell me and I'll see you get a shot right away."

"*Lost in Time*, the folks who run the *Lost in Time* website. It's super private. And I've heard dudes have gone missing there, missing permanent."

Sherrie took rapid notes. "Why do people go missing?"

"You gotta understand. Rich people use that site. They buy services. It's how they get shit."

"Explain 'shit.'"

"Some rich fucker puts up there that he wants such and such a painting. Now, the painting ain't available for sale. People like me, who were invited years ago cause I'm dependable and damn good at what I do, perform him a service, and find whatever he wants. We provide him with it, and he pays for it, big time."

"You mean to tell me, people put ads up for goods they want stolen?"

"That's about it. And someone wanted that scroll, pretty bad."

"How bad?"

"A million dollars bad. And that's all I know. Can I have my shot now?"

Wordlessly, Sherrie reached up and hit the button.

Late that afternoon, Sherrie tried to call Maggie. She was puzzled when she reached Maggie's voicemail, with a notification that the box was full. Sighing, she left work. She'd try Maggie again in the morning.

— CHAPTER NINETEEN —

MONDAY, AUGUST 3

In the small hours of the still-dark morning, Maggie was awakened by horns blaring, engines revving, and ululating cries of exhilaration. Puzzled and wary, she sat up on the cot and was just about to stand when the tent flap was pushed aside and something fell heavily at her feet.

A soft moan came from the shape, and then Maggie was on her knees.

"Reeve," she said, pushing aside her waste bucket and cradling his head in her arms. "My God, what have they done to you?"

"Want the full list? Broken arm, a few ribs done for, and my nose smashed." He laughed, then coughed. "You don't happen to have any water in here, do you?"

"No, I sure don't. Poor baby, I'm so sorry." Tears ran down her face in the darkness.

There was a shout outside the tent, and a furious Finger

brushed his way in, flashlight swinging in one hand. "Where is it?"

"Where is what?" Maggie responded, alarmed.

"The scroll, as if you do not know. I do not know how you got to your guard, but that will not happen again. Now answer me, before I make him—" he kicked at Reeve— "pay."

"Stop! Don't hurt him again!" she cried. "I don't know. It wasn't me—you can search me and the tent. Just don't hurt him any more."

"Rest assured I will do that at first light. For now, we have other plans. You won't get away with it."

"Get away with what?" Maggie moistened a corner of her shirt with saliva, then began dabbing at the blood on Reeve's face.

"Taking that scroll." He shone the light directly in her eyes. She raised a hand in protest.

"So help me, I don't know what you're talking about. There's nowhere else for the scroll to be. Can't you see?"

"I see you think you have succeeded in taking the scroll away from us." He held the flashlight up and aimed it around the tent. As he did so, raised voices came from outside, then sounds of a scuffle. "I am needed elsewhere, but I'll leave you to think about what will happen to you both if you do not hand that scroll to me in the morning." He pushed his way out of the tent and Reeve groaned weakly.

"Reeve! Are you alright?" In the dark, she strained to see him.

"Yes, I think so. Only the tip of his boot caught me this last time." He reached up and gently felt her face. "And you? Have they hurt you?"

"Aside from a slap, no."

"Mags," Reeve said, shifting slightly in her lap, "how the hell did you do it?"

"Do what?"

He reached under his head into her pocket and withdrew the scroll. "Get this back, of course. Felt it bulging under my head," he said, then gasped and choked.

"I wonder how this damn thing got into my pocket? Same thing happened in Nashville after those guys took me. It suddenly showed up in my purse—"

"Don't tell me you don't know how it got to your pocket this time?"

"No idea! I didn't know it was there, till you pulled it out."

"Zeb," he said quietly. "He must have done it. He's here."

"You can't be serious. I knew that boy was trouble—"

"No, he came in the middle of the night last night to warn me not to give the scroll to them." He stopped, unwilling to upset Maggie.

"Not give it to them? Reeve, they'd have killed you. They almost did anyway."

"They'll do worse than that if they get their hands on it. Girl, you've got to hide it. Now."

"What could possibly be worse than killing you?" In the dark, she hugged his head fiercely. "It's been my worst nightmare, being stuck in this hellish place alone."

"Best go ahead and put the scroll somewhere. It's urgent."

"You know something I don't, don't you?" She shivered.

"And you really don't want to know. Can't you trust me?" he said, then sat up and put an arm around her. He distantly realized that the arm no longer hurt, and he could breathe through his nose.

"Why should I trust you?" She challenged him, moving away. "If you have information, you should tell me. They might separate us again."

"Wait just one minute, girl. Why shouldn't you trust me?" He stiffened.

"Never mind. Just tell me."

He sighed. "Maggie, they'll kill our families. They think

you made copies. The Muslims can't afford to have any part of this scroll surface. It negates the basis for their entire religion, according to Zeb. It's something in that scroll."

"Beth," she whispered in fear. She stood suddenly, and felt around her in the darkness. Nothing but canvas and sand met her fingers. Then she had an idea. She got on her hands and knees and crawled silently to the tent opening. She felt the flap and yes, there was a loose string hanging as she'd recalled. The desert had taken its toll on the canvas, and the bottom hem, some several inches deep, was unraveling.

Gently she pulled and tugged on the stitches until she'd enlarged an opening wide enough to insert two fingers. She threaded the tightly rolled scroll upward into the gap, then tightened the stitches. Satisfied, she turned back to Reeve. "That should do it."

"Good for you. You know, I'm hurting a whole lot less now that I'm with you. I was so worried about you."

"Get on the cot and get some sleep."

He pulled himself to his knees. "I'm fine where I am. It's going to be a rough day—you need your rest."

"No, I've slept enough and I'll be fine on the sand. Get your hurt buns on the cot. We might need your strength soon." She curled up on the sand, pushing and digging herself a shallow nest. She spent the next few hours trying to imagine herself on a beach.

Once the sun came up, the camp came to life. People had poured in during the night, and now Maggie heard their voices as they walked by the tent on their way to the mosque for morning prayers. A ragged little girl with a doll clasped in her arms peered at her through the guard's legs then was shooed away by her veiled mother.

Reeve woke with a groan. When Maggie worriedly asked

him if his face was hurting, he told her he had pains in his gut. Maggie herself had severe stomach cramps, whether from dehydration or hunger she didn't know. In pain, she was doubled over on the cot when Finger walked in, a group of men behind him at the tent opening.

"Alright, give it to me, and I'll give you this," he said, and showed them a cold Coke with condensation running down the familiar red can.

Reeve inhaled sharply, but Maggie just shrugged. "Couldn't even keep it once you had it in your hands, huh? Fine terrorist you are," she sneered.

Finger tsked, then backhanded her across the face. Reeve growled and jumped in front of her. Finger grinned. "Don't prefer the civilized method? Well then, time for a lesson in cooperation."

He walked slowly around the tent, examining it for holes. As he drew close to the opening, Maggie's heartbeat increased until she was sure he'd hear it.

He picked up the flap and shook it, and the thread Maggie had pulled came loose and floated to the ground.

Maggie went pale.

He bent and looked closely at the flap, then to Maggie's astonishment dropped it and turned to the guard. He made a motion, and the guard unsnapped his gun and held it to Reeve's temple.

Reeve flinched but remained silent.

Finger roughly ripped off Maggie's filthy shirt. He ogled her breasts in her bra as she held her arms over them. Laughing, he knocked her hands away.

He left her in her bra and underwear while he checked the seams of the shirt. Finding nothing, he took his knife and popped off her bra, and slowly slit her underwear until it fell at her ankles.

Grinning at Reeve, he said, "You're not going to like this

next step at all." He extended his hand, palm flat up, and wiggled his middle finger suggestively. "Of course, Maggie might like it a lot more. You two sure you haven't seen my scroll?"

Maggie went white with horror. Reeve tensed and the guard thumbed the gun safety off before cocking it with a loud click. Tears ran down Maggie's face and she sobbed out loud as Finger kicked her legs apart. He then grabbed her inner thigh and thrust cruelly. Maggie let a bloodcurdling scream as she felt what seemed like half of his dry, filthy hand inside her. She went limp.

Reeve jumped up in a murderous rage. In one swift move, he knocked the gun and Finger to the floor.

Throwing Maggie backward, Reeve leapt out the tent opening, only to be met by a laughing group of men with weapons drawn.

Finger recovered the gun and casually pistol-whipped Maggie's face.

She felt her cheek split and blood run freely down into her ear as Finger threw her clothes at her.

He flipped over the cot, then patted Reeve down.

Reeve's expression was so cold that Maggie shivered. Muscles rippling as he clenched his belly, he stood staring while Finger ran a hand down the back of his pants.

Trembling in fury, his teeth bared, Reeve was pushed out of the tent at gunpoint. Even the well-armed terrorists backed away as he and Maggie were shoved in front of the mosque.

Maggie doubled over and covered herself with her clothes, holding her belly in agony from the harsh intrusion.

She felt like a small, cornered animal. Blood dripping off her cheekbone, she straightened and walked slowly behind Reeve down the path between the white plaster cubes that made up the camp.

The sight of the shooting gallery came as no surprise.

— CHAPTER TWENTY —

TUESDAY, AUGUST 4 —
WEDNESDAY, AUGUST 5

As they were marched behind the smiling line of jugs, Reeve took a quick look over his shoulder. Maggie's expression was blank, and her eyes looked through him as if he wasn't there. He began to whisper "it will be al—" and was rewarded with a rifle butt in the ribs.

Soldiers stepped up and tied them together so they couldn't move, then Reeve heard a sharp command. Other soldiers unshouldered their rifles and aimed. Another command, and they responded with a verbal "hah!"

Maggie was totally still, tied against his back. Waiting for the order to fire, Reeve didn't see his life flash in front of his eyes. Instead, he saw Maggie, laughing at Cocktail's antics. Maggie, a smudge of plaster on her cheek, working on a sculpture; Maggie, in misery the night she'd been so sick.

He felt her, warm and shaking against his back, and suddenly memories of all the flirting, the teasing, and the sexual tension vanished. More than that, all other women vanished. All that was left was a heartachingly deep, real love for Maggie—more real than anything he'd ever thought possible. It was like nothing he'd ever felt. Tears welled in his eyes, and his heart shrank at the waste. As the final order was given, he thought, *oh Maggie*.

Shots went so close to his head that he felt the hot wind through his curls. His legs gave way and he toppled face down onto the sand, Maggie falling with him. He felt slow tears brim and pour down his cheeks as Finger called out, "Next time, the real thing. You have one day to tell us who you're working with in the camp—if you make it another day without water, that is." He barked another command and their ropes were untied.

A row of dunes towered over the shooting range. Knowing the deep sand behind would catch any wayward bullets, the men shot at ease.

Just behind a dune, toward the farthest end of the range, Ebbi whispered to Masood, "There. I told you she'd not be hurt."

Face downward in the scorching sand, Masood didn't respond.

"Masood, did you not hear me? Maggie Purcell is untouched. I saw it with my own eyes. Masood, you may look now, if you are very careful."

No response.

"Masood?"

Slowly his brother turned to face him, tears flowing from his eyes. He didn't speak.

Ebbi grasped him in one long arm and clasped him close,

the thin shoulders heaving as Masood sobbed silently into his shoulder.

"Ebbi," he heaved out. "This is so wrong. All the training we've had, and ... and yet we do nothing. She is the *Chosen!*"

"Have you not seen the guns down there? The very weapons themselves carry other weapons, they are so numerous. Shhh now, shhhh. All will be well."

"I want to go back to Badu Tanar *now*. Please, Ebbi ... Please."

Reeve pulled an unresisting Maggie to her feet in the unrelenting noon sun. Sand flew up in heated clouds as groups of soldiers moved about with purpose.

Behind him, Reeve heard a pathetic bleating noise. As he took Maggie in his arms, the noise grew louder, then was cut off. Just beyond Finger, a group of sheep had been led into the camp and were being slaughtered one by one. Long curved knives glinted in the sun as they rose and fell, and the smell of fresh blood wafted to Reeve's nostrils.

"A honorable feast for all the extra mouths," Finger remarked. "Big party tonight—so very sorry you aren't invited. And tomorrow, we hit the cursed Jews with all our might. Of course, you will be there for that. We're taking your bodies as a gift. How could they not take in two dead Americans? You'll be stuffed with C4 and a timer. The gift that keeps on giving, no?"

Reeve stood and stared, horrified. There was no more time. He had to make a move that night, or they'd be dead— and countless others with them.

Something about the grim set of his mouth reached Finger, who again smiled. "Don't get any ideas. Your guard has been changed, and doubled."

Back in the tent, hours of unbearable heat passed. The

activity outside continued—the clang of steel as vehicles were readied. Laughing men called to one another.

Reeve talked quietly to Maggie of their work in New York, of Beth, even of her mother and her liquor problem. Nothing got through. Seated on the cot, her back hunched, Maggie stared through Reeve. He ran a hand in front of her eyes but she didn't flinch.

Late that afternoon, there was a giggle from the back of the tent, behind Maggie. Wary, Reeve picked her up and sat her near the opening, placing himself between her and the noise. Then the canvas flapped, and a small, dirty brown face peeped at him.

He relaxed—it was just a child. For a while, the face would peep at him, grin widely, then would disappear to the sound of whispering and more giggles. Evidently, there was more than one child back there, he thought with interest. *Too bad I don't speak Arabic.*

The next time he saw the grinning little face, Reeve raised his thumb to his mouth in the universal thirst gesture. The little face frowned, eyes looking at him warily. He made a great show of teeth, then using his fingers, pulled his lips away in a terrifying scowl and followed it with a growl. The eyes grew wide, and again the child giggled. This time, she didn't disappear, simply lay watching him expectantly.

He made more ferocious faces, then smiled and again raised his thumb to his mouth. The child giggled, and in a flurry of whispers and muffled laughter, vanished.

Reeve sat and waited. Had the child gotten the message? He hoped and prayed that if so, the child would not get caught or hurt. Eyes closed in exhaustion, he heard the whispering again, followed by a stream of small grunts.

A half-filled smiley jug was just under the cot, and the child was gone.

He knelt hurriedly next to it, took the top off and smelled

it. Heaven.

Pouring a small amount into his mouth, he felt his entire body open, like a flower to the rain. The water running down his throat was so exquisite that he expelled a long, heartfelt moan.

"Maggie! Water!" She still didn't stir.

He poured some into his palm and raised it to her lips. Nothing. He inhaled, then luxuriously took a deep drink. He filled his mouth, brought his lips to Maggie's, and squirted a sip into her mouth. Her throat moved reflexively, then she took the mouthful. Her eyes grew wide, and to his delight, focused directly on him.

"Is that water?" she whispered.

"Thank God you're back. Let me hold this for you—yes. It's water."

Maggie took another gulp and held it in her mouth. As it ran into the crannies and crevices of her tongue, she felt sand lift and swirl between her teeth. She bent, spat, and took a long deep drink. Then she eyed Reeve.

"Do you mind if I use some of this to—clean up?" she said, hesitating over the words.

"Is now really the time to ..." he caught her embarrassed glance down at herself. Mortified, he continued, "Of course." Then he turned his back, flinching at the sounds of her shorts unzipping. When he turned and saw the bright red blood on her tattered underwear she'd used to clean herself, he paled with rage.

The laughing man would lose far more than a digit before Reeve was done with him.

Reeve sat up half the night, listening to Maggie's quiet breathing and occasional whimpering as she slept. When she made small noises, he placed a gentle hand on her arm and assured her she was safe.

Long after the camp had quieted for the night, the canvas

behind Maggie's cot rustled slightly. Thinking it was the child again, Reeve sat back on his rump and smiled until he saw the blackened features of Zeb appear. Tense, he started forward, but stopped when Zeb put a finger to his lips and motioned at Maggie.

"I see you got water. Good. Here, I brought some stew." He handed Reeve a plastic container. "See that you both eat as much as you can. Then stick the container out behind the tent. There's so much junk back there—"

"Who are you?" Reeve whispered.

"Someone who means you no harm, unlike some you call friends."

Reeve thought a moment. "You don't mean Mohammed?"

"Firm backer of Al Qaeda. That import-export business is the perfect cover. He launders money, brings in supplies. He also delivers up dumb Americans."

"How the hell were we supposed to know? What did he do, plant the virus himself?" Reeve flared.

"Shhh, it's bad news for all of us if I'm caught here. He must have planted your virus, it certainly wasn't me. I would think you would have taken a closer look at his files while you were in there."

"No such thing," Reeve retorted. "We never open a client's files—at most, we scan them. Again, who the hell are you? The anti-terrorist terrorist?"

Surprisingly, the other man grinned, teeth flashing white in his grease-darkened face. "We are friends. Your friends, America's friends. Just be ready tomorrow. Things are going to be hopping."

"Yeah, so I heard earlier."

"What do you mean, you heard? Heard what?"

"The man missing a finger told us about the Israel raid tomorrow." At Zeb's look of total horror, Reeve began to understand. "Christ, you're Israeli."

"Shin Bet. Never mind. It's urgent I pass on this news. I must leave. I'm glad to be helping you. You've just done us a rather large favor." He clapped Reeve on the shoulder and silently went back the way he came.

Morning dawned black with a tremendous sandstorm. The soldiers outside the tent cried orders and tried in vain to cover the vehicles, already knee-deep in swirling sand. Reeve and Maggie coughed and choked in their tent, where the sand flew in through the flap and swirled underneath from all directions.

Reeve finally took off his shirt and covered his and Maggie's faces, and they sat cuddled on the cot as the raging winds finally died down. A thick layer of grit covered both of them.

"Ugh, it's in my teeth," Maggie said, spitting.

"Here, rinse out." He passed her the rest of the water. "Whatever Zeb has in mind, I hope he hurries up. You catch what he said last night?"

"Yes. But Mohammad—how can it be? We've known him for a year."

"Not as well as we thought, evidently."

A sudden roaring noise brought Maggie upright on the cot, rigid. "Reeve, do you hear—"

"Oh shit. Maggie get *down*." At the whining sound of helicopters and then a spate of explosions, he flung himself on top of her. She screamed in mortal terror as the explosions grew nearer and the ground underneath them shook and quivered with each boom.

One particularly loud explosion sent the smiley jug sailing upwards, and Reeve was flung off Maggie into the legs of the cot. She screamed anew when an arm snaked into the tent and grabbed her. It was Zeb.

"Time to go," he whispered harshly.

Quickly, she reached down and slid the scroll out of the tent, Reeve exhorting her to hurry.

She stepped out of the tent into hell. Gunships flashed overhead, big helicopters bristling with missiles, which they loosed at bands of soldiers who kneeled and shot back. The din was unimaginable, as were the torn-apart soldiers she and Reeve ran past. Some cried out, and some simply died.

Clouds of acrid black smoke swirled over dark, new craters. Ahead of her, Zeb shouted into a headset, and a helicopter broke away from the others and headed down at a steep angle. "Now, run!" Zeb called as he stepped aside to let them run past him. "That one is ours!"

But Maggie heard a female scream and saw a mother huddled against a blown apart building, her bleeding daughter hanging limply from her arms. The child's head dangled at a totally wrong angle. Reeve, too, hesitated. Maggie felt his hands as he grabbed the scroll from her and yelled, "That's the child with the water! Run, Maggie. I'll be right behind you."

Maggie ran, pulled by a cold, determined Zeb.

Reeve, scarcely believing what he was doing but determined to try, pressed the scroll lightly against the child's crooked neck, then ran back toward the copter.

He didn't see what happened with the mother and her child, but heard a thin cry rise over the whap of the helicopter. Reeve turned quickly to concentrate on catching up to Maggie. While Reeve had spent precious moments dealing with the child, the man with the missing finger had trapped her.

Maggie fought furiously, with all that the man had done to her fresh in her mind ... the disgusting feel of his fingers in her. He laughed in rage, a mad, harsh sound over the din, and hurled a fist at her face. Zeb, approaching the helicopter hovering just above the ground, was unaware of what was happening behind him.

Then Reeve was upon them, a blind fury welling up from a place deep within his soul. He thrust his fingers into the man's eyes and was rewarded with a bellow of pain. The man dropped Maggie. Instead of retreating, she turned, slammed a knee into his groin then clawed at his face, snarling.

The man known as Finger dropped to his knees and clapped his hands over his bleeding eyes, moaning. With care, Reeve took Maggie by the arm. "We need to go now."

She looked at him through feral eyes, the deep green ringed by circles of black, and he wondered briefly if she'd ever be the same.

Well-sheltered behind the dunes, Ebbi tried in vain to start the Jeep's motor. He had the feeling that the sandstorm had fouled the engine.

As helicopters blazed overhead, Masood sat in the passenger seat, head in hands, unmoving. Ebbi shouted to him over the roar of the copters to try the ignition. He didn't move.

Frantically, Ebbi tinkered with the engine, whipping off his shirt and using it to brush sand from all the parts he could see. Then he raced to the door, jumped in the seat, and turned the key.

Nothing.

He grabbed at Masood and shook him gently. "My brother, you must help me now. There are helicopters with guns! Hurry! You must turn the key when I shout."

Masood raised his head and looked him in the eye. "If I do, will you take me back to Badu Tanar?"

Ebbi expelled air in frustration. "Please do not speak of that now. I will get Father on the phone and you may speak to him. Will that suit? Now, move into the other seat!"

Twenty minutes later, the Jeep came to life with a weak

grumble and the brothers drove back to the nearest village. Ebbi was determined to return as soon as possible to keep an eye on Maggie.

— CHAPTER TWENTY-ONE —

As the helicopter sped away from the camp, Reeve looked at Zeb warily. "I suppose we should thank you. Can you tell us how you managed to be here? What's all this all about?"

"Came to save your skin. Isn't that evident?" The Israeli was now relaxed and friendly, a side of him new to Maggie.

"How do we know you didn't get us into this in the first place?" she asked, eyes narrowed to slits.

"Because we're just about the only ones who have nothing to lose in this affair," Zeb responded.

"Would you like to explain that?"

"You guys are famous—and not in a good way—in certain places. You're all over the news—you and that scroll. The Arabs have declared a fatwa on it, naturally. Not all the motives of Muslim radicals and fundamentalists are theologically sound, but they certainly wouldn't want anything surfacing that could so powerfully unite and strengthen the Christians of the world.

"And a very rich, very eccentric Jewish millionaire in San

Diego has offered a million dollars for it. So you can see that every lunatic in the world will be after it now."

"A *million* dollars? That's news to me. I got ... never mind. I don't get it, though. If the guy is Jewish, what would a thing like that even mean to him?"

"Sammie has a thing for Dead Sea scrolls and Israeli artifacts from the time of Christ. We've heard it's quite an impressive collection," Zeb said.

"Samuel Greene? *The* Samuel Greene? The billionaire?"

A million dollars.

She looked down. The helicopter lurched and bile rose in her throat. Her mind swirled in agony. No amount of money was worth this. She shifted, and a twinge of pain from her crotch brought tears to her eyes.

"The Arabs and the billionaire. That all?" She asked.

"Actually, the Catholic church would love to get their hands on it also, to validate it, as the Pope said in the news yesterday."

"This is all a bad dream!" She shook her head in disbelief, looking at the scrap of leather in Reeve's hands. All the trouble the thing had caused, and no end in sight. It had haunted her for the last few weeks and almost cost her her life.

She stared at the scroll in loathing, and before anyone could stop her, she ripped it from Reeve's hands and flung it straight out of the helicopter's small window.

"Maggie, no!" Reeve shouted.

Maggie stared out the window in silence. At the same instant a hand reached out a window on the other side of the copter and a young Israeli soldier drew in an object, still flapping and fluttering against his bronzed palm. Maggie turned and looked at the soldier in horror. Sobs wracked her body.

Exhausted and drained, tears made muddy rivulets in the

grit on her face. The soldier gently handed her the scroll, and when Zeb asked to see it, she handed it over wordlessly.

The flight was brief, and they were soon joined by a squadron of Israeli fighter jets. Maggie looked up when one flew in close and waggled its wings at her.

The copter deposited them just outside the remote kibbutz of Ein Geddi. Situated close to the Dead Sea, Ein Geddi proved a refuge and place of work for Israelis of all ages. Fields, looking almost falsely green against the desert on all sides, surrounded it.

Maggie headed straight for the bathroom and hurriedly washed the grime from her face. She was in a somewhat improved state of mind when she met Reeve, Zeb, and a group of young people in the Great Room. Smiling people thrust platters of fresh fruit and homemade cheese at them. Maggie and Reeve crunched fruit and drank cider until they thought they'd explode.

Zeb finally showed Maggie and Reeve their rooms, and to their delight, the large showers. Maggie stood under the rushing water for nearly half an hour before at last feeling clean again. She wandered back to the Great Room, now empty except for Reeve.

"We're in deep trouble, wherever we go. We have to make sure we don't bring trouble to anyone else," Maggie said, toweling dry her dark hair. Reeve watched her, only half-listening to her words.

He watched through slitted eyes as she threw her hair over her head and rubbed it. The sight brought back to him his epiphany during the fake execution. He'd been attracted to Maggie for a long time, almost since he'd met her five years ago. There had been plenty of women in the meantime, but none had ever lasted more than a few months.

He looked out the window onto an idyllic scene. Men and women working in green fields, children running everywhere, and the desert gleaming red in front of low mountains in the distance. If only they could stay here. But the fatwa brought danger to these people, too.

The scroll certainly complicates issues already very complex, Reeve thought with an inward sigh. His parents would be appalled if they knew the depth of his feelings for Maggie. His mother had always wanted him to marry black—not out of any obvious racism, more from the knowledge of how difficult a biracial marriage could be. Not that he was considering getting married at all, he told himself hastily.

His mom's attitude was incongruous, considering his own deep blue eyes, courtesy of Grandmère Amelie's own beautiful Grandmère, Ardene. The youngest of seven children born to a poor seamstress, Ardene had entered the New Orleans world of dance halls when she was sixteen.

At that time, it was perfectly respectable for men to meet women in dance halls, buy them an apartment, and keep them separate from their wives. And the man who'd fallen in love with the beautiful Ardene and her waist-length curly black hair had been white, a wealthy Northerner transplanted to New Orleans.

Grandmère Amelie had a portrait of Nicholas Hawthorne, white with cobalt blue eyes, and Ardene DuBois, her hair intricately curled over her high forehead, a single large diamond gleaming at her throat, and love shining from her eyes.

Such obvious and unabashed happiness.

"Maggie, we need to talk," Reeve said.

Maggie poked him. "Have you heard a word I said? I'm *terrified* these crazies will get to Beth and Mom. We need to do something about them. If these kind people will let us borrow a phone, I'll call them."

Zeb walked in with a short brown woman in khaki shorts and a denim shirt.

"Reeve, Maggie, this is Zöe. She'll look after you for a few days, if you agree to stay."

"Though I love the idea, I'm not sure we should," Maggie said, the peace of the green oasis not lost on her. "I'm really worried about my family."

"Maggie, I have a proposition for you. There's a man here, Rabbi Isaac Dolman, who runs the Israel Museum's Shrine of the Book in Jerusalem. He would very much like a look at your scroll. He's fluent in Ancient Aramaic, so he could translate it as well. If you agree to see him when you're rested up, we'll look out for your family in the meantime. I assume you know by now that we're very capable." He had a large grin on his tanned face, his black eyes sparkling.

"Yes, you people are amazing. We owe you our lives. I can't thank you enough." There were tears in Maggie's eyes. "Can we think about it tonight? I'm so exhausted from the ordeal that I can't think straight."

"Of course," Zeb responded warmly. "Take whatever time you need. Nothing moves fast in Ein Geddi, anyway. Oh, I imagine you'll want to call home. We're poor here at Ein Geddi, but feel free to use the phone. We'll present you with the bill!"

Maggie laughed. "Thanks, I wouldn't have it any other way."

That night, the plain little twin beds in which Maggie and Reeve slept felt like the utmost in luxury. They awoke refreshed, and decided that a trip to the Israel Museum would be relaxing. But first Maggie called home.

Beth answered the phone groggily—it was close to midnight there. She was ecstatic to hear from Maggie, who didn't mention much of the past few days, only informed her of their upcoming visit to the scroll museum. Beth was excited and made Maggie promise to call her the moment she had any information, then she went silent.

"Is everything all right at home? How's Darla doing?" Maggie wondered.

"Darla's great ... Mags, did you hear from Sherrie yet?"

"No. Why would Sherrie call me?" A chill went up her spine. "What's wrong?"

"Well, a bad thing happened, but Cocktail saved the day. You won't believe it, Mags. Some man was coming in my window and Cocktail yelled so loud I woke up and called 911, like you always told me—"

"What the hell! Are you alright? And Mom? Is she okay?" Maggie talked past an enormous lump in her throat. She should never have left them.

"Yes, we're okay. I was asleep again ... The man used some gas to knock me out, so I wasn't awake when Sherrie snuck in the window. Mags, she shot him. Got him in the shoulder, right in the kitchen doorway. There was blood on the carpet. Mom was pissed."

Crying silently, Maggie battled to speak normally. Finally she said, "Well, thank God for Cocktail, waking you up like that. And for Sherrie."

"Sherrie's a hero. She came back and interviewed me and everything." Beth's light voice broke. "Oh Mags, when I saw that guy in his black mask ... I'm gonna have nightmares for a long time."

"I'm so sorry I wasn't there, love," Maggie said in tears. Alarmed, Reeve got up, crossed to her, and knelt by her side.

"Is she alright?" he whispered. Maggie nodded, brushing at the tears.

"Mags, Sherrie said if you hadn't already talked to her, you should call her. You got the number and everything?"

"No, give it to me, will you?" Beth read out the number. Maggie scrambled through a drawer until she found a pen, feeling slightly guilty as she did so. "Okay, got it, thanks. I'll call her in a minute. I just have to know that you're okay. Listen, what did Mom do? Was she asleep when Sherrie shot the guy?"

There was a pause. Maggie felt an uneasy prickle on the back of her neck. "Sprout? Are you still there?"

"Yeah. Now Mags, don't go crazy or anything, but Mom wasn't here."

"Where the hell was she? What time did all this happen?"

"It was around three a.m. or so, and I was gonna tell you. She—"

"Get her on the phone. Now." Maggie was seething, her tears turning into rage.

Beth took a deep, shaky breath. "I can't. She's not here. She took this robbery thing really hard, and started drinking sort of early, like after lunch early. Then Uncle Kevin picked her up and—"

"Who the hell is Uncle Kevin?" Maggie was fast nearing the end of her rope.

"He's this guy she met Saturday night at a bar. He's sort of weird, and she's making me call him Uncle Kevin."

"That's just perfect. Some total stranger. God!" She took a deep breath.

Beth tried to change the subject. "Hey Mags, Mom and I read the news, although it wasn't all news to me, was it?" Her voice was proud.

"No, it sure wasn't. You did great. You're talking about the scroll, aren't you?" Maggie asked, voice taut.

"The thing put out by the Muslims where the scroll is to be destroyed—Maggie, there were riots in London and Paris. The Muslims were in front of the US embassies and demanding we give the scroll up. They're threatening a holy war."

Maggie tried to speak and couldn't. Her throat closed with fear for Beth. This scroll thing was snowballing far out of control. She cleared her throat finally. "We're really going to have to think about our next move—all of us. But enough of that for now. Your appointment is when, tomorrow morning? Is Darla going to take you?"

"Yeah. She's just great, she really is. But Mags, I feel so much better—do I really have to still go?" Her voice quavered.

"Yes, although I'm delighted you feel better, sweetie. Reeve and I are kind of stuck in Israel for a bit. Our passports were lost, but it's nothing awful. It'll only take a few days to replace them … That's right … I love you, too." She hung up, enraged with her mother all over again. Beth was alone in the night with a burglar, the very thing Maggie had feared.

The morning dawned fresh and clear, and Ebbi's Jeep was functioning well as they rattled down the track behind the camp. Masood hadn't spoken much since the day before. He had a lost look to him that Ebbi didn't like.

Soon they were climbing the dune, following their own footsteps from the day before. Masood broke the silence. "Ebbi, something is wrong. I hear nothing."

"It's mid-morning, Masood. Perhaps the soldiers are resting."

They maintained silence themselves as they climbed the summit of the dune. Panting slightly from the effort, Ebbi cautiously poked his head over the top.

The camp spread before them in the sunlight, peaceful, quiet, and seemingly deserted. Ebbi slid part way down the dune in shock. Masood scrambled down after him.

"What do we do now, brother? Where could they have taken her?"

"Perhaps they did not take her anywhere," Ebbi said. "We should go down and have a look."

He raised his head above the top of the dune. Nothing

happened, so he scrambled to his feet and held a hand out to Masood. Masood stood, then stumbled forward, and a shot from somewhere below went right over his head. The brothers quickly fell back to the safe side of the dune.

"We had best go back to the village and call Father," Ebbi said glumly. "I do not know how to explain this."

Maggie, outraged, detailed Beth's call to Reeve. His jaw dropped. "Your mom hooked up with some dude in a bar? And brought him home? Are you kidding?"

"Not a chance. He also told Beth to call him 'Uncle Kevin.'"

"Well, you never know. The guy could be great. Weren't you hoping she'd hook up with someone?"

"I guess, but from a damn bar? I don't know. It's too new and too weird. Not to mention it's the middle of the night and they've gone off and left Beth completely alone." Still upset, she blew her nose.

"He may be a really good guy, though," Reeve said uneasily. "At any rate, there's not a damn thing you can do about it from here."

"Maybe I should call Darla, have her spend the night. I hate the thought of Beth being all alone."

"For all you know, Anna could be home in the next ten minutes."

"I hate this, I really do. And there's so much else we need to focus on. We need to call Todd, tell him about Mohammed. I don't think Xcorp needs that kind of association." Maggie stood slowly and walked toward a nearby bathroom.

"All this, and you still think of your job. Todd really doesn't know what he has with you. He just completely escaped my mind. But a deal is a deal—we go to the museum first. And the very next thing is to look into our passports. I don't reckon we'll ever see anything we left in Egypt again. Lord, I'll miss that laptop," Reeve said bitterly. "It has my life on it."

"I'm so sorry. It's all my fault," Maggie said from the open bathroom where she stood splashing water on her face. "Do you think it's going to be difficult to get the passports replaced?"

"It's not your fault, kiddo. This whole thing has taken over both of our lives, and personally, I wouldn't have it any other way. This is an unbelievable honor for me, to be associated with that scroll. About the passports, I assume it'll take a few days," he said, considering. "They have to have a procedure in place for lost passports, especially with the war. It might take a while due to heightened security, but we'll figure it out."

"With no ID whatsoever?" Dabbing her face with a towel, Maggie was doubtful. "I'm sure we'll need copies of our birth certificates. I can get Sarah from work to get into my apartment. Where's yours?"

"My mom and dad have a copy. I'll call them as soon as we find out exactly what we need. You about ready? Zeb just pulled up."

"Would you go ask him to wait five minutes? I have to call Sherrie, see what's really going on back home."

"Sure, but don't be too long." He walked out the door.

Maggie consulted the paper and dialed. Sherrie answered, even more groggy than Beth had been.

"Sherrie, it's Maggie Purcell. I'm so sorry to get you out of bed, but I just talked to Beth, and I'm so worried I can't stand it."

"Wow. Maggie. I've been trying to call you since yesterday."

"Yes, I wasn't near a phone. What on earth is happening

there? I hear you got the guy?"

"Yeah, sure enough did. Nailed him in the shoulder." She exhaled loudly into the phone. "Spent all day today on him, too. You won't believe the weird crap he came out with."

"Are Mom and Beth really okay?"

"Yes, I promise. Beth has a little headache from the gas the guy used—nothing major. Anyway, the guy was after the scroll. Turns out he was a member of this private website where super-rich people advertise art works they want. The site members steal the things and sell them for the advertised cost. Maggie, the scroll is up there for a million bucks."

Maggie went silent. A million dollars. The fine hairs lifted on the back of her neck. Could it be that the scroll was what Reeve thought it was? And what did it mean if the scroll was really written by Jesus? She shivered.

Unbidden, an image slipped into her mind: Jesus on the cross hanging above the dais in the church she'd attended with her father. The statue was bronze, and had very realistic tears flowing down the bearded cheeks. She'd had such a calm, safe feeling there, such a difference from the acrimonious fights that shattered any peace her own house might have known.

But the money. Responsible for Beth's bills, Maggie was severely in debt. The money would free her from that load, and she could put Beth in a private school. It would ensure Mom and Beth could move to a better, safer part of town. It would—

"Maggie, are you still there?" came Sherrie's voice.

"Yes. Sorry, my mind is a mass of confusion. This is the second time I've heard a million dollars. Seems Samuel Greene made that same offer."

There was a sharp intake of breath on the other end of the line. "How did you know that, girl?"

"My Israeli friend told me about Greene, and other jolly

things like the Arabs declaring a fatwa, and the Pope also wanting in. Sherrie, it's a nightmare."

"Well, if you swear you'll keep it quiet … I tracked down the owners of the *Lost in Time* website. Made a few threats, and you won't believe—Samuel Greene is behind the web offer as well."

Maggie breathed in sharply. "You have to be kidding." Samuel Greene was a notorious billionaire, living on the West Coast in a virtual castle after his program, BalanceSoft, became the accounting software of choice for everyone from small businesses to large corporations. She could understand his making the offer that Zeb had seen, but for him to be associated with a website for thieves? The idea was outlandish.

"Serious as a heart attack, sister. Listen, before I forget. I reckon I've taken a real interest in Beth. She's just adorable. You heard about this Uncle Kevin character your mom is hanging out with?"

"Yes, just, although, Beth didn't say much."

"Well, just for kicks I ran him. He's been divorced twice, been hauled into child support court several times. Lives in an apartment—doesn't even own his own house. Kind of odd for a dude in his fifties."

"Oh God, I wonder if Mom knows that. As much of a snob as she is, I can't see her dating someone like that."

"Takes all kinds. I believe I'm going to keep a much closer eye on your house while you're gone, although, what with you and the scroll being all over the news, I don't reckon anyone else will hit your house looking for it."

Maggie thanked her profusely for all she'd done, and hung up.

The drive to Jerusalem took only forty minutes, and the land surrounding the road was mostly desert. Maggie leaned her head back and dozed until Zeb announced they'd reached their destination.

"Look, the museum's dome is shaped like the top of the first jar in which the first Dead Sea Scroll was found. Isn't it beautiful?" Zeb said.

"It looks like a giant white nipple," Reeve cracked.

Maggie poked him. "You *would* think that. I think it's simply stunning."

They descended steps into the cave-like structure. Right in front were two large jars—the first two found, Maggie read from a plaque. As they stood there, a small old man with an enormous belly, bright black eyes and heavy glasses approached them. "Zeb! So glad you could make it."

"Hello, Rabbi. Maggie and Reeve, meet Rabbi Isaac Dolman." They shook hands and the rabbi added, "Please, call me Isaac. We don't stand on ceremony here." He smiled under his traditional Jewish yarmulke.

He gave them a brief tour of the museum, and Maggie was fascinated by how a simple goat boy had come across the old jars with the scrolls in them. They saw the twenty-seven-foot-long Temple Scroll, the longest scroll found. The writing was very similar to that on her own scroll, Maggie found. The material looked exactly the same, down to parts that, eroded with time, looked burnt.

Finally, the Rabbi led them to his large, cluttered office. Maggie, seeing the man's intense excitement, handed over the scroll without a word.

"To think that I lived to see such a thing," he said, hands shaking as he accepted the old document. "My father was in the camps along with my mother and three sisters. We had such difficult times, such pain, such agony. Excuse me, I know I'm rambling, but this could be a real miracle."

He crossed to his desk and sat, motioning them to seat themselves on a couch across the room. "Make yourselves comfortable. Would you like a refreshment?"

"No thanks, we're fine." Maggie said. "I'm terribly sorry about your family."

"It was many, many years ago. Had I not been so young, I too would not have survived." Tears brightened the old black eyes. He straightened his shoulders and took in a deep breath. "Have you had the scroll looked at?"

"Yes, an old professor of mine snipped off a piece and sent it to Oxford for testing. The results were positive. I think he said it tested to around two thousand years old, and the ink was made from gum and something black." She looked at Reeve with hesitation, and he stared back at her, expressionless.

"Lampblack?" the rabbi asked.

"That was it."

Reeve bit his lip and stood, restless, to examine a bit of scroll set in a glass case near the door.

"Excellent. Oxford is one of the foremost research institutes in the world for Carbon-14 dating," the rabbi said with enthusiasm. "Indeed, they dated many of our own scrolls, so they are well-prepared, nu?" He looked down and pursed his lips, unrolling the scroll. "And the translation? Has anyone done that for you?"

"No," Maggie said. "We were hoping you could help us with that."

"May I?" he gestured down at the scroll. "My father spoke nothing but Aramaic. He was from what is now known as Kurdistan. All of us spoke it growing up, and we," he paused and took a deep breath, "we used it in the camps to pass messages."

His eyes teared again behind the thick glasses. He removed them and dabbed at the moisture with a finger. "Once back home in Israel, I taught myself written Aramaic and became involved with the scrolls, as you see."

Warily, Maggie regarded Reeve's back as he gazed down at the display. She had a deep curiosity that vied with her reluctance for Reeve to be any more intent on keeping the scroll.

"We're sorry to hear that, Rabbi," Reeve said at last and turned where he stood. "That was a disgrace to mankind— those camps."

"Yes, it was." He sighed again. "So many years ago, nu? But now, look what fortune has brought my way."

"Please continue, Rabbi," Reeve pleaded. "I'd be fascinated to know what our Lord had to say."

"If indeed it was him," Maggie muttered. Reeve stiffened and sat on the far end of the couch, nearest the rabbi's desk. Confused but sensing the tension, Zeb, in the middle of the couch, looked from one taut face to the other.

"Is there a problem?" the rabbi asked.

"No, Rabbi, I'm just tired and my brain is wandering," Maggie said with haste. "Please translate what you can. I've been wondering what this scroll could possibly say. Perhaps it's like some of the others—a list of household items." Reeve expelled his breath audibly. She stiffened and held her head high. "One way or the other, for all the trouble this scroll has caused, I'm fascinated to find out what it has to say."

Faintly, very faintly, she heard low chanting. She glanced around the small room. No one else seemed to notice. She drew in a slow breath, and Reeve looked at her curiously.

The rabbi replaced his glasses and concentrated on the scroll. After a moment he turned on a very bright lamp and moved it to the center of his desk, then arranged it until there was a wide pool of light illuminating the old scroll.

The chanting swelled. Maggie shook her head to dispel it.

He read for a moment, then frowned. Then he made tsking noises. Lost in the scroll, he said nothing until Maggie prompted him, "Rabbi? Could you read it aloud?"

He looked up with a start. "Fascinating. Most utterly fascinating. I'm sorry. I'm all catched up, don't you say?"

"Caught up," Maggie corrected him with a smile. The chanting abated, but now she could hear a low, deep drum beat.

"At any rate, parts of the scroll are eroded away by age and missing. But much remains. Indeed, more than I ever thought possible."

He took a deep breath and began.

"Dear child,
Our father has bid me leave word that thou might readest in days to come what thou hast done to cause thy God to turn his face from thee and what thee might doest to redeem thyself. All is not lost, yet thou hast worshipped other Gods before me. Thou hast created ... this part is illegible ... *invoking My name.*

"Thou shalt revile false prophets as well as those who would profit from our Church. Only I am Alpha, I am the Son of ... again, unclear. Sorry.

"There are cities of gold where hideth treasure beyond compare, all in my name, whilst within a short distance, others starve and liveth upon what they must beg.

"Thy beliefs in the utterance of mere words to save thy soul is repugnant unto me. Thou shalt be judged on thy actions as well as thy words. Thou shalt invite me to dwell in thine heart, where I shall stay with thee until the end of time.

"In these things do I guide thee, as thee are to enterest the age of the Sons of Light.

"Cleave thee to these teachings and see strife and ill feelings wane by the day. The heavens themselves will open and I shall look upon thee and deem thee good.

"As thee read this scripture, time will run swiftly until ... this part is also illegible ... *are performed on Earth. Those who believe in and accept Me into their hearts will become Mine earthly Family, and once again live in the Garden, separated from*

thy brethren who chose not.

"*Above all, respect and hold dear she* ... I can't make that out ...

"*These things I pray for thee to take to thine hearts and make them yours* ... Another large illegible splotch ... *Signed,*

"*Son of Man.*"

— CHAPTER TWENTY-TWO —

THURSDAY, AUGUST 6

Rabbi Dolman stopped, and explained that the final signature was next to an irregularly shaped blotch that continued a good distance down the scroll. He wasn't sure if anything further was written there.

Reeve was frozen, tears in his eyes. He slowly turned and looked at Maggie, and she saw something new in his eyes.

"Reeve?" she said, her voice trembling with uncertainty.

"'Respect and hold dear she ...'" he quoted softly. "Maggie, girl, that has got to be you."

In her ears, the chanting built to a crescendo, then suddenly cut off. For a second Maggie sat, astounded and confused. "Have you lost your mind? He was probably writing about his mother—" She stopped, aware of what she'd just admitted. Unsettled, she crossed her legs and felt a small twinge, reminiscent of her ordeal in the desert.

Quickly, she changed the subject. "'Cities of gold.' The

only thing that comes to mind is the Vatican. Reeve and I visited Italy last year on business. The Catholics won't like that one."

"And then," Rabbi Dolman said, "it might not be the Vatican at all. It could be construed that 'false prophet' refers to Mohammad, though, at least in part. No wonder the Muslims are at war." He gently ran a finger over the ancient writing. "This is simply the most marvelous thing." He felt in his pocket and withdrew a card, passing it to Maggie. "Would you do me the immense favor of a call, before you make a decision on the scroll? Once before, in the fifties, we were able to buy four scrolls that came on the market. I feel we would be the best place for this scroll? After all, it came from here."

"I have no idea where this scroll originated," Maggie said. "I got it in France. You might be aware of a certain man in California who's made an offer of a million dollars for the scroll—"

"And she's already decided to take it," Reeve interrupted.

"I've decided nothing. I'm keeping my options open. After all the incredible things I've gone through because of this scroll, I deserve compensation," she said, anger in the defensive hunch of her shoulders.

"And I agree," the rabbi said. "Just give us time to match that figure. I hope we can at least do that."

Maggie turned the card over, then put it in her own pocket. "Rabbi, thanks for the time and the offer. I'll call you before I dispose of the scroll, but I have to warn you, the man in California has made it clear he would top all offers. Thanks so much for the museum tour. It's added a depth to my understanding."

The rabbi rummaged under a stack of papers and withdrew a book called the *Making of the Scrolls*. "Please, take this as a memento."

"Thank you, rabbi. That looks fascinating." Maggie stood and stretched.

Reeve stood and walked to the door. "And the translation. I've wondered so long what He could have written, and now we know—"

"Well, we know a great deal," the rabbi gently interrupted as he also stood. "There's a large portion of the scroll that makes no sense to me, as I said. Look, here at the bottom. It curves right around these characters, where he signed 'Son of Man.' It's a pity this part didn't survive as well as the rest."

Something stirred in Maggie's mind and she frowned slightly, then shook her head. "I bet his quill stopped up and that's where he got it flowing again. I love fountain pens, and that's happened to me, too."

The rabbi grinned. "Perfectly possible. Imagine, the hand of Jesus tapping the parchment in irritation."

Maggie smiled. "If it's Him. Well, we've taken enough of your time. Thanks again for all the help."

The bright domes of Jerusalem shone in the sun as they made their way back through the bustling, modern city. Reeve pleaded to see the Garden of Gethsemane and was delighted to see the ancient hillside, twisted olive trees much the same as they were in Jesus' day.

Reeve was awestruck to hear that many of the trees were two thousand years old and might have been alive when Jesus spent his final night there, in prayer. Still, there were the steps that Jesus had climbed on his way to Caiphas' house for the first part of his trial.

Reeve laid a hand on the gnarled bark of an olive tree, still warm from the sun. Could Jesus have leaned on this same tree the night before he was crucified?

The Dome of the Rock glowed golden as they finally made their way out of the old city.

Zeb made one last brief stop at a news kiosk, then handed

Reeve the previous day's *New York Times*. In the back seat, Maggie was huddled against the window in total exhaustion. She wondered how long her body would take to recover from the ordeal at the camp.

Then she heard Reeve make a small gasp of surprise, and she leaned forward to read over his shoulder. To her horror, her own face was featured prominently on the newspaper's front page.

"Oh God, Reeve, that's my college photo. This is such a mess. What's wrong with people?"

"Girl, you just don't get it," he said, reading. "'Maggie Purcell is in possession of what could be the holiest of holies in the Christian world, a scroll written by Jesus Christ himself. Rumored to be out of the country on business, she couldn't be reached for comment.'"

"What am I, chopped liver?" Reeve wondered with a grin.

"This isn't funny. Now everybody'll know what I look like. I'm thinking of dying my hair blond before we go back." Upset, she leaned back and fought tears. "They'll never leave me alone now."

"Mags, you got to think positive. Right, Zeb?"

"Right. I know it's been quite a time for you. But you said yourself, good could come of this, Maggie."

"That's an understatement," she said, sniffling. Zeb reached into the glove compartment and handed her back a tissue.

Reeve, still reading, sucked in his breath. "I don't believe it. Mobs have assembled in Paris. Muslims are rioting, claiming the scroll is false and should be destroyed. Christians are facing them, singing hymns. Lord, what a mess."

"And bound to get worse," Zeb muttered. Maggie, still sniffling, shook her head.

Reeve turned a page and kept reading. A short while later, he said, "Well, here's something interesting. Your friend

Achmed's daughter was interviewed, Mags. It's pretty neat. She knows how the scroll was found. Listen to this. 'My fiancé at the time, Faod, was working on a dig at the Lascaux caves. The lamp on his helmet caught on a protruding rock, and it pulled out. That's when the scroll was revealed.

"'He tried to sell the scroll to my father, but my father contacted his old school friend, a member of the Sons of Light who had originally created and protected the Dead Sea scrolls. Ebrahim Sotudeh sent his sons to Paris to investigate the scroll, but my then fiancé determined to steal the scroll back from my father. Faod went to *Ancienne Écriture* and surprised my father as he was selling calligraphy to Maggie Purcell.

"'I can only guess that my father meant to protect the scroll, making sure Maggie Purcell had it.'"

Maggie sniffed. "That poor man. I'll never forget how he died."

Back at Ein Geddi, a surprise was waiting. Mohammad Ishtara had, inexplicably, sent a large box with all their belongings. Reeve greeted his laptop like a long lost child. For her part, Maggie was delighted to find their passports stuffed into the spare purse she'd thought gone for good. In with her passport was a brief note from Mohammed: "I never meant it to go this far."

Maggie looked at it for several seconds and felt her eyes begin to water. At least one decent thing had come from the entire experience: their friendship with Mohammad hadn't been totally false.

Reeve compressed his lips, took his cell phone, and excused himself to make a few calls. Maggie went to their small room to have a nap. She tossed and turned restlessly, seeing the newspaper article over and over again. A deep, sinking feeling in the pit of her stomach informed her that nothing would ever be quite the same again on their return to the States. And big decisions had to be made.

Just before six that evening, Reeve woke her from a fitful sleep. As he entered and sat on the foot of her bed, the din from the hungry young people lining the long tables came through the door.

"I got through to Todd," he said, and looked out the window.

Maggie yawned and sat up, hugging her knees. "What'd he say?"

"I wish I had better news, but it is what it is. Maggie, he's let you go."

She froze. "You have got to be kidding. I get kidnapped to a terrorist compound and that asshole fires me?"

"The moment we left for Cairo, he hired someone—in your place—before the kidnapping ever happened. I'm really sorry."

"What about you?" she asked, bitter.

"Me, I'm fine. Can't let go the only black face he's got, can he?" He reached out to her tentatively, not sure how she'd react.

She pulled away and curled herself into a small, pained ball. He heard her voice catch with sobs. "I'm so sorry, sweetie," he said. "You got so much on you right now, and then this."

"It's just unbelievable. I really don't know what I'm going to do. What can I do?" She said through tears.

"Let us get back to the States, and I'll make a few calls. I have a few ideas, but I don't want to say anything until I'm absolutely certain."

"You're so good to me. You know that?" She sat up and

looked directly into his dark blue eyes.

"And why wouldn't I be good to you?"

"I don't know," she mumbled. "I don't know much of anything anymore."

"Now, can we possibly talk about what you're going to do with the scroll?" Reeve asked.

"This makes it all the more important I do the right thing, Reeve. Even if I'm beginning to think … if you knew the debt I'm in right now from Beth's bills. There's no end in sight."

"I want you to at least meet a friend of mine in New York, Father Phil Ramsey. I've been going to his church for the last three years, and we're pretty tight."

"Sure, I'd be glad to talk to him. For now, though, let's make reservations and get back home."

— CHAPTER TWENTY-THREE —

FRIDAY, AUGUST 7

After an emotional farewell to Zeb, who promised to come see Maggie and Reeve in the States, they caught a flight home the next day. For Maggie, the flight was anticlimactic— she heard no chanting, had no visions. She slept nearly from takeoff until an hour before they landed.

Reeve was reading a magazine that he hastily hid when he realized Maggie was awake. "Hi there. You sure slept soundly."

"I know. I drooled all over my shirt," she said with a smile. "That's the best I've slept in days. It must be that we're finally on our way home."

Reeve stretched his legs into the aisle and groaned. "I'm not made for plane travel."

"You make a decent pillow, though," Maggie admitted.

"Got to be good for something. Now that you're awake and a captive audience, can I ask you a question?"

"Sure."

Having thought this over for most of the trip, Reeve took a deep breath and began. "I've been working since I was fifteen. I know I've told you that. I've also salted away damn near every dime I ever earned. I have close to half a million, if you include my IRA. I'll give you every penny if you agree to donate that scroll to a church."

Maggie reddened. "You make me sound so greedy for holding out for a good price. It's not me that I'm thinking about: aside from a tiny Social Security check, I'm my mom's only means of support. I *have* to do what's best for them."

"Not greedy. I just don't think you understand—"

"*What* don't I understand? That you believe this thing was written by Jesus Christ? Who's to say it's not a fake from the same time period? Such things were done, you know."

"You don't get what this scroll can mean to millions of Christians. It validates the entire Christian religion: it's proof positive that Jesus lived, and what he thought."

"It's not proof of anything, except the proof you assign it. How are you going to validate his writing?"

"Maggie, why can't you see what's been happening around you? Are you that blind? I pressed that scroll against a dying child in Egypt and—"

"And you saw what you wanted to see. How do you know she was dying? You take so much on faith. I'm sorry. I just don't see it. And I have to do what's best for my family. If I could do this for you, I would. But Beth comes first. She has to."

A bell chimed softly and the pilot came on the intercom welcoming them to New York. Maggie brought her seat upright and turned toward the window.

Reeve stared at the back of her black hair, helpless. Never in his life had he imagined such a state of affairs. The most holy object ever found, and Maggie had it— Maggie, whom he longed for with a fire he'd never known with any woman. She had it, and she was prepared to turn it over to a greedy, selfish millionaire. He expelled air in a harsh sigh.

There had to be a way to stop her.

Customs at JFK went smoothly, although the lines were long. Maggie and Reeve followed the crowd to the Air Train. They got their baggage and were ready to leave when Maggie came to an abrupt stop.

"What's all that happening outside?"

Concentrating on pulling their bags, Reeve looked ahead to the exit door. There was an enormous crowd standing just in front of the taxi stand. TV cameras sprouted alongside people pushing onto the sidewalk from the road.

"I have no idea. I'm not sure I want to go out and get in the middle—"

"Oh my God. Look at the poster that lady's holding."

He squinted, eyes grainy from the long flight. Then he gaped. "Oh no. 'God Bless Maggie Purcell.' I should have guessed this would happen. You're even on the cover of *Newsweek*, although I wasn't going to tell you that until we got home."

"What do we do now?" she said, voice shaking, her nerves frayed. "I'm not leaving this airport in that mess."

The crowd outside spotted her through the large windows, and a roar went up. They rushed to the window and screamed. Terrified, Maggie backed up to the turnstile for baggage retrieval. As if in a nightmare, she saw one old man fall forward and the uncaring crowd trample right over him, his mouth open and screaming in a high voice she could hear right through the window. A woman in a blue hat spotted her and pointed, and the crowd converged on her.

Maggie screamed and lost her balance, falling into Reeve.

269

He grabbed her and turned her away from the windows. "Hold it together now. We'll get out of this."

"May I help you?" A policeman materialized through the crowds inside the airport, most of whom had stopped in front of the doors, bemused.

"Yes, I think you can," Reeve said. "That crowd outside is waiting on my friend here. Is there a quieter way out of this terminal?"

The policeman looked out the window, then gazed at Maggie. "Oh, you must be … Yes, come right this way."

They followed him gratefully to a small lounge where Reeve phoned a limo service—the privacy was worth the extra cost. The policeman gave the service specific instructions.

Maggie was totally silent during the short wait, and Reeve watched her, worried that she'd go blank again as she had in the camp. Her complexion was pallid white, her green eyes focused on nothing.

Finally, they were taken to a side exit where a long black limo waited. Maggie got into the back, followed by Reeve. As the limo drove off, Maggie ignored the crowds still buzzing in front of the terminal, and though necks craned at the passing limo, the tinted glass hid their identities.

Maggie felt like disappearing into a hole and pulling it in after herself, as her mother often said. She couldn't conceive of the sheer number of people screaming her name. "Reeve. Shit. I forgot to tell the cop about that poor man …"

"I'm ahead of you. Told him when I walked back out to the bathroom."

She fell silent again in horror.

"Mags, you know I'm always here for you."

"I do. You're the best. I'm only sorry—"

"Don't worry about that now. Things often have a way of working out. We're on our way to meet a friend of mine. I didn't think it was too great an idea to head directly home."

Maggie inhaled. "I never thought of that. God, Reeve, what am I going to do if they know where I live?"

"I'm sure they know, unfortunately. You're listed."

Silent sobs convulsed her throat. She leaned her head back and began to think. For the first time, the realization hit that everything had changed.

She was jobless—not that she'd miss Todd and his sexism, she thought bitterly. All the same, it was what she was used to. Working at Xcorp with her friends, the travel, and of course the paycheck and benefits—gone.

And it was all due to a rampant gang media. If they hadn't published sheer supposition as facts alongside her name and picture, much of this wouldn't have happened.

She shivered, remembering that scene at the airport. Those faces all packed together and gaping at her. Such need—a need she didn't begin to understand.

Has the whole world gone mad? she thought miserably. New York was cloudy, hot, and dank outside the limo's tinted windows, a huge change from Israel's clear blue skies and pure air.

She drew a deep breath. That camp. The children running around, burnt black by the sun, rags hanging off their thin bodies. The mentality it took for someone to violently thrust his hand inside her in the name of what? Allah couldn't look favorably on that—not to mention the plan to kill two innocent people, stuff their corpses full of explosives, and thereby slaughter hundreds more innocents.

Not even Reeve was the same. He'd become a brooding presence, studying her when he didn't think she noticed. But she noticed, a tiny flame of anger licking upwards in her chest. He was a fine one to dictate what should or should not be done with the scroll. He had a solid job, a warm, loving family, and, as she'd just found out, a more than sizeable nest egg.

She noticed the lights glowing dimly in the Queens Midtown tunnel. Night was falling over New York, bringing with it a thin rain that meandered down the windows in tear-like ribbons. As much as she'd miss New York, maybe now she'd be able to move closer to Beth.

Soon the limo made its way down to the Village. Surely, Reeve wasn't taking her to his place.

To her surprise, they drove up to a small church—the Church of the Immaculate Conception, Reeve informed her as he held the door open. It looked to be at least a hundred years old, Maggie thought, stepping stiffly out of the limo. There were gargoyles leering from above dark stain glass windows. Maggie shivered a bit in the rain and hurried up the sidewalk after Reeve.

He took their bags and pushed on one of the enormous wooden doors. Although organ music swelled from some-where up front, the church was empty.

A black priest hurried down the aisle toward them, smiling. "Reeve, my son, you're here. And you must be Maggie. Come back to my home and I'll make you both a cup of hot tea." He hugged Reeve and warmly clasped Maggie's hand.

"Father Phil, this is Maggie Purcell. We're grateful you allowed us to come here. Our reception at JFK was unex-pected, to say the least."

"So I understand. It's been all over the news. That doesn't please you?" he asked over his shoulder as he led them to the back of the church, behind a curtain, then up a musty set of stairs.

"Not at all," said Maggie, aghast. "A poor old man got trampled in the crowd outside JFK. I'm sure the news didn't show *that*."

"Isn't that awful? Well, here we are. Reeve, you get Maggie settled while I go see to the tea."

The living room was comfortable with several old, deep

couches facing a bay window that looked over a little garden behind the church. The walls were a rich warm burgundy against which several paintings of New York hung, and Maggie heaved a sigh of relaxation as she let herself fall into a recliner next to the couch. A knock at the door came shortly after, and the priest bustled back in to answer it.

"Hello, hello! Come in, Neal. Maggie and Reeve, meet Dr. Neal Price. He's part of a small proposition I have for you, if you don't mind listening." He looked at Maggie, deep-set brown eyes shining under a cocked brow.

"Certainly, Father. Reeve has told me what a good friend you've been to him."

"Very well, then. Neal is very well-versed on ancient scriptures in the Church. If you'd let him have a peep at the scroll, we can get down to business, so to speak. While he's doing that, might I ask you a few questions?"

Stooping as he set a tray on the old coffee table, he pushed aside several stacks of papers and an open book to do so. He turned on a floor lamp.

Dr. Price, a well-built man in his forties, sat on the couch nearest Maggie. He had very pale skin and a long face under a shock of ginger hair. His grin was warm.

Maggie shook his hand, then brought out the scroll. The priest's eyes widened at the sight, then continued pouring tea from a plain white teapot into matching cups.

Dr. Price took the scroll and unrolled it on his lap. "This is a beautiful thing. I appreciate the opportunity, Maggie. It certainly has the proper look and feel of the age, Phil," he said to the hovering priest.

Satisfied, the priest turned and sat himself in an old leather armchair facing the couch, casually swiping a cat to the floor as he did so.

Dr. Price fumbled a small pair of reading glasses out of his pocket and placed them on his nose. For moments, he perused the scroll, muttering softly to himself.

"Maggie, how are you feeling about all this?" the priest asked as he took a sip of tea. "It must mean great changes in your life."

"Mostly horrified," Maggie admitted openly. "You wouldn't believe what I've gone through because of this scroll. It's been a nightmare, and there's no end in sight."

"But if it is what it seems to be, it's a thing of wonder, wouldn't you agree?"

"It's fascinating, from one perspective. But I'm the one who has to live with it, and the people desperate to get it away from me. It's already caused me to lose my job. There's not much wondrous in what's happened to me so far." She took a deep, calming breath.

"I realize it's been difficult, but it's a miracle really, if it proves out. So many people's lives will be changed, just by its existence."

"It's certainly changed mine, and not for the better."

"I realize that, and this leads me to the small proposition we have for you. The Church will only recognize the scroll if our own experts are able to examine and test it. Therefore, we'd like to invite you to Rome for a few weeks. You'd have your own private apartment in the Vatican—a thing of beauty, I'm told. You would be secluded while we work out what the scroll really is or isn't. What do you think?" He leaned forward, and his teacup rattled on its saucer.

"I appreciate the offer, but it's out of the question. I need to get to Nashville to check on my little sister."

"Mags," Reeve broke in, "I'm sure we could see to Beth while you're in Rome."

"Except I'm not going." Exhausted, Maggie was direct. "I've had enough travel to last me a lifetime. The scroll has been validated already by Oxford University, and the head of the Shrine of the Book in Jerusalem has compared it to scrolls there. It's all checked out, as far as it can be. I don't see any reason—"

"Mother Church would be able to compensate you well for the scroll, should it test out to her satisfaction," Dr. Price inserted smoothly.

Maggie shifted uncomfortably in her chair. Was this the real reason Reeve had brought them to the church? She shot him an accusing glance and he shrugged at her.

In the resulting silence, Father Phil stood abruptly and said he'd put on another pot of tea. Over the protests of the others, he took the tray and crossed quickly back to the kitchen doorway.

"I've had several offers for the scroll," Maggie said. "I don't feel the need for further verification, and it's absolutely out of the question for me to travel again. I need peace and quiet, and I have to see to my sick sister. I'm sorry."

"I'm sorry as well," said Dr. Price, "and Father Phil will be disappointed. While I'm here, though, do you have any questions about the meaning of the scroll? I believe I can translate for you."

Glad to move, Reeve stood and walked the short distance to the couch. He sat next to Dr. Price, and the priest came hurrying back in with a fresh platter of tea. This time, he'd added a plate of sugar cookies, all of which he placed on the coffee table before sitting back in his chair with a quick glance at the door leading to the church.

Maggie also stood. "Father Phil, may I use your restroom?"

"Certainly. It's just down that hall to the right," he replied, pointing.

She walked around her chair. The dark, narrow hall stretched back to his bedroom. She noted the beautiful flowered quilt on his bed as she entered the bathroom.

In the dark, she fumbled for a light switch and finally felt a string hanging from the ceiling. She gave it a pull and a bulb came on over the mirror above the old, ceramic sink. She used the facilities, then washed her hands. Throwing water on her face, she studied herself in the rippled glass.

Her eyes were red and puffy, the green irises looking cloudy and dense. Even her skin looked murky. She rubbed more water over her face and sighed. They'd have to find a hotel for tonight, as costly as that would be. No way she'd chance going home or to Reeve's place, the addresses of which could well be public knowledge. There was no question of staying with the priest, if he should offer. She wasn't comfortable here. Everywhere she went, people wanted something from her.

Leaning over the sink, she looked into her own eyes. What did she want in all this? Life to be as it was. And if that couldn't be, at least the means to ensure Beth's comfort and safety.

Uncertain, she looked at her tired feet. Lately, she'd felt something different, a pull from the scroll. It almost seemed warm, like a living thing, when she handled it. What if ... ?

When she was young, church had been a refuge from the screaming fights between her parents—a cool, dark sanctuary filled with wonderful music, and that face. His face on that statue was so kind.

Her heart gave a peculiar lurch, and time seemed to slow. What if ...?

She would no longer deal with people who were single-mindedly after the scroll, she decided. There really was no question about what she should do with the scroll: call the rabbi at the museum in Israel and make arrangements to get it to him as soon as possible, no matter how angry that made others. He could nearly match the billionaire's offer, and it would leave Beth set—hospital bills paid, and maybe even a vacation. Beth had always dreamed of coming to New York.

A tendril of anger curled deep in her belly, and Maggie

frowned. What right did the others have to decide where the scroll was going, no matter how well-meaning they were? No one, possibly excepting Reeve, had suffered as she had. She dampened her hair with water and slicked it away from her hot face.

The anger grew. It was time she was back in control ... of her life, of her future. Determined, she pulled at the light cord and opened the door.

" ... she's unbelievably stressed. It's been a horrific couple of days," she heard Reeve's low voice. "Just give her—"

"Don't give me anything. I appreciate your offer, but the scroll is mine to dispose of, and I've made my decision. Unless your church can match the sum Samuel Green and the rabbi offered, it's going to the rabbi."

The three faces stared at her, speechless.

Suddenly, she'd had enough. "I didn't think so. I'm done here. I need some air." Tears blurring her exhausted eyes, she strode by the couch and back to the door. Before anyone could move, she snatched up the scroll and was through the door, pulling her bag behind her. She walked hastily up the aisle of the church, lit by lights at the head of every pew.

The night air was thick with rain, and a heavy fog swirled over the street as she moved out of the old church, her bag's wheels catching briefly on the stone stoop. A bus approached, and its headlights arced bug-like through the dense fog. She slowly stepped onto the cement walkway leading to the street—and found herself surrounded. Priests in black robes, at least eight of them, their white collars gleaming in the light rain, materialized through the fog. *This can't be happening. What do they have in mind?*

She moved to walk through them and they closed in around her tightly. In her rising panic, she moved backwards, and bumped into one standing solidly behind her. The rest gently moved her toward the street, where a large van was waiting, doors ajar.

She called out to Reeve, but the church's doors remained closed. In desperation and anger, she lashed out with a foot. One of the priests grunted and dropped back, but another quickly took his place.

She began to flail at the dark figures with her fists and feet, feeling a sudden rush of rage. She wouldn't go down easily this time.

Then two figures raced out of the dark, and they fought by her side with eerily quick movements. She caught an elbow to the stomach and abruptly sat on the pavement, breathless.

Suddenly, the priests disengaged, ran to the waiting van and were gone.

Maggie sat back on her haunches on the wet sidewalk, exhausted but exhilarated. This time she'd fought her own battle. The two men who'd helped closed in on her, and she looked up.

"Do I thank you or are you here to attack me, too?"

"Neither one, Miss Purcell. I am Ebbi and this is my brother, Masood."

Reeve ran out the front of the church. "What's happening here? Maggie, are you okay?"

Panting, she sat on the curb. "Just fine, no thanks to you and your friends."

Speechless, for once, Reeve lifted a hand to hail a cab as Father Phil walked slowly out the door. Halfway down the front walk, Reeve turned on his heel to face his priest. "Why?"

"All for Mother Church," Father Phil replied. "All for Mother Church."

— CHAPTER TWENTY-FOUR —

Later that evening, the four sat in an exquisite suite at the Plaza Hotel. Reeve had appeared in time to see Ebbi and Masood, side by side with Maggie, banish the last of the priests. He was horrified by what had occurred.

Now Maggie ordered several meals from Room Service, including a large platter of fresh fruit for Ebbi and Masood. They had yet to divulge their interest in the affair. Maggie refused to hear any more until they'd all had something to eat.

While they waited for the food, Ebbi discussed Paris with Maggie. Reeve sat apart, next to one of the enormous windows that overlooked the darkness of Central Park. This latest encounter had taken something from him, something he didn't fully understand.

He'd trusted Father Phil, both as a friend and a representative of the Church Reeve so revered. That the man would betray him and his faith in such a fashion was almost unfathomable.

A soft knock on the door interrupted his thoughts. Maggie

rose to admit room service, and begged Reeve to join them at the large table the uniformed men set up. He waved a hand in dismissal. The very thought of food caused nausea to churn in his stomach.

"Come on ," Maggie exhorted him. "You have to eat. We haven't had anything except those sugar cookies at Fath—"

"Don't remind me," he said in misery. "Mags, I am so sorry. I don't know how you can forgive me." The sight of black-clad priests surrounding Maggie, fighting for her life, the two young men fighting deftly next to her, had nearly given him a stroke.

"There's nothing to forgive. You had no way of knowing that man's plans. I never thought you did."

"Still, it's my fault. And if those two hadn't come along when they did—how did you two happen along right then?" he asked, curiosity making a small dent in his depression.

Masood looked at Ebbi, who responded, "We did not happen along. We are behind you for weeks now."

Reeve surged to his feet and Maggie held up a quelling hand. "Let them speak. They've earned it."

He sat down, his back stiff with nerves.

Ebbi looked at Reeve. "It is not our intention to harm you, nor take from you what you have. We are to watch only. But tonight Maggie was alone. We could not let those persons take her."

"Who are you, then?" Reeve asked warily. "What do you want from us, from Maggie?"

Maggie, slicing into an enormous Porterhouse steak, groaned as the scent of perfectly grilled meat hit her nostrils. "Can't this wait until after we eat? Reeve, the other half of this monster is yours. I just heard it moo. It's exactly the way we love it."

"I'd rather know more about these two, if you don't mind."

Mouth full, eyes closed in bliss, she nodded.

Ebbi's darkly tanned face became serious. "Some things I discuss must remain private, is understood?"

Maggie nodded.

"Several thousand years ago, my tribe wrote Dead Sea scrolls. There was split in the tribe over, ah, change of opinion. Then Romans attacked Qumran and killed most. Some escaped to Africa where we founded Badu Tanar, a village in Ethiopia. Thirteenth tribe took us, and we established the Sons of Light enclave.

"Others scattered to save what they carried, and we lost touch. Through years, we look everywhere for signs of our people and the Scrolls. The Paris shop owner called my father and told him what his daughter's fiancé had found. My father was certainly interested—it sounded like a Dead Sea Scroll. We went Paris to see and when we arrived at the shop, there was gunshot and you ran out back. First, Masood thought you shot owner.

Maggie nearly spit a mouthful of green beans onto her plate. "Me?! Me?"

"Masood had not see others enter the shop, but I did. The Tribe has us following you ever since. And now, we have offer for you.

"We know you are tired of all this trouble, and perhaps you agree to come to Badu Tanar to just relax. Maggie, it is beautiful. It is the Mouth of the Nile—jungle, big cats, and palm trees. Very different from New York, from even Israel."

Maggie stopped eating, entranced. "I'd love to. But my sister Beth is very ill—she has leukemia. I need to be near her. But one day I'll certainly take you up …"

"Badu Tanar is but a hundred miles from Addis Ababa, capital of Ethiopia. There we have advance hospital. They cure my aunt of breast cancer," Ebbi said.

"And it is so beautiful," Masood said longingly. "I never

knew it was so beautiful until I have been away for nearly a year. Maggie, the trees there have spirit. Your sister, she will love Badu Tanar. We have baby baboons in our village."

Maggie cut a piece of steak and chewed slowly, considering. "You know, Reeve, we can't very well stay here. The news is out that we're back. Life will be awful here and in Nashville. I don't know how I'm going to afford it—"

"This is premature, but I got news for you. My friend Hiro—you remember I told you about him? How he taught me tai kwan do?"

She nodded and he continued. "Hiro is coming back to town. Of all things, he paid a surprise visit while we were in Nashville that last time."

A slow understanding dawned in Maggie. "Oh my God. You got a phone call from him while we were driving to Nashville, didn't you?"

He frowned. "And I so tried to be sneaky."

Maggie burst into laughter, something inside her loosening.

"Anyway, Hiro's business is rocking. He's opening a New York shop. They're going to be building a huge enterprise website in English, a new search portal for their clients. Hiro's looking for a lead developer in charge of security. Pay one-fifty K per year and better yet, a ten grand bonus to set you up a home office wherever you like."

Maggie stiffened and put down her fork. "No way. It's too good to be true. What about benefits? Do you know?"

"Full boat. Taki Enterprises is known in Japan for their flex benefit packages— Hiro has told me a thousand times."

"I'll take it," Maggie said, amazed and relieved. Her appetite came back and she attacked the steak with gusto.

"Does this mean you're not going to—" Reeve said, his voice hesitant.

"I don't know what I'm going to do." And then she did

know, at least her next step. "But I know what I'm not going to do. Oh my God. You will have to excuse me. I need to make a fast call." Maggie laid down her fork, distressed. "Reeve, this isn't going to be easy."

"It's going to be okay, girl. What can he do, after all? Throw a tantrum?"

Maggie stood and walked to the door, cell phone in hand. "I'll be right back." She walked into the high-ceilinged hall and down to the elevator. Elegantly clad people filled the lobby, dining early before a show. The doorman held the door for Maggie as she passed into the brightly lit New York night.

She crossed to the wall separating Central Park from the street and walked until she spotted a bench. Body aching from jet lag, she sank onto to it and flipped her cell phone open.

He answered his office phone on the first ring. "Royce Stevens."

"Hey there, this is Maggie." She heard a slight intake of breath. Sighing to herself, she forged on. "I've made a decision regarding the scroll. It's going to the Shrine of the Book in Israel. It's only right. Things have happened— amazing things. Knowing what I know, I could never sell the scroll to someone who would just hide it away. I'm very sorry."

At first he didn't respond. "I suppose there's nothing I can say to change your mind. My friend will be very upset indeed." His voice was taut.

"No, there isn't." Suddenly a thought occurred to Maggie, a connection she hadn't made until now. "I don't suppose your friend is Samuel Greene, the billionaire?"

"How did you discover that?"

"He didn't really offer *half* a million, did he?"

A gusty breath came over the line. "No, he didn't."

Maggie felt a flush of anger rise to her cheeks. She started to say something to Royce, then thought to herself, why bother? Evidently he'd been offered the same million dollars that had been specified on the website Sherrie had found. In deciding to keep half of it, he might well have ruined the deal. Would she have accepted that large a sum much sooner?

"It's just as well," she said now. "The scroll is with me, and that's where it will stay until I turn it over to the museum."

Royce slowly replaced the phone in its cradle. Such an opportunity, lost. He didn't imagine he'd ever have access to that kind of money again.

He spied the picture of MaryAnn and the kids. Picking it up, he frowned. There was no real reason for him to require that sum of money. As a tenured professor, he'd always made a decent living, if not one that could afford a house on the Sound.

Hmmm. That was an interesting thought, a new thought. Slowly, he placed the photo, face down, on the desk in front of him.

As Maggie walked back into the suite, Reeve spoke up from his chair. "Everything okay?"

"Yes, it's over. The scroll stays with me for the time being. About this Badu Tanar, how can I possibly afford *that* now?"

"Remember your new job," he said. "I will stake you for a month, a few months if you like, in Badu Tanar. It's just what you need after the time you've had. I'll come with you the first few weeks at least, if you don't mind? Todd owes me three weeks of vacation this year." Suddenly shy, he looked down at his feet.

"With the new job, I guess we'll be fine. And I wouldn't

consider going without you. Now, let me call Nashville and get Beth up here before the news hounds figure out who she is, if they haven't already."

Several hours later, Maggie was curled up on her bed dialing Beth. As late as it was, nearly one a.m., the girl answered her phone immediately.

"Hi Maggie! You're back!"

"Hi cutie. How're you doing?" Maggie asked.

"I'm hanging in. Things are better. Darla's all over her cold and was here today, and—well, I have other news, but it's gonna wait."

"Wait for what? You little devil—"

"Mags, this once, it's your turn to trust me. In fact, you'll be seeing me soon. I'm coming to New York," she said grandly.

Floored, Maggie didn't respond at once.

"Yes, as a matter of fact you are. That's why I'm calling you." A loud squeal into the phone had Maggie laughing through her next words. "But how did you—"

"I'm serious, Mags. I'm not going to say a word till I see you. But this is the biggest ever! Totally radical!"

"Well, sweetie, I want to take you to a place called Badu Tanar in Africa. Do you still have your passport from Bermuda two years ago?"

"You bet! I know right where it is."

"Well, you don't have the shots needed, but you can get those in New York. My life is fairly out of control now, but I might have a new job, Beth! Where I can work from wherever I am! Including an African village with Internet dial-up, if need be."

"An African ... Mags are you serious? What about Mom?"

"The village is a hundred miles or so from one of the best

285

hospitals in Africa. It might take some persuading, but you're definitely going. I'm going, and I'm not going without you. I have some new friends from there. They saved my bacon earlier tonight ..." At the small gasp, she hurried to add, "No, it's all good. We're safe and at the Plaza Hotel. Anyway, they say that Badu Tanar has baby baboons, Beth. In the streets."

"Mags, I hear a noise." Her voice went quiet, scared.

"Hang up and dial 911, sweetie. Oh lord—"

"Never mind. It's Mom and Uncle Kevin! Uh oh, she knows I'm on the—"

"Maggie, honey, is that you?" came Anna's slurred voice over the phone.

"Hi, Mom." Inwardly Maggie sighed. This wasn't the best time for a conversation.

"Do you know your sister wants to come see you in New York?"

"Yes, she just told me. Sounds like a great idea. How is she, health-wise? Didn't she have a treatment yesterday?"

"Yes, she had the chemo, but she's doing great. Really great. Kevin and I feel she desherves ... deserves ... a little trip to New York."

"I bet you do. Well, that's settled then. I'll make arrangements to get her here soon, possibly tomorrow. Is she well enough to travel? Can you handle getting her things packed for a nice long stay?"

"Yes indeed. You won't believe your eyes. Then Kevin and me, we're going to Florida for a few weeks. Do you know how long it's been since I've had ..."

"Mother. What about Cocktail?" Maggie worried about the beautiful white bird.

"Darla's seeing to him. They're the besht, best of friends. He's not so bad. He's kind of cute."

They made plans for what Beth would bring to New York, and Maggie hit her Internet travel site to make arrangements for Beth to fly to New York the following day, then she fell into bed like a dead woman. Just before she went to sleep, she realized she'd said nothing of Badu Tanar to Anna. She grinned. Perhaps it was for the best.

Saturday afternoon, the crowds were dense in the large greeting area at JFK. Maggie was glad she'd thought to tell Beth to meet her near the bottom of the escalators.

She wasn't so glad about her thin disguise of sunglasses and floppy hat hastily bought at a boutique in the Village. They weren't working at all. She heard murmurs all around her.

"Look, honey. Isn't that the girl ..."

"It's her. She's the one ..."

"I wonder if she has the scroll with her right now?"

Reeve, who also heard, put a protective arm around her and pulled her close. "It won't be long now. Hang in. I'm looking for Security."

"Reeve, I'm really not liking this. My gut is in my throat. How much more time do you think?"

He consulted his watch. "She landed ten minutes ago. She should be coming down that escalator any second."

Maggie uselessly pulled the hat lower over her eyes and edged through the crowd closer to the foot of the escalator. The murmurs grew louder, and one large woman in a bright blue sun dress finally said, "Excuse me, but are you Maggie Purcell?"

"No I'm not. If you'll excuse me." She looked away from the woman.

"Yes, you are. I saw your picture on the news last night. Hey, can I see the scroll?" Insistent, the woman moved closer to her.

Maggie huddled against Reeve. "Leave me alone."

"Well, I never," the woman huffed. "You'd just think—"

Maggie reached an arm out and brushed the woman aside. "Excuse me, but you're blocking my view. I'm waiting for someone." Then the chanting started again, low but insistent. She tensed. *Not now.*

A sole drum began to beat.

And then she saw her.

The chanting swelled with hundreds of new voices chiming in, and the drum beat deepened until Maggie was nearly deaf with it.

Wearing a tube top and a pair of tight jeans, Beth stood at the top of the escalator scanning the crowd. She held back and the stream of people behind her accumulated as she looked for Maggie.

Maggie, forgetting her wish to remain anonymous, waved both hands over her head. Beth spotted her and broke into a huge grin. The chanting grew so intense that Maggie saw brief spots in front of her eyes ...

She watched as Beth hefted a large backpack onto her shoulder and ran lightly down the stairs, hair streaming behind her.

Time stood still. The breath left Maggie's chest. The chanting abruptly stopped, yet the sole drum beat continued. She gasped and sagged against Reeve, who had gone completely rigid.

The child was glowing with health.

Her hair had grown back and shone in the bright airport lights.

Maggie fell to her knees, the tile cool beneath her.

Tears streaming down her cheeks, she didn't notice as the crowd gasped collectively and moved away.

A long roll of thunder sounded over the busy airport, and suddenly the lights dimmed, then went out.

Maggie knelt in the dark, stunned senseless. *How could it*

be? The small, wasted body showed distinct evidence of curves. Through her confusion, one truth was evident: Beth was healed.

The thunder increased and the crowd muttered. A scream rang out near Maggie. Oblivious, she remained still as the truth gradually sank in. There in the darkness, tears began to flow, and her heart opened in wonder.

Reeve—he'd been right all along.

Still frozen with shock, she moved her head back until she was staring upwards in the stygian darkness.

So it was that white light, a single ray falling from above, picked out her pale face, then widened until it blanketed her kneeling figure. Maggie felt an incredible warmth, a deep love emanating from the brightness.

Heedless of her surroundings, she pitched forward onto her face. "My Lord, forgive me, for I have sinned. I have not believed."

Her words dropped into a deep silence in the airport. A child laughed, a joyous sound that echoed in the stillness.

Then a deep voice surrounded Maggie: "Behold my daughter, for she carries the Word of my Son. Behold her, for she is good. There is no shame, daughter. All will be well."

— CHAPTER TWENTY-FIVE —

TWO WEEKS LATER

Maggie lay on a brightly colored blanket. Reeve sat next to her, his back against a tree, eyes on her face.

Next to her, a picnic basket contained the remains of their lunch: a kiwi salad, sausage sandwiches, and a large hunk of Beth's chocolate cake.

Just beyond the blanket, a deep blue pool stretched to Tississat Falls, incredibly beautiful and surrounded by mist. The Mouth of the Nile was their favorite picnic location, the normally hot African afternoon cooled by tons of falling water.

Reeve sprawled, half-propped on an ancient baobab tree, his hands lightly playing with Maggie's dark hair, his eyes closed. Maggie plucked a piece of saw grass and held it under his chin, tickling him lightly.

"You're really a devil," he said lazily, giving her dark hair a faint tug.

Maggie looked up at him, his head back against the enormous trunk, the slight breeze from the pond blowing over his tight black curls. Her fear twisted knots deep inside. It was almost painful, his beauty and the peace she now felt.

With Beth a healthy, happy girl, the need to sell the scroll was gone.

Whatever she did, she would do with the aid of prayer. She wasn't sure what He had in mind for her, but she was positive that He would let her know. She had a niggling feeling she was missing something regarding the scroll, but no matter how she concentrated, it was just out of reach.

She'd thought Badu Tanar would answer her questions—the young Masood had assured her that "all things make sense in Badu Tanar." On arriving two weeks ago, she'd met their elegant, silver-haired father, the head of the village.

He was so proud of his sons, it was a joy to see. And the ceremony held last week! Maggie was delighted to be the guest of honor at Masood's Coming of Age. She had never seen a spread of food like that. And the drums, the chanting. Those were very familiar to her, and a thrill had gone up her spine.

She became yet more certain that Badu Tanar would hold answers for her.

So far, though, all she'd done was to attend the clinic daily—she, the scroll, and Reeve. Increasingly large crowds showed up for the daily meetings, where she prayed and laid her hands on those who were sick.

Not always with the best results, she thought ruefully. Often she performed a healing, but occasionally, the person was healed of all pain, only to be returned to his Maker.

The true miracle was that, when their family member crossed to the other side, none of the loved ones blamed her. Instead, there was a great rejoicing when agony left their pain-wracked faces for the last time.

Ebbi's father, Ebrahim Senior, arranged the crowds for her. Strangely, it was his careful sculpting of the crowds each day that revealed yet another of the scroll's properties: Maggie did not have to personally touch each person. As long as there was a chain of people, with Maggie touching the first one, healing would flow along the chain.

Maggie wasn't certain where her future lay, but she hoped to travel and share the wonders of the scroll with Christians world-wide, and heal as she went. Already, donations were pouring in that would enable her to do just that.

For now, she was content to lie in the shade and watch Reeve's perfect profile. She harbored a deep fear that, soon, he'd go back to the States. The past two weeks had been almost charmed in their tranquility. She and Reeve had explored several nearby villages. Beth had discovered a world where healthy, brown children ran through dusty streets chasing baby baboons. She never wanted to go back.

"Wow, something big leaped over there," Reeve said.

Maggie leaned forward and looked. Sure enough, an enormous feline form arced through the spray just under the falls. Reeve exclaimed again and pulled himself to his feet. He held a hand out to Maggie, but she disregarded it and stood on her own.

Reeve took a step toward the pool and heard a muffled curse. He turned in time to catch Maggie as her feet stumbled over a root and nearly pitched her into the icy water.

Hands on her shoulders, he stood for a moment looking into her deep green eyes. She tried to pull away, as always. But this time he tightened his hands and drew her to him. "No, you don't. Not this time," he said under his breath.

Maggie's heart beat faster. Caught with nowhere to go, she leaned back against his hands, looking up into the serious blue eyes. Her heart skipped a beat. *What was he doing?*

And suddenly his head lowered, blocking out the sun. And his lips were on hers, hard and demanding. Her breath caught in her throat and she felt her legs go weak, then his arms tightened around her. She melted against him with a soft moan, and his lips went gentle.

His lips played around her own, kissing and nibbling. Breath coming faster and faster, Maggie wrapped her arms around his neck to maintain her balance. And still his lips nibbled and wandered, from the corner of her own lips along her jawline.

Then Maggie leaned back briefly, brought her hands to his face, and trapped him while she kissed him deeply, tongue questing between his full lips.

Reeve's head spun and he almost lost his balance as Maggie's small form wrapped itself around him. He returned the deep kiss and plucked her off her feet, then sat against the old baobab with Maggie curled in his lap.

He planted a series of kisses on her small nose, then tasted the saltiness of tears.

Alarmed, he pulled away slightly. "Am I hurting you?"

She snuggled closer. "No. No. I am just so happy. I never thought …"

"Well, I had a pretty good idea," he said, voice smiling. "It just took you long enough to come around, girl."

"I know, and I really …" her words were lost as Beth came running down the overgrown path.

"Maggie! Maggie, come back to the house. I learned something pretty neat in school today!" Beth's face was filled out and darkly tanned.

"This better be good, sprout," Maggie grumbled with a grin.

"Yes, I saw you smooching. It's about time! I wouldn't interrupt unless it was really important," Beth smirked. "Come on! You just got to see this."

Reeve stood, pulled Maggie to her feet then collected the basket. "Can you get the blanket, Mags?"

"Sure. We better hurry. She's dancing around like a nut!"

They walked back down the dusty path toward the tiny village of Badu Tanar. Small houses, each painted pink, red, or white, lined the road. Though deceptively simple, each dwelling had satellite TV and an Internet connection, as decreed by the tribal elders.

Maggie and Reeve were staying at an elder's own home, a two-storey pink stucco house directly on the town square. As usual, Masood and Ebbi were working at their father's office across the large square.

Reeve opened the gate to the courtyard and ushered in Maggie and Beth. Beth skipped ahead. "Mags, get the scroll and meet me in my room."

Maggie pushed the door to the house, left unlocked, and walked back to her large white bedroom. The house was pleasantly cool, with its two-foot thick mud walls.

The scroll lay on her desk. She picked it up and walked across the hall to Beth's room.

"Alright, monster. What's all this about?"

"Mags, I had my first Geography class today. The teacher was showing us Africa on the overhead, and something just clicked in my brain. Let me see the bottom of the scroll."

Maggie obligingly laid out the scroll on Beth's lap and stood back, interested.

"Okay. Oh my. I was right. Here's my Geography book. Give me a second to find … alright, here it is. See the bottom of the scroll, near His name? What we thought was a big ink blot?"

Maggie peered down and nodded, confused. "Yep."

"Look at my book, Maggie. That's not a blot at all. See the coast of south Africa?"

Maggie took the book and looked, then gasped. She

looked at the scroll.

The irregular blotch wasn't just a simple ink blot. Now that she had something to which to compare it, it clearly showed the coastline of South Africa. *Fascinating.*

She looked more closely and her breath caught in her throat.

Just near the indent of a bay, there was a discernable five-point star.

"What is that? Where is that? Could it be the City of Gold?" Maggie asked, pulse pounding.

"Tanzania, I think," Reeve responded, bent over her shoulder. "Yes. See that little blotch? That's the island of Zanzibar. How did I never see this before?"

"But what about that star?" Maggie asked excitedly. "Where is that?"

"I've looked all over the net, and the nearest city I saw was Bagamoyo," Beth responded excitedly. "It's a little village southwest of Bagamoyo! Can we go, Maggie?"

"One day, we can. First there's a world of healing to be done."

Photograph: C. L. Casey

Cat LeDévic graduated from MTSU with a degree in Computer Science. A longtime technical writer, she has lived all over the world, including Europe and the Middle East. She modeled in Paris and attended the American Academy of Dramatic Arts in New York. She had a small part in the cult classic movie, 'Porky's'. Her love of computer technology and interesting people prompted her to purchase www.jokersupdates.com, which has grown into an international community from which she draws much creative inspiration. *The Scroll* is her debut novel, and the first of a trilogy. Cat currently resides in Nashville with her father, 3 temperamental Siamese cats, and a St Bernard with a drooling issue.

Visit the author at www.CatLedevic.com

Printed in the United States
54484LVS00001B/4